I M⬤RRIED J♥E

SHERRY MYRICK

Fulton Books, Inc.
Meadville, PA

Published by Fulton Books 2021

Used by Permission from Jean Ann Willis
Dinosaurs in 1990's and Cinderella stepsisters have nuts

April 1988 Jonathan and Jamie Myrick
I looked to see if he was looking before I done it.

All jokes of the characters Elijah were told by
Jonathan Myrick at the age of eleven years old and
the Winnie the Pooh joke. Origin not known.

All characters are fictitious even though I had the privilege
of working with inmates from the Hamilton Prison on
work release at Russellville, Alabama chicken plant.

I, Sherry Myrick, am the only songwriter of Grandma's
Lullaby. It was written for Ezmah Annie Bruton
Portwood, aka Mamaw Portwood, for her 98th birthday
September 10, 2010, It is copyrighted Library of Congress.
SRu-1-065-062 June 20, 2011. Also songs mentioned of
Backroad 48 are copyrighted by Library of Congress.

ISBN 978-1-64952-438-6 (paperback)
ISBN 978-1-64952-440-9 (hardcover)
ISBN 978-1-64952-439-3 (digital)

Printed in the United States of America

Chapter One

Debra Allen's' strong voice echoed "Break These Chains" through the speakers of Sacora Haynes's radio from her favorite country station in Mobile, Alabama. Sacora had packed all the last things and had them on the front porch. She had already moved what she was able to keep from her home of the last ten years. Sacora had released her Porsche and ownership of her home to her ex-husband, Barton Haynes, with an exchange for some financial return. She was standing on the steps waiting on the movers to put these last boxes in the truck when Barton Haynes parked in the driveway in his Porsche.

Out stepped his new wife-to-be, Rachel Bracken, and she screamed at Sacora, "Get out of my house, you—" Barton immediately kissed her to hush her from saying what she had intended and from being any more rude than what she was.

Sacora's college roommate came to the rescue, Julie Johnson, and motioned for Sacora to go to her Volkswagen Bug after the movers had finished all the boxes on the truck. Julie waited until Sacora had not been looking, and she flipped Barton and Rachel an unkindly choice of her fingers.

Sacora had been with the wealthy, spoiled, narcissist Barton Haynes since she was twenty. She married him at twenty-two years old after college graduation even though he was ten years older than her. After ten years of marriage, he decided he would start another life with Rachel.

Sacora, being a college graduate, a social worker, had accepted a job with Mobile County Department of Human Resources. Her salary would not supply the income or supply the lifestyle that her marriage to Barton had, so she was moving her things into storage and an apartment closer to her office in Mobile.

Julie called Sacora on her cell phone, and they stopped to eat at the local McDonald's. Julie asked her why she was keeping these things with nowhere to put them. Sacora answered, "Anything and everything I have, Rachel can't sell." While eating at McDonald's, Sacora and Julie talked about college years taking Sacora's mind off her heartbreak.

Sacora had met the truck at the storage unit and placed the last few things in order she wanted it to be. Julie was waiting at the apartment, putting things in the kitchen, when Sacora walked through the door.

Julie joyfully announced, "By supper time we will be ready to cook and eat our first meal in your new home." With this, Sacora busted into tears. Julie immediately put her arms around her and just waited until the breakdown was over. Julie did say, "I can only imagine."

Sacora went into the kitchen and finished putting up the things she knew she would need, with quiet tears falling. With the last box emptied and sat outside the door, Sacora asked Julie, "And what did you have in mind for the first meal here?"

Julie answered with, "Sloppy joes or order us a pizza."

Sacora said, "I guess I'm cooking sloppy joes." The sloppy joes were the best, and the two girls enjoyed the night remembering the years before Barton Haynes.

Julie did mention over and over, "This is why I NEVER MARRIED." Sacora agreed. Julie's life would not be able to include a spouse. This would be the first Saturday night in Sacora's apartment, one to remember.

Chapter Two

Julie had spent the night with Sacora and hugged her friend good-bye the following Sunday morning. Julie, an attorney for the plaintiff, had a big week in court and needed to rest and be ready for the ordeal. Sacora was so grateful for her company and assistance this weekend but also for the work she did on her divorce from Barton.

After Julie left, Sacora's phone rang. It was her mom, Samantha Hill, asking how things were. Her parents, Samantha and Corey Hill, were in South Africa on a missionary trip that they had planned for two years. Sacora had convinced them that she was a big girl and could take care of herself through the transition of divorce, getting employment, and moving to her apartment. Her parents were expected to stay another six months in South Africa. Sacora would be fine; she convinced them to stay as they had planned.

Sacora started moving boxes around in the living room and neatly put things up and away. After she had completed her goals in the living room, she started unpacking her work clothes. Monday morning would be a new experience for her. Out of college with a degree in social work, she never worked while married to Barton. So here it was, life without Barton.

She finished putting up her clothes ready for the week coming. After a long, hot, relaxing bath, she finished putting towels and cloths away in the bathroom. Looking around with satisfaction of progress, she was surprised how much she had advanced in settling in her apartment.

Ready for bed, setting the alarm on the clock, Sacora fell asleep faster than the night before. When the clock had sounded, Sacora looked at the nightstand to turn it off. This was a new experience for her awakening with an alarm clock. She looked at the pictures Julie had suggested to put by the clock, them of happier days at college. It being the month of May of 2019, summertime, one of her favorite seasons, Sacora usually made her days to Orange Beach, so it was all such a change.

Sacora immediately started her morning with coffee but no breakfast until McDonald's on her way to work. Her clothes were ready to jump into after her bath. Her plans for lunch were to eat at a fast-food place close to her office. Out the door she went on her planned schedule.

At her office, she was introduced to her superior, Mr. Calvin Hamilton. He made her feel so welcomed and had an outstanding, warm smile. Sacora settled into her office space, and before lunch she had taken on her first case.

Mr. Hamilton had given her some information on three children: three-year-old girl Aylassa Blaine, six-year-old girl Alisha Beth, and nine-year-old boy Elijah Chance Malone. The children's mom, Autumn Malone, had just recently died of cancer, and the children were in foster care until further notice. The mom's boyfriend had been sentenced for some time in prison for selling drugs.

Sacora made her way in the Mobile lunchtime traffic to an individually owned hamburger cafe. One hour for lunch, she still couldn't get the children off her mind. On returning back to her office, she started all paperwork required by Alabama law for the children. Soon five o'clock had arrived, and she made it back to her new home. The apartment was surrounded with some memories but more hope for a new beginning.

Sacora decided on a homemade chicken tossed salad and rested still with the three children on her mind. She prepared for another day and did sleep soundly.

Chapter Three

Sacora had been dreaming when the clock sounded. She was in a huge white house hearing children laughing loud. She could feel so much happiness in her heart in her dream. She turned the clock off and put her mind back to reality.

Remembering her dream off and on while getting her bath, she still felt different in her attitude and mood for her new beginning. She decided to put the toaster Julie had bought for her to use. Frozen waffles and sugar-free maple syrup with plenty hot butter was the start of her day with coffee. Jumping in her favorite dress and heels, out the door she went. From a distance, she could see her Bug needed washing soon. Being married to Barton for ten years, cooking, cleaning, and car maintenance were always hired work.

Sacora made way to her office and sat down to start working on the assigned case from yesterday. She handed Mr. Hamilton the papers she had collected and completed as he had instructed. Mr. Hamilton smiled and spoke to her, "Nice work for your first day. This is what we needed. I will get back with you on the follow-up details."

Lunchtime seemed to come quickly, having spent time refreshing her mind on Alabama law for children. Eating lunch at the close McDonald's, she could hear children's laughter and see a bus of third-graders on a field trip. Her attitude and mood seemed to be improving through the adjustments she was making.

Lunchtime was over and back to her office, Sacora's heart melted. She saw a two-year-old girl and her eight-year-old brother sitting on a bench at another social worker's desk. The little girl had a cast on her arm, and her brother had his nose broken. Sacora's mood immediately became full of sadness with sympathy. The children's parents were intoxicated and on a drug high and went into a violent rage, causing severe injury to their children.

Five o'clock was here. The two children were taken to a foster home hours earlier, but she still couldn't get them off her mind. The dream she had awaken to this morning seemed to be tugging at her mind on her way home.

Julie called as soon as Sacora went through the door of her apartment. She said, "Barton has filed a motion for you to sign over more money to him. If you get summoned, don't do anything until I can put a stop to whatever technicality his attorney is using. I'm out of Mobile for two weeks on a case and will be in touch with you when I am back."

Sacora said, "Yes, Julie, I will. I have already been more than civil, fair, and reasonably considerate. I know I am not willing to give up any more."

Julie answered, "I agree. No one else would have behaved the way you have and accepted the loss of money and not being material-istically interested. The divorce settlement is so over. In days you are eligible to marry again. Sacora, I will see you soon. Goodbye."

Sacora said goodbye to Julie with the thought of what Barton and Rachel had scammed up now. She decided to change out of her dress and heels into a cool summer shirt and shorts and went to eat at a seafood restaurant. She indulged into her shrimp and steak. On her way to the parking lot after paying, her mind went to the five children she had been introduced to this week. She wondered what they had for dinner. Supper was probably what they called it.

Samantha Hill called and interrupted her thoughts. Sacora answered, "Hello, Mom. How's everything in your world?"

Samantha answered, "It is wonderful. I'm sure it is just as hot in Mobile as it is here. Your dad and I are wondering about your progress in adjusting to your new life. Are you still moving on with a new beginning?"

Just then Sacora's dad interrupted with, "Hey, my sweetie pie. I know you are doing great with being independent. Your mom has been a great teacher. We miss you and will be home in a few more months. Love you, my treasure."

Sacora answered, "I love you, Captain. I do miss you, Dad, and can't wait to see you."

Samantha returned to the phone, "Sacora, I know you have everything under control, but we will still come home when you say so."

Sacora said, "Mom, I am okay. I am doing the chicken thing and just winging it. I have thought about Thanksgiving and Christmas holidays. Barton always dictated my holidays. Would you and Dad still be interested to spend these holidays in the Smokey Mountains?"

Samantha said, "Yes, honey, that sounds good to me. What about you, Corey? Our captain said yes, Sacora. I will talk to you again soon, and I love you."

Sacora said, "Great, <om, talk to you later about it. I love you."

After a few minutes scoping out TV programs, she decided to prepare for tomorrow and call it a day.

Chapter Four

Sacora woke without the alarm clock this morning. Day three, hump day of her new beginning. She jumped into cool khaki pants, a white lace shirt, and a sky-blue blazer with matching heels. Ready for work, breakfast at McDonald's and time to enjoy it.

Sitting at her desk for thirty minutes, putting paperwork together for the new case she has been assigned, she heard a loud voice say, "Sacora Elizabeth Hill Haynes." Sacora looked toward front of the office, and there stood a police officer. She walked up to him knowing it was the motion that Julie had told her was coming.

Sacora looked at him with a smile and said, "Yes, I am here." She handed him identification, and he handed her the paper to sign, and she took the documents after signing. She looked at the summon and realized this was not anything from her divorce, nothing from Barton.

You are hereby requested to appear at the will reading of Mrs. Elizabeth Louise Clark Baker. The scheduled date of Monday, May 13, @ 10:00 a.m. at the office of Atty. Angela Faith Mays.

Sacora looked at the name and decided this was her mother's mother. Her grandmother she had never met or had a conversation with, but she was named after. When her parents married, the relationship with her grandparents was dissolved by their decisions. They did not agree with a mixed marriage; her mom marrying her dad was strongly disagreed with. Sacora's parents started a life of their own without their blessings or association with them from that moment on.

Sacora noticed the address was not far from her office, and she discussed with Mr. Hamilton her coming in at lunch on Monday. He agreed and would make arrangements for her to make her time up in the future weeks.

Sacora called her mom at lunch. "Mom, did you know Grandma had passed? I got summoned for her will reading."

Samantha said, "No, I did not. Are you going?"

Sacora answered, "Yes, ma'am, it is on Monday. I am going to lunch, Mom, I will talk to you later. Love you."

Samantha said, "Goodbye. I will talk to this weekend when we can talk longer. Love you."

Sacora went to lunch with questions and being puzzled. What had Ms. Baker left her in the will? Samantha Hill was an only child, but it still was not making sense to her at all.

Sacora finished her day. Five o'clock had arrived. She went home and made a chicken salad for dinner and thought about her Grandmother and the situation. Monday would answer all her questions, she thought.

Julie called and asked if she heard anything from Barton. She said no but informed her of the will reading of her grandmother.

Julie let her know of her concern and promised to stay in touch. Almost one more week and she would be returning to Mobile.

Sacora did not have a peaceful sleeping night. But the days toward Monday were coming.

Chapter Five

Thursday and Friday have come and gone with the usual days of work, lunch, and dinner. Saturday is here, and a sunny day but cooler. Sacora decided to go to the beach that was closer to her apartment to save on time and gas in her Volkswagen Bug. She stopped at the seafood restaurant and enjoyed being alone with her thoughts of her grandmother after she dropped her dry cleaning off at the cleaners near her apartment. Was it normal to be more curious of what her will was to her than to be thinking about the passing of Ms. Baker?

Sacora finally made her way to the beach, swam in the waves, and then settled down on the sand for some sun and to think. Samantha Hill called and interrupted her thoughts of questions.

"Hey, my sweetie, how are things with you today? Are you still thinking about your grandmother?"

Sacora answered her, "Yes, ma'am, I cannot get it off my mind why she would have me summoned to be at the will reading and why she did not notify us when she was at her last days."

Samantha answered Sacora, "She was loaded with pride and would have had to put it aside to make contact with us. But I do admit when she acknowledged that she was my mom, she was a good one."

"I can't imagine how difficult it has been for you both through these years of missing one another. I don't know how I would have made it through life without you and Dad," Sacora said.

Samantha got quiet and finally spoke with humor, "Yes, but my life with your dad and you has been more important, full of happiness for me, and what a prize Captain has been. There he is coming through the door." Samantha handed the phone to him.

Corey spoke with laughter, "Hello, my treasure. What has your mind tossing about?"

Sacora answered him with, "Just thoughts of Grandmother's will reading on Monday." Sacora decided to change the subject. "Hey, Dad, did you know that my divorce from Barton was finalized on Thursday?"

"That's great, now you can think about moving on with whatever you think will make you happy. Goodbye, Sacora, we will be home in November and we will plan our holidays in the Smoky Mountains."

Sacora had told them goodbye and put her phone down on the towel by her. She stayed on the beach for a couple more hours and then headed home to her apartment. She decided it was a sloppy joe night and cooked herself some for tonight and tomorrow, Sunday's lunch.

Sunday morning was very peaceful, and she gathered up clothes that she needed for the upcoming week. She took a stroll in the local grocery store and bought some things for dinner after work. Sacora was still living on a budget. Barton's settlement wouldn't come into her possession until after two more weeks. She hoped his motion would not intervene any of his funds.

Sacora finished up the sloppy joes and got ready for tomorrow. The day that had been on her mind for days. She set the alarm clock, tossed, and turned all night.

Chapter Six

U p and wide awake before the clock went off. Sacora decided to get ready by her routine schedule and indulge in McDonald's breakfast and coffee. She made it to the office of Atty. Angela Faith Mays by nine thirty. She announced to the secretary that she had arrived for the reading of the will of Ms. Baker.

The secretary said, "Ms. Mays is here and ready. No one else is mentioned in her will."

Sacora made her way down the hallway to Ms. Mays's office. Ms. Mays introduced herself to Sacora as the attorney for her grandmother. She made the comment that Sacora had some of her grandmother's facial features.

Ms. Mays took her driver's license as form of identification and recorded her number on the document that Sacora signed and dated. First thing Sacora was handed an envelope with handwriting of her name on it, Sacora Elizabeth Hill Haynes.

Ms. Mays started to recite the will, and Sacora's head started spinning. She had left all her possessions to Sacora. A home on the outskirts of Mobile where her mom was raised, stocks, and savings bonds. The home had some furnishings, but some rooms were empty. Fifty acres of land, mostly pasture land, and a well-kept barn was also part of the home.

Ms. Mays said, "Sign this as I have read and instructed you of what is now yours." Ms. Mays also handed her the keys to the house and gave her directions to the location. Sacora nodded, and still dazed, she finished signing all documents and stood up to leave when Ms. Mays said, "Congratulations, and don't forget your letter."

Sacora still had two hours before going back to work. She decided to grab McDonald's for lunch and sit and read the letter, consuming the thoughts of what was hers.

Sacora had put her hamburger and fries and drink on the table. She opened the letter and started to read it:

> *To my granddaughter that I never held in my arms, never kissed your cheeks or told you that I loved you. I now know the cost of foolish pride seeing you as a grown woman and I have not been a part of any phase. It took years for me to realize that it took a devoted mother to raise such an independent minded person as your mom is, to be nontraditional in starting life or making a life for herself. Now after all these years I know I have paid the price of being narrow minded and racists as I have missed out on a wonderful person. Signed, Elizabeth Louise Clark Baker.*

Sacora was in tears as she could feel the regret in her words. She finished her lunch, still too emotional to talk to her mom. It was best that her parents didn't hear tears in their conversation. They would come home early.

Sacora took the keys to the house out of her purse and rubbed the worn places in them to touch some sort of connection with her grandmother. Still uncertain why she attempted to make things right after all these years and why she was the recipient of all her known possessions.

Sacora went to work immediately on her assigned case when she went to the office, attempting to take her mind off her grandmother's letter and her present situation.

Five o'clock had finally gotten here, and Sacora called her mom. "Mom, I did go to the will reading of Grandma's, and she left me all of her possessions, the home where you grew up, and surrounding land. The letter she left me is very touching, and I will take a picture of it and send it to you by text."

Samantha said, "Okay, Sacora, I never understood her reasoning or thinking of avoiding you, but it is what it is. I am peaceful with her decision of acknowledging you in some form after all these years. I know you are still on a budget, sweetie pie, and I won't continue to add to your phone bill, but I am here or can come home when you say so. We love you, Sacora, and so proud of the adult you have become. Goodbye."

Sacora said, "Goodbye, Mom, and I do love you and Dad. I will be fine until you return home in November."

Chapter Seven

Sacora spent the next days of pondering on the new adventure coming her way, a new home, and with her directions, it showed twenty minutes from her office from the other side of Mobile. She couldn't wait until Julie called to tell her of the will of her grandmother and the new options she had. Most of all, still no information of Barton's intentions.

Finally it was Friday and the last day of work, and Sacora's plan to visit the homeplace she had inherited on was Saturday. Maybe Julie would be home tonight as she had planned on.

And as Sacora had hoped, Julie called, "I am home. And yes, I will go with you tomorrow to check it all out."

Sacora answered her with, "I am so glad you are going with me. I have been anxious about what is awaiting for me."

Saturday morning, Sacora was up without an alarm clock. She met Julie at McDonald's for breakfast. Sacora decided she would drive the Volkswagen Bug and Julie would navigate. The girls ate breakfast but mostly caught up on the details of the will, and Julie was just as puzzled as Sacora why she was the one who inherited everything.

On the way to the homeplace of her mother's, the song "Who Says You Can't Go Home" by Bon Jovi and Jennifer Nettles came on the radio. The girls sang along loudly, enjoying each other's company and being optimistic on the day.

Finally they reached the homeplace of Sacora's mother. It was a huge white house, kept up with vinyl siding and a dark-brown tin roof. Sacora fell in love with the house immediately. Sacora grabbed the keys from her purse and stepped on the front porch. She noticed the porch went around the house and had an entrance/exit door on each side.

Sacora and Julie went in the front and looked around at the surroundings of the large living room. Sacora had assumed some or most of the remolding had just been done. Her mother never mentioned or described what Sacora was seeing. She looked in the kitchen, such a large room with new cabinets and appliances. The dining room was newly painted and furnished with a table, chairs, and china cabinet. The wood floor had been refinished, shining with a new coat of polyurethane. Two bedrooms on the right of the living room and the same new paint and refinished floors in both. Ecru color on the walls, Sacora knew her furniture in the storage building would be great in these bedrooms. The bathroom and the hallway were also painted and with new flooring. All of Sacora's things she had kept from her home with Barton would be perfect here. Julie said, "Let's check out upstairs." The girls went up the new carpeted stairs and looked around. Three bedrooms and a bath here and up one more flight of stairs an enormous one bedroom and bathroom. Everything had been finished, except the bathroom was not completely painted.

Sacora was pleased with the house and looked out the window on the top floor and saw a barn. She said to Julie, "Let's go see the barn." The two made it to the barn and looked around. Sacora said, "Mom never said anything about the barn or the house being so nice, with bedrooms and bathrooms on all floors. She talked about three bedrooms on the middle floor and an attic on top, where she would play on rainy days. My grandfather's office was downstairs and my grandmother's sewing room. Mom's room was the one on the left upstairs with a large closet." Sacora looked around at the barn and noticed stairs and started up to look around. Julie followed, and they were impressed at the view around the windows of land and the house. Sacora said, "I can't wait until my mom and dad sees this."

Chapter Eight

Julie and Sacora went back to the house and locked everything up. Sacora turned around and looked one more time and thought about the reasoning her grandmother would have left her such wonderful gifts. In the car, Julie said, "Congratulations, and what for lunch or dinner?"

Sacora answered, "What about Olive Garden to celebrate?"

Julie said, "Great, I have not been there in a while."

At Olive Garden, Sacora's thoughts and conversation went straight to her plans on where she was putting the furniture in the house. Julie commented occasionally on some ideas of the pictures in the living room. Sacora was relieved of the bathroom items she had saved in storage from Barton's. What she had in the apartment would be the last items she would have moved.

Julie reminded Sacora that her settlement from Barton should start in a few days, if not this week. It would be perfect timing too. Sacora would be paying movers again hopefully for the last time. Not paying rent on the apartment and the storage units would be a large amount saved also.

Julie said, "Sacora, I have got to go on home and unpack. Tomorrow is church and lunch with Mom." Sacora told her goodbye with a hug and thank you.

In the apartment, Sacora looked around and thought about where these things would go in her new home. She looked in the kitchen and the kitchen in the house was three times larger. It would still feel empty.

Sacora got ready to search things out on TV when Samantha called, "Hey, sweetie, how did it go today?"

Sacora answered, "It went fine. It is a nice place, Mom. I can't wait for you and Dad to see it."

Samantha asked, "Are you still doing okay? What are your plans for the house?"

Sacora answered, "I plan on making arrangements Monday to move in by this weekend. Every room has been painted with new flooring. The dining room has an enormous table, chairs, and china cabinet full of china. The bedrooms are perfect for the furniture I kept from Barton's."

Samantha said, "Okay, we will still be in touch. Love you, honey."

Sacora said, "Goodbye, Mom. I do love you and Dad."

Sacora slept soundly after her day and woke to another day of wonder about the house and the barn. She did her usual shopping and made preparations for another week at work.

Sacora went through her clothes from the dry cleaners, sorting her pants and skirts for work tomorrow, her mind constantly on the plans and the visions she was seeing about the house.

Sacora turned the clock off. It was Monday, and she enjoyed her long, hot bath and taking her time to dress, her mind still on the house. She made it to work and focused on the cases she had started last week. Lunchtime finally, she called the movers and gave them the address of the storage units and the location of final destination of the house. After setting a date of Saturday and time of noon, she finished lunch from Subway and returned from lunch, back to work. Today she would be finishing some documents on the three children she had worked on her first week, Aylassa, Alisha, and Elijah Malone. Her heart went out to these three children. To lose their mom and home at one time was such an adjustment she could relate to.

All week Sacora worked on moving into the house and focused on where the movers would be placing the furniture when she was not working on cases in the office. Every day was business for Sacora to take care of.

Chapter Nine

Sacora woke to a gorgeous June day in Mobile, Alabama, the Saturday she would be moving into her new home. She went to pick up Julie, and they went through the drive-through window of McDonald's and sipped on coffee all the way to the storage units. Sacora unlocked each one for the movers to fill their trucks with the furniture she treasured. After all units were emptied, Sacora and Julie went to look in each one to make sure nothing was left behind. Now to the house to put all the furniture in its place.

Sacora had given instructions for furniture to each room in the upstairs' bedrooms. Even the one bedroom on the top floor had furniture placed and bathroom of teal towels and washcloths. The three bedrooms were furnished with furniture and boxes of sheets, quilts, and pillows. The bathroom was red, and there were towels and pictures. Sacora knew she had a lot of work to do putting everything in its place. They decided to stay the night in one of the bedrooms and go home tomorrow.

Sacora and Julie worked until midnight. Looking around it was becoming a home, her home. The bedroom by the living room would be hers in the future with the furniture in her apartment. The bathroom would also be with the items in her apartment's bathroom.

Sacora put towels and washcloths in the bathroom and tried out the tub. A long, hot bath, and then she slept in the bedroom across the hall from her mother's room. Julie took another bedroom by side Sacora and showered in the very top bathroom. Everything seemed to be ready to use. Sacora put the towels and cloths in the washing machine and then the dryer and was pleased with the laundry room.

Sunday morning was welcomed with more to do. Sacora and Julie warmed water for instant coffee in the microwave and was pleased with the flavor. Julie had brought some Pop-Tarts, and they ate those while thinking of what came next in settling down. No furnishings in the kitchen yet, they ate in the dining room.

Sacora knew she needed to be back at the apartment around four o'clock to get ready for her week of work and Julie was also needing to be home. So they finished what was started and locked all doors, setting the alarm system. Looking at the front of the house from her Volkswagen Bug, Sacora was still in disbelief that this was hers, free and clear. Sacora said to Julie, "No woman will ever say to me again, 'Get out of my house!'"

Sacora and Julie ate at the local Kentucky Fried Chicken on the way home after getting some groceries. Julie was ready to be home and told Sacora goodbye. Sacora went home to her apartment. In the apartment, she thought she hadn't resided here long, so it shouldn't be a big adjustment to move her things into her house.

Assorting her clothes and shoes for the coming week, Sacora decided to look in the kitchen to estimate how much space she would need in boxes to move her things herself to the kitchen in her house. The Volkswagen Bug would only carry a few things at a time, and Julie's sports car was out of the question.

The bathroom towels, cloths, etc., should go in the Bug without using boxes. The living room furniture should be able to go in one small truck, and she could do without this for a few days, until the rent was due again.

Sacora set the clock and fell asleep thinking about the yard/lawn and what she could do with it and make it her home. She slept until the clock alarmed.

Chapter Ten

The alarm clock sounded, and Sacora jumped up, ready for Monday. She enjoyed the long, hot bath and sipped on coffee thinking about the change that was coming. She dressed in the skirt, blouse, and heels she had set out last night. She looked at her hair and decided it was time to make a visit to Ginger Jackson and Sandy Flippo's salon for her deep conditioning and straightening. Ginger Jackson and Sandy Flippo were her mother's first cousins but were more like sisters. Samantha was an only child like herself.

Too excited to eat breakfast, she drove on by McDonald's. First thing in the office, more paperwork for the Malone children, Elijah, Alisha, and Aylassa. After the documents had been scanned and emailed to Mr. Hamilton, Sacora saw an email from Wells Fargo Bank. She checked it, and yes, her money had been deposited into the assigned account for IRA and the interest into her checking account, which was expected to be deposited each month. Sacora could breathe a little easier with the financial break.

At lunch, she called the salon and talked to Ginger and scheduled an appointment for this Saturday after lunch. This would give her time to pack some of her kitchen treasures for her new home. Their salon was closer to her new home than the apartment.

Back at work in her office, she had another issue to prepare documents for an elderly couple to leave their home and reside in the nursing home. They didn't have living children, and Sacora's heart went full of sympathy for them and could relate of not having children herself. This was the only disappointment from her marriage failing.

After she finished all the documents, Sacora handed these to Mr. Hamilton. Her day was over, and she decided to eat dinner to have a celebration. Her divorce was over completely with the deposits today. What Julie was expecting Barton to have in a motion, she was not thinking about tonight.

Sacora called Julie, and she agreed to meet her at their favorite seafood restaurant. The girls left all their troubles behind, work and life, and enjoyed the music and conversations of remembering the past of college days.

Julie hugged Sacora and said goodbye. With this celebration tonight, Sacora had so much peace and hope for the future when she returned to her apartment. Making her final choice in clothes and shoes for tomorrow, Sacora was pleased with today's events.

Tuesday and the rest of the week were contributed to Elijah, Alisha, and Aylassa Malone and the elderly couple leaving their home. Saturday morning, she slept until nine o'clock and put her dishes stacked in dish cloths to keep them from breaking. With more space in the tote she had, she put the silverware and some cooking spoons. This would be all that would fit into her Bug.

After she packed the tote into the Bug, she was off to the salon. Sacora was excited to see Ginger and Sandy. She had not seen them in a while and needed to catch up on the latest.

Ginger greeted her with, "Come on in, child, and we will get you started with a deep conditioning of coconut oil." Sacora sat down in Ginger's chair, and the oil felt cool while Ginger was massaging it thoroughly.

Ginger said, "What man would not want to woller in all this hair, have that gorgeous face pressed against his face, and those big ole boobs?"

Sandy interrupted, not looking up from the hair she was drying, and said, "We get the picture, Ginger, Barton is a loser."

Sacora looked at them both in the mirror and said, "I have wondered what Rachel has that I don't. Maybe Barton decided he wanted children after all."

Sandy broke into her thoughts and spoke loudly, "I will tell you what she has that you don't, and that is dishonesty, plenty of it. She is out to get what she can from him, and then she will leave him high and dry. I tell you, she is a scam artist, and he will regret that he let you go and all the materialistic things she will take from him."

Sacora said, "Thank you. I do hope that is the way it all ends. I have a new home and life now that I am anxious to get settled into. I need to have some work finished on my house. Do you know of a reliable man to call on?"

Ginger said, "I sure do. Joe McCarley. I will give you his number. He is the man we call on constantly. The salon and home has always got something needing repairs."

After Ginger finished Sacora's hair, she hugged them both and took the business card of Joseph C. McCarley. She excitedly told them goodbye.

Chapter Eleven

S unday morning, Sacora called Julie, and they went to church with Julie's mother.

They had lunch at Olive Garden with leftovers to take back to her apartment. Sacora told them, "I should be completely moved into my house by the end of June, if not first of July." Sacora suggested a Fourth of July celebration at her new home. Julie and her mom agreed it was a great idea. Sacora was thinking it might keep her from missing her parents so bad. They were in a remote area of Africa with no cell phone service.

In her apartment, Sacora looked around and decided on what she could take with her in her Bug after work tomorrow. She packed the Bug down as much as she could get it to hold. No rain expected, she put the large bathroom picture across the back seat with the windows down enough to hold it. Three inches of the picture on both sides of the Bug were hanging out the window. The other boxes were in the floor and back seat.

Sacora was ready to call it a weekend and ready for Monday morning. Sleeping very good even though with things on her mind. Up before the alarm clock and ready in her chosen clothes and shoes, out the door in the Bug with her things loaded down. She went through the McDonald's drive-through with the picture extending from the windows.

Making it to work on time with putting her things in the bathroom tonight at her new home in the back of her mind, the first thing on her list of cases were the Malone children, Aylassa, Alisha, and Elijah. The foster home was closing. The retirement of the workers were to be at the end of the month of July. Sacora was to prepare all paperwork needed for the transfer to the foster home in Baldwin County, Foley Alabama. This just broke her heart, another major adjustment for these children.

After lunch, she had finished all the documents and handed them to Mr. Hamilton. He smiled and said, "Sacora, I can see the interest you have in these children. You know, you have a large home for just you. Would you be interested in fostering these children? Now that they are transferred to Baldwin County, you would qualify to submit application to foster them and keep your job here. We would help you find schools for the older children in the fall and day care for the three-year-old."

Sacora responded and said, "Yes, I am interested in these children. It will be something I am going to consider and think about."

Mr. Hamilton added, "I know you would be good for them and good to them."

Sacora went back to her desk absorbing the compliment Mr. Hamilton gave her. Yes, she would be a good candidate to give these children a dependable home and parenting. Yes, she had resources to meet all qualifications.

Sacora put these thoughts aside and continued on the case of the elderly couple and decided to make a visit to the nursing home tomorrow before going to check on her home. Finally five o'clock, and Sacora finished up organizing her desk for the next morning and out the door to her new home.

Her drive was slower to give consideration to the picture hanging out the window but still made it with good time. She unlocked the door after setting the alarm system to enter through the front door. She put the picture in the bathroom first and then unloaded all the other things to the bathroom she had decided to use as hers. When Sacora had finished all the unpacking from her Bug, she went to the kitchen to start working on her final move with everything. She noticed a large place of water coming from the faucet and knew that the faucet needed to be replaced.

Sacora reached in her purse to look at the card Ginger gave her of Joe McCarley. She called the number, and when he answered with,

"Hey, this is Joe, leave me a message," Sacora did. At her surprise, he called back within five minutes.

Sacora gave him the address and filled him in on the idea that she needed a new faucet. He asked her, "Do you have a certain kind in mind?"

Sacora answered with a chuckle, "Yes, one that will work and not leave a puddle of water anywhere."

Joe asked, "What are the color of your appliances?" Sacora gave him a detailed description, and he said, "All righty, I will be there with a new kitchen faucet in thirty minutes or as soon as I can."

Sacora said, "Thank you and goodbye."

She went to the downstairs bathroom to finish putting up towels and looking at where the picture should go and how to hang it without it falling or damaging the wall.

Chapter Twelve

L ost in her thoughts, she heard a loud sound of music coming toward her home. She asked to herself, "What is that?"

Sacora went to the front door, and out stepped a man from an older truck with dents and signs of days' use of maintenance. He grabbed something from the back and walked toward her with a limp.

He offered his hand to her and said, "I'm Joe McCarley, and you must be Sacora Hill."

She answered, "Yes, I am. What kind of music did you have playing in your truck? I have never heard it before."

Joe answered, "It was the Foo Fighters. You have never heard of Foo Fighters or their music?"

Sacora said, "No, I listen to country music."

Joe smiled and said, "I guess that is why you have not heard their music. I don't think it would be played on a country music station. I have brought a kitchen faucet that I think will work and coordinate with your kitchen appliances."

Sacora walked in lead to the kitchen and stopped quickly. Joe stopped, but not in time to avoid bumping her. Sacora screamed and pointed to a squirrel in the kitchen. She jumped up and down, ran to the front door to open it, and then still screaming, she ran to the stairs. Joe did some motioning, and the squirrel ran out the door.

Joe spoke first, "I don't think he had planned on staying long. I did not see any luggage."

Sacora replied, "I'm glad you were here, I would not have handled it well being alone."

Joe grinned and said, "Well, if you say you handled it well, I guess I will take the compliment. So now I will replace the faucet. I will get it together and try it out before I leave."

Sacora, looking around in the kitchen, watched Joe when she thought he was not paying attention to her or watching her. She spoke without thinking it through, "I am having a Fourth of July gathering with my friends if you and your family would like to come."

Joe answered, "Well, it would be just me. I am divorced with one daughter, and she won't be visiting me until around the middle of July."

Sacora smiled and said, "Okay, I will let you know. I have your number."

Joe finished and turned the faucet on. It worked, and Sacora paid his fee and watched him walk back to his truck. She waved a small motion, and he nodded as he started his truck.

She had bought a salad to have in her apartment when she made it back for supper. She decided to call it a day, locked everything up, and checked the alarm system. On her way back to the apartment, she thought about today's events and decided to call Julie.

Julie was supportive on fostering the children and agreed with Mr. Hamilton that she would be good for them and to them. Julie's first question about Joe was, "You think he is attractive, don't you? I know you, Sacora."

Sacora did answer, "Yes, I do."

Sacora said goodbye when she got to her apartment to eat her salad and to think about what she would do next if she went to Baldwin County to apply for the foster position of the Malone children. Where would she put the children's things, as in what bedrooms? Sacora kept thinking as she gathered her clothes and shoes for tomorrow.

She slept with things on her mind and was awake before the clock sounded. She was up and out and to McDonald's for coffee and breakfast. Still with so much to think about, she sat at her desk and then finally went to Mr. Hamilton's office.

Sacora asked him, "You were talking to me yesterday about fostering the Malone children. Where do I apply?"

Mr. Hamilton's smile was such a compliment on her idea. He said, "I will check in on it and let you know what to do next. I know you already have a home ready for them."

Sacora went back to her desk and thought, "YES, I CAN DO THIS."

Chapter Thirteen

The last Saturday of June was here. This morning, Sacora met the truck and movers with a smile. She was moving everything out of the apartment and to her new home, final home. Sacora had the vacuum and some cleaning supplies left to clean after the truck had left. These few things she would carry in her Bug.

While the men were moving her furniture, she stepped outside and looked at the door. She thought to herself, "The person who moved in here is a totally different person from the one moving out." She looked around and made sure everything was on the truck before she went to clean for the final minutes.

Her heart was so anxious with the new home and the change in her life. She was putting in the back of her mind today the hope of fostering the Malone children. She had gotten to focus on finishing the adjustment of settling in her house. Mr. Hamilton had prepared all necessary paperwork for Baldwin County Department of Human Resources and had submitted them yesterday. She was waiting on a scheduled inspection of her home and would focus on that event when it was time.

Sacora had closed the doors and took one more last look. She vacuumed first and put the vacuum in the Bug. She cleaned the kitchen and then the bathroom. The movers had given her an approximate time her furniture would be arriving. She had made quick time cleaning and loading her Bug that she would go through a drive-through on her way and not have to leave once she got to her new home.

Sacora was still a few minutes earlier than the movers and had the alarm system off with the doors open. She was ready to place her furniture and all her bathroom supplies. Sacora thought she would settle everything in the bedroom first and then the bathroom. The movers placed furniture as she instructed. She had boxes of towels and washcloths placed in the living room and all her hygiene supplies in the kitchen. She thought this would make it easier to place in the bathroom.

Sacora looked into the truck to confirm everything had been placed in the house, and she signed a form that all her furniture had reached destination and the truck was leaving empty. She closed the doors and took a long, deep breath and started finding sheets and quilts to make the bed. She had planned on working on settling in until midnight.

Midnight came too soon, and she worked thirty-five minutes longer before indulging in a long, hot bath. She did relax and accomplish some thinking on her plans of the Malone children. She would place Alisha in her mother's bedroom, Aylassa in the bedroom downstairs, and Elijah in the bedroom upstairs across from Alisha.

Sacora felt this day to be a productive day and slept with peace until the sun woke her up. The first morning in this room, the sun shined in her face with a pleasant warmth. She was up and to the kitchen for coffee and a bowl of oatmeal before she continued placing all the newly moved things into the bathroom and in the bedroom.

Sacora was placing some winter clothes and shoes in the closet of the bedroom she had chosen for herself. There was a small chest in the corner. She picked it up and sat it in the bedroom to look inside. There she found old newspapers of her, birthday announcements, and her wedding announcements when she married Barton. Her parents always included her grandparents in all announcements. Her mom would always have the opinion, "They avoid us. We did not avoid them."

Also in the chest were old *Winnie the Pooh* books. Samantha would often talk about the moments her parents would read these books to her. This chest Sacora would always treasure. It was the only connection she would have with her grandparents.

Chapter Fourteen

Sacora took a break from moving her things into the bathroom and walked out on the porch. She looked at the clear blue sky and felt the warm Alabama sun. Her thought was to enjoy this Sunday of ninety-eight degrees with water. She looked at her Bug and decided to wash it after she finished the bathroom cleaning.

Sacora showered to remove the bleach and pine sol smell and dressed in denim shorts and a halter top. She covered her face and arms with sunblock and put the tube in her purse for more if she needed it. She locked everything up and started toward the car wash she had seen on her way toward town. Sacora was trying to remember the last time she washed a car. Barton always had the car maintenance contracted out.

Sacora put coins in the machine and started washing her Bug when she heard a voice behind her. "Hey, how many times did you go through kindergarten?" She turned around and saw Joe McCarley.

She answered, "Just once. What makes you ask?"

Joe smiled and said, "washing your car is just like coloring. You start and finish in the same place. The hot sun is drying the soap quick, and it has to be rinsed immediately. After you rinse, start on another place."

Sacora smiled looking at Joe and said, "Thanks, I haven't washed a car in years."

Joe came to the Bug and started washing and said, "If you will rinse after I wash, and we will knock this project out. I'm finished with my truck."

Sacora looked at this truck and said, "Yes, it looks great."

When the Bug was finished with a shine, Sacora moved her Bug to the vacuum. Joe got on the passenger side, and Sacora on the driver's side, and they worked on their sides and finished vacuuming when Joe asked if she would like to walk to the small Dairy Queen and have lunch with him. Sacora said, "Sure."

They both were still wet from the car wash and ordered and ate on the tables outside. Sacora noticed across the street a car lot and spotted a van on the front row. She was looking at it when Joe asked, "What are looking at?"

Sacora replied, "I'm looking at the red van across the street."

Joe asked, "Why would a single woman want a van?"

Sacora smiled when she answered, "I have submitted paperwork to foster three children, and I need a van for school and whatever."

Joe smiled in return and commented, "I wondered why you didn't have children."

Sacora suddenly went serious with her explanation. "After Barton and I had been married for a while, five years or so, I had tried to have a family. After some months, I was diagnosed with endometriosis and was forced to accept losing all hope of having a family of my own. And then after some time, he left me for another woman, Rachel."

Joe responded with kindness and said, "I'm sorry, Sacora." Holding out his hands, Joe continued to speak, "These hands have touched a football time after time, high school, college, and pro, making rememberable touchdowns for years. When these hands touched my newborn daughter, I had never felt such joy, and that is what I named her, Joy. Her mom wanted some kind of snuddy name, Catalina Celeste or something, but I wanted Victorious! She did agree on Victoria Joy. I'm sorry you never felt that feeling in your hands. I also know that some people are never in love. My ex-wife was always looking for the next man with more money and status in lifestyle."

Sacora replied with, "Thank you, Joe. I am hoping to foster the Malone children. I think I can be good for them and to them. I feel for them and never met them, just through paperwork. Their mom died with cancer, and I can relate to losing a family with no control."

Joe said, "If you are finished, let's go over to the car lot and look at this red van. I take it red is your favorite color in automobiles."

Sacora answered, "Red is my favorite color in everything."

Joe and Sacora looked at the van, a new model with ten thousand miles on it and would seat eight. Plenty of room for car seats in the rear seat and storage in the back. Sacora smiled and said, "I might come look at it tomorrow after work and test drive."

Joe nodded and asked, "Would you like for me to come along? If you would, call me. I should be finished tomorrow around five o'clock."

Sacora smiled and answered with, "Yes, that would be great."

Chapter Fifteen

Sacora nodded bye to Joe and went to her Bug and took a last look at Joe going to his truck. She wondered why he had a limp but did not ask. On her way home, the clouds started moving in for a storm. She decided to wait until tomorrow after work to buy groceries and have a salad later tonight.

Sacora made it home before the first drop of rain fell. On the porch, she turned around to look at her Bug, shining even in the cloudy sky. It had been an unusual afternoon. She turned off the alarm system and unlocked the door when the first lightning flashed and the first sound of thunder came. Inside, she returned to the bedroom and felt the relief of accomplishment of settling down for the weekend.

Turning on the TV for company, she thought she heard something on the porch. She went to look, and there was an older dog on the porch taking shelter from the rain. Sacora looked closer to conclude it was a female Labrador retriever with one blue eye and one brown eye. Her ribs were showing as if she hadn't eaten in days. Sacora took a look at her opening the door, and in she came finding a comfortable place on the floor. Still wet from the rain, Sacora took a towel to dry her off. The dog seemed so friendly and weak. Sacora could see the spade scar and knew at some time this dog had been very loved and cared for. The only food Sacora had to offer was leftover soup in the refrigerator. She put it in the microwave and waited a minute and then gave it to her. She ate it willingly, but her movements reminded Sacora of her childhood days of Winnie the Pooh's character Eeyore, so she named her Eeyore. The dog even seemed to like the name as she answered when Sacora spoke it. Sacora looked at the dog and gave her a sponge bath so she could stay inside. Eeyore acted like she had been a house pet. She never attempted to jump on the furniture and was content with the blanket Sacora put on the floor. She seemed to know the house. She was waiting in the kitchen for a bowl of water when Sacora went to the refrigerator for her salad.

Sacora ate her salad with the TV on. Still another few days until she could talk to her mom and dad. So far a lot of things have changed—she settled in her new home, had a dog, and had met a man. Wow, "met a man" sounded unreal after a broken heart from Barton.

She put her thoughts aside and gathered all her things for work tomorrow. Eeyore went to the front door after drinking water, and Sacora opened it. Eeyore did her business and was back in quickly from the storm. She was still weak from no food, and Sacora put her blanket closer to the kitchen and her water bowl for the night before she closed the door to her bedroom for the night.

Monday morning was started with the sun shining bright, and Sacora opened her bedroom door remembering to look for Eeyore. Just as Sacora thought, Eeyore had not bothered anything through the night and was standing by the front door. She went out, and Sacora started getting ready for her day at the office. After she was dressed, she decided to put on the porch a bowl of milk and bread with another bowl of water. She would get proper dog food this afternoon when she would buy groceries. Sacora made sure Eeyore was on the porch with water and a blanket before she left for work. She thought to herself that she enjoyed having a dog as a companion again and hoped she would be there this afternoon when she made it home. It was in her childhood years since she had her dog, Nike.

At the office, Mr. Hamilton received an email stating Sacora was entitled to be a foster parent for the Malone children. His smile was so big with the announcement. Sacora asked him, "What comes next?"

He answered her, "The next step is inspection, and I know you have this covered with moving in your large home."

Sacora smiled and asked, "When will this be arranged?"

Mr. Hamilton said, "I will let you know. It should be scheduled sometime next week. The foster parents have agreed to postpone retirement until the children are placed in the next foster home. I am predicting it should be soon."

Sacora smiled trying to hide the butterfly feeling in her stomach. She kept telling herself, "I can do this."

Chapter Sixteen

F ive o'clock on Monday was finally here. Sacora checked her phone, and she had a missed call from Joe. She returned his call to get a voice mail, and she left a message that she was going to the car lot to test drive the van. Sacora went to Dairy Queen across the street first and grabbed a burger and fries before going.

By the time she had finished her burger and fries, she looked up and saw Joe drive in the car lot. She got in her Bug and made it to the car lot, meeting up with Joe. A salesperson came out to greet them and gave them the keys for a test drive and got in the back seat, Joe in passenger front seat, and Sacora driving.

Sacora smiled and said, "I think this is perfect. What do you think?"

Joe said, "Red is your favorite color, and it does have a nice-sounding motor. I will check it if you want me to at the car lot."

Sacora nodded. Sacora asked the salesperson, "What kind of gas mileage is predicted?

The salesperson answered her, "On average, twenty-one miles to a gallon."

Sacora made the turn into the car lot and parked. Joe got out and looked under the hood and was impressed with the condition. She handed the salesperson the keys and stood back and looked. She asked the price and if she could take it home today. The salesperson carried her to the financial manager.

Sacora was handed a list of different prices and information. She read through it and asked, "Is this the closing price, thirty-two thousand five hundred nineteen dollars?"

Financial manager said, "Yes, it is, and then the financing charge, plus gap insurance and etc."

Sacora said, "This is what I'm asking, how much do I write the check to purchase the van now?"

The financial manager looked at her and handed her another paper for her to read. "This is the amount of check." Sacora took the checkbook out and wrote the check. The salesperson looked at the financial manager when he spoke, "I will call the bank and confirm payment. I will be back, and you can wait here."

Sacora went to where Joe was standing by his truck. She said, "I have bought it but don't know how I'm getting my Bug and van home."

Joe said, "I will follow you home in the Bug and will pick you up in my truck. I can bring you back when they have it ready for release tonight. If this is okay with you."

Sacora agreed. The salesperson came to where they were standing and said, "The check cleared, and we will have everything ready in one hour."

Sacora said, "We will be back then." Joe left in his truck and Sacora in her Bug. They both made it to the driveway, Sacora parking her Bug. Sacora got out, and Joe got out and opened the passenger door. Sacora climbed in and said, "Thank you. This is very sweet of you to take me."

Joe said, "No problem, it is on my way home. If you will, text me and let me know when you are home and settled in." She agreed and said goodbye.

At the car lot, all papers were ready to sign, and Sacora started driving the van home and remembered to stop for groceries. The back seat was perfect for Eeyore's dog food and her other bags.

As she said she would, she text Joe, and he responded with good night. Sacora carried in the bags to the kitchen. She looked for Eeyore, and she came on the porch ready to see her.

Sacora poured out some dog food and opened a can of Pedigree. Eeyore ate it quickly and then lay on the kitchen floor, only moving once to the water bowl.

Sacora decided to call it a day and started gathering her things for work tomorrow. Still wondering if inspection would be soon, she could and would take care of that next.

Chapter Seventeen

Today was another beautiful day of sun and cooler temperatures. Sacora was up and looking for Eeyore to open the front door. Eeyore went out, and Sacora put more dog food on the porch for her and a water bowl. She looked in the driveway and looked at the red van, thinking about how much her life had changed within just a few weeks.

The Fourth of July was this week, and she had planned on a celebration with her friends this weekend. Still a few more days that she could talk to her parents. Julie should be calling within a few days, returning home from her research on a case.

Sacora put her thoughts aside and finished getting ready for work. She cooked some french toast and coffee, slowing down to enjoy it before heading out to the office. She drove the Bug and made it to the office with plenty of time to enjoy the gorgeous weather.

In the office, Mr. Hamilton came to her and said that inspection would be two weeks from Monday. This would give her days to finish on things she thought she would accomplish before inspection and after the Fourth of July celebration. One of the first projects would be finished, the painting of the upstairs bathroom and finishing the finessing of the bedroom.

Sacora, finishing her day, stopped by the hardware store. She bought some paint brushes for the paint that was still in the bathroom. She also purchased a doghouse for the back porch, which Eeyore would need while outside on the days she was working.

Sacora, remembering she was driving the Bug, told the clerk that she would be back to get the doghouse. Behind her was a voice that said, "Sacora, I can put it in my truck and take it to your home after I finish my next service call."

Sacora turned around, smiled at Joe, and answered, "Yes, that would be nice."

Joe put the doghouse in his truck and said, "I will see you later." Sacora told him thank you and bye and headed home. She went through the drive-through at McDonald's for her quick supper. She ate on her way home. Her plans were to finish painting in the bathroom tonight.

Just as she got home, Eeyore was waiting by the front door and wagging her tail. Sacora could see she was beginning to gain some of her weight back and having some energy. Her ribs were not showing like they were the first day she had come to live with her. The first thing was to give Eeyore some dog food, and she changed clothes to paint in.

Sacora gathered all the brushes and headed to the stairs, Eeyore following her. She picked up the radio to turn on while she painted the baseboards, sitting on the floor. She had just got started when the radio disc jockey announced, "This is a new group from Russellville, Alabama, Backroad 48." From the first sound of the piano, Sacora's attention had went straight to the music. Stopping her painting, just listening to the music and lyrics, Sacora related to the words of "He's Never in Love." The second verse was what got her attention the most.

There was a time I wouldn't believe, he would touch someone else married to me.
I was the last to know he's a womanizer, I discovered on his phone he's such a liar.
(Chorus) Girl he's telling lies to you, and you are wearing a face of a fool.
And your best ain't ever gonna be good enough, he's never in love.

This was what Joe was saying about Barton and his ex-wife. Some people are never in love, no matter how much love they are given. Sacora's heart suddenly felt so much peace realizing that Barton's relationship ending with her was not her decision. That was when the disc jockey announced another song from their CD, *It Wouldn't Me*. And this song definitely said it all, "It wouldn't me that said you could end our love." The radio played all the songs from the CD titled *Your Dog Stays with Me*. Sacora was a fan after hearing all the songs. The love song "Talk to Me" was also a favorite. By the time she had finished the painting of the baseboards, all the songs from the CD had played. She turned off the radio and looked at Eeyore and said, "We are finished. Let's go downstairs and wait on Joe."

After a few minutes downstairs in the kitchen, Sacora heard the loud music of Foo Fighters and knew Joe was here with the doghouse.

Chapter Eighteen

Sacora went to the front door to greet Joe. He went to the back of his truck and asked, "Where would the beautiful ladies like me to set this?"

Sacora answered, "I would like for it to be on the back porch."

Joe smiled and said, "Yes, ma'am."

Joe drove his truck to the back porch and set the doghouse up where Sacora had wanted it to be. He looked at Eeyore and said, "Is this okay with you?" He gave her a few pats on the head and then looked at Sacora as he spoke, "I will be heading on home now."

Sacora asked, "What do I owe you, Joe?"

Joe answered, "Not a thing. I was already this way with a service call. No problem at all."

Sacora smiled and said, "Do you have plans for Saturday? I am having a small gathering at four o'clock with some friends for a Fourth of July celebration. I would love for you to come."

Joe nodded and said, "Yes, I would love to. See you then."

Sacora smiled, nodded, and waved goodbye before she went in through the back door. Eeyore didn't pay attention to the doghouse and followed Sacora through the back door.

In the living room, Sacora sat down to think about Saturday, and Eeyore sat on the blanket close to Sacora. Just as she was making a list of what she would need, she had a call from Julie.

Sacora said, "Hello. Are you back in town?"

Julie said, "Yes, I am, and ready for the weekend. Are you still having a Fourth of July celebration?"

Sacora answered, "Yes, I am. And I am ready to see you."

Julie said, "I have just a few more things to do at my office for this case, and then I will be ready for Saturday. I think I will try to be there around two to help with what I can do to help."

"That sounds great, and I will see you then," Sacora said smiling.

The week went on with Sacora getting her home ready for the inspection and her gathering on Saturday. Her thoughts were going round and round for all the changes in her life. She drove the van on Friday so she could buy new decorations and groceries for her Fourth of July celebration.

At home finally on Friday afternoon, she started putting the new decorations on the back porch with table and a few chairs. She decided to wait until in the morning to decorate the table. Reaching a point of stopping with getting ready for tomorrow, she fed Eeyore more canned Pedigree and took a long, hot bath. Eeyore was waiting for bedtime too. Sacora went to sleep quick, and so did Eeyore.

All at once, Sacora opened her eyes to the sunshine shining through the window. Up and out, dressed and ready to work on the other decorations. Sacora drank her coffee and ate some toast while thinking about the front porch decorations. She did put the table-cloth on the back porch table and the arrangement for centerpiece with more decorations on the railings. On the front porch, she put some banners of flag prints on the railings.

Julie came at fifteen minutes before two. She looked around and said, "I think you have everything decorated nicely."

Sacora said, "Thank you. I was hoping you would help me cook the hot dogs and hamburgers."

Julie said, "Sure. Where do we start?"

Sacora answered, "In the refrigerator I have everything."

Julie and Sacora started cooking the meats and then put all the buns, ketchup, mustard, mayonnaise, pickles, cheese, tomatoes, onions, lettuce, and silverware on the table on the back porch. Sacora and Julie had everything under control just like they always had. Sacora took the boiled hot dogs and put them in the oven to roast to give them extra flavor. Four o'clock was getting close.

Sacora left Julie for a few minutes to shower and change into some shorts and her favorite red-white-and-blue T-shirt. Anxious to know if Joe McCarley would actually come, she decided not to say anything to Julie about him.

Chapter Nineteen

All the food was ready, prepared for the Fourth of July celebration with Sacora and her guests. Julie being with her was such a joy. The hamburgers were the last to be placed on the flag-printed platter and set on the tablecloth. All at once, Julie said, "What is that loud music?" Sacora's heart and stomach fluttered. Joe was here.

Sacora attempted to act calm and spoke to Julie, "That is Joe McCarley, and his favorite music Foo Fighters."

Sacora then noticed he had parked in the driveway. She went to the front door and motioned for him to come inside and walk through the house to the back porch. He looked around and said, "This is nice, and the food smells great." It wasn't too much longer that all the guests she had expected were gathered laughing and enjoying the celebration of Fourth of July.

Julie looked at Sacora, "Do you know who he is?"

Sacora said, "Yeah, he's my friend Joe McCarley that fixes all my broken things."

Julie nodded and spoke again, "He is Joseph McCarley. Played college football with the Florida Gators and went pro with Miami Dolphins. That is where he got hurt, total knee replacement, but still couldn't return to football. And I will tell you one thing more, Sacora, he could be fixing your broken heart. I see the way he looks at you. Bam, girl, go get him."

Sacora spoke, looking at Eeyore, "Julie, it is too soon after Barton. I don't think I could trust my heart right now. I'm starting a new life, new home, new dog, and maybe fostering children that needs me and I definitely need them."

Julie said, "Look at me, Sacora, this is me. You can have all these things and Joe. Barton treated you terrible, and you kept on loving him. This is a great guy, never heard anything bad on him even when he played football for the Dolphins. You can't compare a great guy to scum."

Sacora smiled. "Yes, you know what is on my mind without me telling you. I would love to have a family but gave up on that thought a long time ago. I will just let it be friends right now. I do need someone to help me with this house, and it seems he is always dependable. But, Julie, if it is to come to more, you will be the first to know."

Julie said, "Yes, ma'am, I will hold you to that."

Julie's mom came through the door and asked, "Where are my girls?"

They both went to her and started talking when Joe came in. Sacora introduced him to her, and they all started small talking. Julie said, "It is time to start our celebration."

Julie waited to everyone was assembled around and sang the national anthem. Sacora's uncle Owen said the blessing, praying for Sacora's parents also to have a safe trip home. Eight o'clock, and everyone was leaving for the fireworks show in Mobile.

Joe said, "Sacora, you had a nice Fourth of July celebration. Thank you for the invitation. The food and company was great. I am needing to get home early. I have a large job scheduled for in the morning first thing, so I'm calling it a day. It is nice meeting you, Julie."

Julie looked at Joe. "It is nice meeting you. And you taking care of our Sacora is greatly appreciated."

Joe said, "It is my pleasure."

As Joe walked away with his limp, for the first time Sacora didn't wonder why. And yes, it had been a great day. After cleaning up and finding a place for the new decorations in the closets, Julie and her mom were the last to leave.

Sacora petted Eeyore and said, "It has been an awesome day, and you have a full stomach from all the leftovers. Let's call it a day too."

Sacora had settled Eeyore down for the night and started thinking about Julie's advice before she fell asleep. Could she start completely over? Could she have some chance at having a true love relationship with Joe? Was it too soon? Sacora's last question in her thoughts, "Is Julie right? Does he look at me different?" She fell asleep not answering any of these questions.

Chapter Twenty

Sacora woke to a beautiful day of sun shining in her eyes. First thing of finding Eeyore and opening the door for her, she then sipped on hot coffee. Looking at the kitchen water faucet and thinking about Joe, Sacora started asking the questions again to herself. Sunday morning had been such a beautiful morning to awake to. She went outside to sit on the front porch. She was thinking about the sound of Joe coming toward the house with Foo Fighters music in the driveway and how much her life was changing. Julie was never wrong in the past about her opinions of people in Sacora's life.

Sacora changed her thoughts, looking toward the barn and wondering what her grandparents had thought about putting in it when they built it. It seemed like it was designed for something other than cattle. She decided to take a walk and look again at the unique design. Her intentions were to take her mind off Joe McCarley.

Eeyore had followed her, walking beside Sacora. Sacora went in, and looking around, it seemed to hit her that this might have been designed for sheep. It looked like a place to sit the lambs on the table for shearing. Sacora decided she didn't know anything about sheep other than what she had seen on TV.

Sacora and Eeyore went back to the house, and she fixed hamburgers from the leftovers of yesterday's celebration. Eeyore was excited to eat some more leftovers. Ice cream was still in the freezer, and Sacora was finishing it when her cell phone rang. It was Julie.

Sacora answered, "Hello, what are you doing today?"

Julie replied, "I am going to the beach. You want to go?"

Sacora said, "Yes, I do!"

Julie said, "Okay, would you like to meet me at my place and we will go from here?"

Sacora said, "I will be there as soon as I can."

Julie said, "I will see you then."

Sacora showered and dressed in denim shorts over her swimsuit and a halter swim top with plenty of sunblock. She met Julie with a smile, and the girls started on their afternoon at the beach. The swim in the ocean and the warm sun was relaxing. The laughter and visit with Julie was an overtime break due. The girls went to get a burger and fries when Sacora saw in the window of Generous Hearts Thrift Store two cribs with linens and quilts. It took a minute for her to comment to Julie.

Sacora spoke excitedly, "Julie, let's go in here and look at these cribs. They are so beautiful. I will need cribs already set up for Aylassa when the inspection is done."

Julie said, "Yes, they are beautiful."

Sacora went in and asked about the price of everything, cribs and linens. The price was very reasonable, and Sacora decided to buy both of them and then decide which one to return. The saleswoman gave her information to bring it back with the receipt of the one she decided not to keep.

Sacora's next question was how she was going to get them home. Julie said, "I know a good-looking man with a truck. Just give him a call or text."

Sacora said, "I'd rather not, Julie. He has already done so much for me."

Julie grabbed Sacora's phone and went outside to call Joe. When Joe answered, Julie told him it was her, not Sacora, and that Sacora needed help with moving two cribs from the thrift store to home. Joe said he knew where they were and would be there in an hour or so. Julie said she could take the linens and quilts in her car.

Sacora and Julie went to eat while waiting on Joe. Sacora was anxious of getting the cribs set up for inspection and seeing Joe again. Julie could see her anxiety and attempted to change the subject of waiting on Joe with her conversation of the barn and the plans Sacora might have for it.

Joe came as he had predicted an hour later, and the girls went to meet him. In the store, Sacora used her debit card, and the saleswoman had bagged all the linens and quilts and handed them to her and Julie. Joe was looking at the cribs and disassembled them to fit in his truck without any kind of damage.

Julie said, "Sacora, you will have to ride with Joe. I don't have room with the quilts and linens."

Sacora looked at her and whispered, "Sure, that was your plan all along."

Chapter Twenty-One

J oe had the cribs firmly attached in the bed of his truck and asked Sacora, "Are you ready?"

Sacora climbed into the passenger seat, and Julie was grinning when she placed the remaining bags in her car. The ride home with Joe was pleasant, and he turned the Foo Fighters on with "There Goes My Hero." Sacora had actually began to enjoy their music.

At home, Eeyore met Sacora, and she was ready to go in the house. Sacora turned off the alarm and unlocked the door. Eeyore went in first and then Sacora and Joe. Sacora showed Joe where she wanted the cribs in the bedroom next to hers. Sacora said, "I will go back and get the chest of the crib I decide to keep. I do like them both."

Joe said, "Just give me a call and I will meet you there."

Julie came in with the quilts and lines. Sacora took them and went to the laundry room and started the washer. Julie went to look in the bedroom and said to Sacora, "Good decision. These look good in here."

Sacora pointed to a corner and said, "I will put the matching chest there."

Julie said, "It will be nice for Aylassa."

Sacora said, "I thank you, Joe. I'm thinking inspection will be sometime this week, and this is the last thing on my list. I will text you on what I'm keeping and the chest I will need."

"Sacora, just let me know. This week I will be working in the area, and the hardware store is where I will be buying my supplies. It won't be out of the way."

Sacora smiled a huge smile at Julie and whispered, "Thank you."

Joe stood up and looked at the girls and said, "They seem to be sturdy enough for a toddler. I have secured both of them, but it won't be any trouble to disassemble and take back to the store the one you want to return. I will be on my way. I will be looking for the text or call."

Sacora said, "Thank you. I will let you know what I decide to keep and purchase the matching chest."

After Joe left with the music of Foo Fighters playing loud, Julie said to Sacora, "He is a nice guy. And yes, this was some bother for him to do."

Sacora said, "I will make sure Eeyore is all right, and then we will make it to your place for me to get my Bug. And yes, I'm avoiding your discussion. It was nice of him to bring the cribs to me and offer to bring the matching chest one day next week."

On the way to Julie's, Sacora did smile a lot and laughed with Julie about everything. It was such a break from getting ready for the inspection. Sacora told her good night and started home. Good thoughts were on Sacora's mind and a happy smile on her face. When she made it through the door, Eeyore was ready to call it a day. Sacora made her regular routine of getting ready for Monday. She slept well with the list for inspection completed.

Monday morning was another beautiful sunny day. Sacora went outside on the porch to sip on her coffee and think about all the changes just in a few weeks. She took care of Eeyore and dressed quickly after her long, hot bath. She made good time for McDonald's breakfast. Butterflies in her stomach, the breakfast tasted good, and it seemed to settle her nerves.

At the office, Mr. Hamilton smiling asked Sacora, "Are you ready for inspection? It is scheduled for this afternoon if that is okay with you?"

Sacora smiled and said, "Yes, what time?"

Mr. Hamilton said, "Today at two, and I will arrange for you to leave at lunchtime."

Sacora smiled and said, "Thank you. It will be great to leave after lunch. I should have everything ready."

Sacora finished her emails and told Mr. Hamilton she was leaving. Sacora never thought about her coworkers telling her good luck and showing so much support and encouragement as they did when she left.

Chapter Twenty-Two

Sacora stopped at Burger King and enjoyed lunch, making a plan for the last details of her home before the inspection. She was finishing when she got a call from Julie.

Sacora answered, "Hello. What's up in your world?"

Julie giggled and said, "Not much, just had a moment to ask you if you had heard from human resources today about the inspection?"

Sacora said, "Yes, it is today at two o'clock. I'm headed home now."

Julie holding a subpoena with a motion in her hand about Barton's next dirty move decided to keep it to herself until after the inspection was over. She had a few days before Sacora would be served. The motion was for Sacora to release her percentage of Barton's trust left from his grandmother. Julie would object to this motion and hoping the judge would also.

Julie said, "I think you are ready and good luck with getting what you want. I would love to hear about it. Call me when you can."

Sacora said, "Thank you for your support and encouragement Julie. I'm nervous about it but ready. I will talk to you this afternoon. Goodbye."

Sacora turned off the alarm and unlocked the door. Eeyore came to the porch and went inside. Sacora poured out her some Pedigree food and looked around while she was eating. She decided to put some Pine-Sol in the toilets for a clean smell. Everything else was still clean and looked pleasant. Two o'clock was long, drawn-out minutes anyway.

The human resources representatives of Baldwin County were punctual, and Sacora answered the door with a smile. The ladies introduced themselves, Rhonda Hines and Lisa Gilbert. The tour of Sacora's home had begun. The ladies were carrying notebooks and pens and began recording immediately, beginning with the porch. Within forty-five minutes or so, the summary of their visit/inspection was read to Sacora.

The living room is nicely arranged for toddlers and the older children, large enough for playing. The kitchen appears to be safe with adequate cleanness. The dining room is furnished with plenty of room for the children. The bedrooms are furnished for children with safe and clean quilts and linens. Cribs are found to be safe for the toddler. The bathrooms are clean and sanitized for the safety of children with compatible supplies for a toddler.

Sacora smiled, and Ms. Rhonda Hines said, "We need an authentic form from your veterinarian, stating that your dog has had all updated shots, rabies, and etc. Also the form needs to state that flea and tick prevention is being used to eliminate infestation of any kind while in presence of the children."

Sacora answered, "Yes, ma'am. I can take care of this immediately. Maybe today before five o'clock."

Ms. Gilbert said, "When you have the form, scan it, email it to us, and we will keep it on file. The follow-up visits instructed from your veterinarian can be submitted the same way."

The ladies left with a pleasant attitude and also said, "Congratulations."

Sacora called Eeyore to her. "Did you hear that? We have passed our inspection. Now to get you to the veterinarian before he closes today."

Eeyore climbed into the Bug, and Sacora started out to the veterinarian's clinic. Eeyore was very cooperative with the examination and shots. Within minutes, she had the form ready to email to Baldwin County in the morning. Sacora told the staff thanks and made it back to the Bug with Eeyore, not minding the rabies tag jingling from her collar.

Sacora called Julie. She was beginning to leave a message when Julie called her. Julie spoke first, "How did it go?"

Sacora said, "It went fine. I passed inspection and have a form they needed on Eeyore. I should hear at the end of this week what happens next."

Julie said, "Congratulations. I hope everything goes well, Sacora. You have always wanted children."

Sacora answered, "Thank you, Julie. Yes, I have, and maybe it will work out for us, me and the children. I will go now, Julie, and will talk to you later."

Julie said, "Bye. I will see you as soon as I can."

Chapter Twenty-Three

S acora went through her night with butterflies in her stomach. She gave Eeyore more Pedigree and started fixing herself some soup. She didn't think it would be wise if she ate heavy or a lot tonight. Inspection was over. Everything so far was good. She would tell Joe what she decided on the returning of the crib and what chest she would be bringing home. Saturday morning, she would go to the thrift store and make arrangements for what she would decide.

Sacora slept restless and was awake before the clock. She stopped by the bedroom and looked at the cribs again before letting Eeyore out. She still couldn't decide. Even though she needed one, she liked them both. Alisha will have the room of her mom's, and Elijah would be across the hall. Their arrangements were finished. No more planning. Sacora was ready for work and sipping on coffee. She was thinking, "What next?"

At the office, Mr. Hamilton was smiling. He said, "Sacora, I have been informed the inspection went well. All your medical requirements were taken from the file of your employment. All the file is lacking is the form from the veterinarian on your dog."

Sacora answered, "I have it to email. I will take care of that sometime today."

Mr. Hamilton smiled and said, "Great. I have the other documents you were needing for the elderly couple in the nursing home."

Sacora said, "Yes, I will send them this morning."

The office was quiet today with everyone busy. Mr. Hamilton broke the silence when he came to Sacora's desk and said, "Baldwin County's HR wants to know if they can bring the children here on Friday to you. This will give you the weekend to settle them in, and

Monday you can have the day off so we can arrange for day care until school starts."

Sacora said, "That will be great. I can use the time for them to get to know me. I am hoping it will work out for us."

Mr. Hamilton said, "I think it will, and so does Baldwin County's human resources. I will respond with approval to bring the children here on Friday."

Sacora went on working on the case she needed to have finished by Friday. This postponed her anxiety on the children coming until later. She decided to go to the local Walmart and purchase a car seat and pull-ups for Aylassa on her way home.

Finally five o'clock, and Sacora went about her business at Walmart. And again, she could not decide on a car seat, not knowing the weight of Aylassa. She bought two, one with larger weight and the other smaller. She would put these in her van tomorrow after work. She had bought more soup for her supper tonight and was ready to call it a day.

Sacora was home. Ready to see her, Eeyore was waiting on the porch. Eeyore ate dog food, and Sacora settled in with her soup and turned on the TV. Sacora was thinking about her parents and how she was looking forward to their visit in Africa being over.

Julie called. Sacora answered, "Hello, Julie. What's going on?"

Julie answered Sacora with bluntness, "Sacora, I have a copy of the motion that Barton is sending you. I think you will be served by Thursday. It is requesting that you waive all of the rights you have on his inheritance of his grandmother's trust account/fund. This will be released to Barton on or before his forty-fifth birthday. I had not known about this or I would have included it in the divorce settlement."

Sacora said, "Julie, I did not know about it either. We will just go with what we know and see what comes next. He is selfish, and with Rachel helping his ideas, I don't know what will be next."

Julie said, "I agree. I will take care of responding to the motion, and we will see what the opposing attorney rebuttals."

Sacora said, "Okay, Julie. I know you will do the right thing."

Julie said, "Goodbye, and I will keep in touch. Let me know when you are served so that I can send in my response."

Sacora said, "I will, Julie, and good night."

Sacora sat musing thoughts of just what money it might have in the balance of this trust fund for Barton wanting to file a motion on. Sacora went back on finishing her night and getting ready for tomorrow's list of things to do. The night of sleep was extremely restless.

Chapter Twenty-Four

J ulie had predicted that Sacora would be served on Thursday. The first thing on Thursday morning, a young woman had come to the front of the office with the summons. Sacora showed her identification and carried the documents to her desk to read some of the motion. It was requesting that Sacora release her interest in Barton's trust fund left from his grandmother. Julie had already informed her of her intentions.

Sacora called Julie and left a message that she had been served. Sacora assumed she was in court and would hear from her sometime around lunch. She went back to her cases preparing the paperwork for Mr. Hamilton to review and sign. When she carried them to Mr. Hamilton, he was smiling and spoke with encouragement. "Sacora, Baldwin County Human Resources will be here with the Malone children tomorrow after lunch, approximately one o'clock. I think you should be finished and will be able to take them home and start making your adjustments. Monday, we will have arranged day care for them starting on Tuesday, until school starts in August."

Sacora was smiling in return. "Yes, this will be great."

Julie called her at lunch as she thought. Sacora answered immediately. They discussed the issue, and Julie finished the conservation with, "I will have a response to the opposing attorney on Monday." Sacora finished her lunch and went back to her desk. She had a few minutes to think about her preparations for tomorrow. She had both car seats in the van ready for Aylassa and pull-ups. If she needed anything else, it would be their first trip to Walmart. She had bought groceries last night for cooking suppers/dinners. She wasn't sure what their favorite meals were but had a start until she was given the opportunity to ask.

Anxiety was making an appearance tonight as she was leaving work. This would be her last night of an empty home. Sacora decided to eat out with Julie and take her mind off the situation that was making her so anxious. Julie could always handle the conversations to make her anxiety go away. She needed to be calm and think tomorrow.

Sacora said goodbye to Julie and went home. Eeyore was waiting for her food and attention. Sacora fed her and talked to her for a while and then went to put a bag in the van of what she thought she would need tomorrow for the children in case she needed to visit Walmart before going home.

Another restless night of anxiety and little sleep, Sacora was up before the clock and started her day. She had her coffee on the front porch knowing that this was the last morning of being alone. Ready for work and to McDonald's drive-through, she was at work a little earlier. Sacora finished her paperwork and decided not to go to lunch until she had the children.

It was a long morning, and then one o'clock came with the sound of Ms. Rhonda Hines talking to children. Sacora could hear their sweet voices answering her. Mr. Hamilton came to the front and greeted Ms. Hines. To his surprise, there were two more children than expected. Ms. Hines introduced the children. "This is Elijah, Alisha, and Aylassa Malone. This is Jeremiah and Sadie Walters." Ms. Hines looked at Sacora and said, "As of today, we have needed to relocate Jeremiah and Sadie. I know you have the space and furnishings for them. Will you please also foster them?"

Sacora answered, "Yes, I will. I do not know anything about them, but I can give it a try."

Ms. Hines said, "I have the paperwork, and Mr. Hamilton and I will take care of everything. We will fill you in on needed information on Tuesday when you return to the office."

Sacora said, "I will be ready to discuss it after the weekend with them." Sacora looked at the children and spoke affectionately, "I am Sacora Hill, and you will be staying with me for a while. My van is this way. Do you like Walmart? We need to get some things for Sadie and Jeremiah. Looks like Aylassa, Alisha, and Elijah have what they need for the weekend, but you might see something you would like to have."

Sacora could tell the children were as anxious as she was but attempted to stay focus on what needed to be taken care of. She instructed the older children to buckle up, and Aylassa was buckled up in the larger car seat, and Sadie, the smaller one. She looked in the reviewer mirror and thought five children, "Now, today, all at once?"

Chapter Twenty-Five

S acora made it to Walmart more calm than she would have ever thought. She looked at Alisha, Jeremiah, and Elijah and spoke firmly, "I will get Aylassa out first and then Sadie. Alisha, will you hold Aylassa's hand while I get Sadie?"

The boys were strangers but did stand by Alisha and Aylassa. Sacora put Sadie on her hip and took Aylassa's other hand. She looked at Sadie and asked, "How old are you? Jeremiah, how old are you?"

Sadie answered first, "My am two years old."

Jeremiah answered, "I am eight. I will be starting the third grade in a few weeks."

Elijah spoke, "I will be going to the fourth grade this school year. I am nine years old."

Alisha added, "I am six years old, and I will be in the first grade in a few days."

Sacora asked, "Do you like shopping for school clothes and supplies?"

Alisha answered, "I love it. My thing is shoes, I love shoes."

Aylassa said, "I am tree. I don't go to big girl school with Alisha yet."

Sacora said, "We will go in Walmart and find what we need for the weekend. Jeremiah, you and Sadie need some clothes, and we need to get snacks and meals of what you like."

Jeremiah answered, "Yes, ma'am. I like anything, but Sadie wants to eat only macaroni and cheese."

Sadie said, "My like macaroni and cheese."

Sacora put Sadie in the seat of the cart and Aylassa in the basket. She got another cart for the items she would be buying, and the boys agreed to push it for her. In the boys' section, Sacora asked Jeremiah, "Do you know what size underwear and pants you wear?"

Jeremiah answered, "Yes, ma'am. I need size eight underwear and pants and size ten in shirts for the length. I like the shorts and shirts on the five-dollar table."

Sacora smiled and said, "Let's go look and see what we can find to take care of this weekend."

Jeremiah chose matching shorts and shirts with Sacora and added a comment, "These match my shoes too. I like neon colors with black."

Sacora said, "Sadie needs diapers and clothes too. Do you know what size for her?"

Jeremiah answered, "Uncle Luke bought this size for her in diapers, and in clothes, he bought her size two toddlers."

Sacora said, "Okay, let's look at this table of three dollars for pants and shirts."

Sacora picked up an outfit, and Sadie said, "My like red."

Sacora was amused with her liking the same color as she did and a two-year-old recognizing the color red in clothes. Sacora thought, "What else do we need?"

They went to the grocery section, and this was the first time Elijah spoke. "I would like to have fish sticks and tartar sauce."

Aylassa said, "Yes, I would like that too."

Alisha said, "I like pizza and pot pies."

Sacora said, "Sounds good, and we will buy this and macaroni and cheese for Sadie. Jeremiah, is this okay with you, or would you like something else?"

Jeremiah said, "Yes, ma'am, everything is my favorites too."

Sacora started putting things in the cart when she got a text from Joe about returning the crib and purchasing the matching chest of the crib she decided to keep, the first time today she had actually thought about it.

She text him back with, "*I am keeping both cribs and purchasing both of the matching chests. I have two toddlers now.*"

Joe text, "*Okay, I will be in touch tomorrow.*"

Sacora responded, "*I will go to the thrift store right after I leave Walmart. I will purchase them and will be ready to pick up. Thank you!*"

Sacora looked at the children and asked, "Everybody ready to go? Do you have what you need for a few days?"

The children saw the ice cream freezer, and Aylassa asked for ice cream sandwiches. Sacora put them in the cart, and Elijah pointed to a gallon of different flavors. This was added in, and then everyone was ready to go.

Chapter Twenty-Six

Sacora checked out and paid the two hundred sixty dollars and started out the door. Jeremiah took her hand and pulled it to get her attention.

Jeremiah spoke so sincerely, "Thank you, ma'am. I'm very grateful for what you bought me and Sadie."

Sacora answered, "You are welcome. Will you help me put this in the van in the back?"

Elijah said, "I can help too." And he did. The two boys acted like gentlemen, and Sacora smiled with accomplishment. This was finished.

She told the children to buckle up, and she put the toddlers in their car seats. She started to leave when she got a call from Julie.

Sacora said, "Hello, Julie. I am leaving Walmart and headed to the thrift store."

Julie asked, "did you get your children today?"

Sacora answered, "Yes, I did, and I will introduce them to you soon."

Julie said, "I am anxious. Congratulations on finally having a family, and I will try to see you tomorrow."

Sacora said, "I will be looking for you, bye."

Julie said, "Bye, little Mommy." She giggled before ending the phone call, and Sacora also laughed some.

At the thrift store, Sacora put Sadie on her hip and held Aylassa's hand. Alisha followed close by, and the boys were behind Alisha. Sacora went in and paid for the matching chests and a matching rocker for the girls' room. Sacora also bought a PlayStation 3 and games for Alisha and the boys. She left Joe McCarley's name on the Sold label to be picked up tomorrow.

Sacora went through the routine again of buckling the children in the van and headed home. She asked the children what they wanted to eat tonight. Sadie said, "My wike macaroni and cheese."

Aylassa and Alisha said, "I want pizza."

The boys agreed with Aylassa and Alisha, and Sacora said, "All right, that is what I will be cooking."

When Sacora pulled in the driveway, the boys' eyes were wide with excitement. The barn was commented on as awesome. Elijah asked, "Can we play there?"

Sacora said, "Yes, only when I am there with you."

When she parked at the house, Alisha said, "You have a beautiful home."

Sacora said, "Thank you. It is your home too."

Alisha said, "Only for a while, and then I will have another one."

Sacora's heart felt touched how this little girl had gone through so much since her mother passed.

Sacora got out, and the older children went to the porch waiting on her. She put Aylassa and Sadie on the porch and turned off the alarm and unlocked the front door. When Sacora motioned for them to come in, they followed, and the children were looking around the living room. Jeremiah spotted the TV first and asked if they could watch TV while she cooked the pizza. Sacora said, "Sure."

Sadie and Aylassa went to the kitchen with her. All of a sudden, Sacora remembered Eeyore had not met her on the front porch and went to the back porch to call her. Eeyore came to her ready to eat. Sacora opened a can of Pedigree and put it in her bowl.

Aylassa was first to Eeyore and asked, "Can I pet the doggie?"

Sacora said, "Yes, you can. Wait until she eats. She is hungry."

Sadie said, "My not right now."

Aylassa stayed at distance until Eeyore had finished eating, and Eeyore took to her immediately. Elijah and Jeremiah heard Eeyore barking and came running into the kitchen excited to see a dog.

Elijah asked, "We have a dog too?"

Jeremiah asked, "Can we take her to the barn to play?"

Sacora said, "You can, but I have to go too. The pizza is almost ready. Come with me, and I will show you the bathroom downstairs for you to wash your hands."

The children washed their hands, and Sacora got antibacterial wipes to clean Aylassa's and Sadie's faces and hands. The girls made faces but was ready to eat. The children went to the dining room table, and Sacora put pizza on their plates.

Chapter Twenty-Seven

After the children had eaten, Sacora realized she had not eaten since breakfast. She decided to eat soup, something light. She was heating up her soup, and the children went to the living room watching TV, the Disney channel. Sadie came back to the kitchen and said, "My wike macaroni and cheese, please."

Sacora said, "I will fix you some. Would you like to sit down with me when I eat my soup?"

Sadie said, "Yep, my will eat mine macaroni and cheese."

Sacora carried her soup and crackers to the dining room and put Sadie in a chair by her with her macaroni and cheese.

Sadie was talking again about Wuke. Sacora could not understand most of it but did figure out she was wondering what he was eating. Jeremiah came into the dining room to check on Sadie. Sacora asked Jeremiah, "Who is Luke that Sadie keeps talking about?"

Jeremiah answered, "He is our uncle." That was all he would say and returned to the living room.

Sacora asked Aylassa and Sadie if they were ready for a bath and pajamas. Alisha said that she was too, so Sacora put the girls in the bathroom and gave them toothbrushes and started the bathtub water. Sacora had to pay close attention to the temperature of the water, not too hot. The girls participated and were so pleasant that it did not take long before they were in their pajamas. The boys wanted to finish the Disney show they were watching before they called it a day.

After the show had finished, Sacora had told them, "Go get your Walmart bags, Jeremiah, and your bag, Elijah, and go with me upstairs to the bathroom." The boys did, and Sacora showed them how to work the shower and the sink faucet to brush their teeth. Sacora said, "I will be back to check on you soon. Call me if you need me before then."

Jeremiah said, "Yes, ma'am, I will."

Sacora left and could hear both shower and sink faucet going. Alisha was sitting on the couch watching another Disney show, and Sadie was falling to sleep beside her. Sacora picked Sadie up and rocked her some in the recliner, singing "Grandma's Lullaby." She went to the girls' room and put Sadie in her crib. This was when she realized that she had seen this baby before. This was the two-year-old she had seen in her office on the first days of her employment with the human resources. Sadie had a cast on her arm, and Jeremiah had a broken nose. Sacora whispered low and soft, "You are safe now, baby. You will be as long as you are with me."

When Sacora returned to the living room, Aylassa was barely holding her eyes open. Sacora asked if she would like to rock some before she went to her crib. Aylassa said, "Yeah, and I wanna hear that song again." Sacora sang "Grandma's Lullaby," and when she fell asleep, she put her in her crib.

Alisha asked Sacora, "May I please sit with you and watch my TV show?"

Sacora said, "Yes, you may."

Sacora was wondering where Alisha and Elijah were taught such politeness and manners but would ask later. Elijah called Sacora upstairs, and she went holding Alisha's hand. Sacora said, "This is your room, Alisha, and you will need to get your bag from downstairs and bring it in here."

When Alisha went downstairs to get her bag, Elijah asked her, "Where do I put my dirty clothes?" Sacora answered, "I will take them and, Jeremiah, give me yours and I will put them in the washing machine."

Alisha came up the stairs, and Sacora showed her to her bed. She turned back the covers with one hand, the boys' laundry in the other. Alisha said, "Wow, such a nice big bed. Do I have to share it with someone?"

Sacora kissed her cheek and said, "No, ma'am, this is for just you."

Alisha said, "All right then, good night."

Sacora said, "In the morning, you can put your things in the dresser too. It is yours also."

Alisha said, "No, thank you, Sacora. I won't be here long enough. I will just keep it in my backpack."

Sacora, puzzled, answered her, "Okay, see you in the morning. Good night."

Chapter Twenty-Eight

S acora closed the door, leaving a small crack for the hall light to shine through. Elijah and Jeremiah were ready to see their rooms. Dressed in pajamas, hair still wet, Sacora asked if they would like to use a hair dryer while she put their clothes in the washing machine.

Downstairs in the laundry room, she started the washing machine and went to the bathroom and gathered the girls' laundry. She put their clothes in the washing machine with regular laundry detergent. She could hear the hair dryer and started back up the stairs. Elijah was ready to see his room, and Sacora showed him. He had a similar reaction to his room as Alisha.

Elijah said, "Where is Jeremiah's bedroom? Is he not sharing with me?"

Sacora said, "No, he has a room to himself."

Sacora turned his covers back and said, "Hop in and sleep tight. In the morning, you can settle your things in the dresser. Good night, Elijah."

He said, "Good night."

Sacora left his door open with a small crack also. Jeremiah had come from the bathroom, and Sacora motioned for him to follow her to his bedroom. She opened the door and said, "This is your bed, and in the morning you can put the things I bought you in the dresser." Sacora turned back his covers and said, "Sleep tight, good night, and I will see you in the morning."

Jeremiah responded with, "Thank you. It is a nice bedroom, and I will put my things in the dresser before breakfast."

Sacora left his door opened some and started downstairs and checked on Alisha and the girls before going to run her bath.

Suddenly it all hit her, and she sat in the bathroom floor with a full-blown anxiety attack. Sacora spoke to herself, "What was I thinking? I have a house, five children that I am responsible for." Eeyore came quietly to her and licked her toes, and Sacora spoke softly, "And yes, a dog. A house, five precious children, and you, Eeyore."

Sacora pulled herself together and enjoyed her bath. Quietly she dressed and put her clothes in the laundry room, changing the children's clothes to the dryer. She checked on the babies again and put Eeyore's water bowl with fresh water and made way to her bed, under the covers with a sigh of relief. She thought, "I made it through my first day of being a mommy. This is a day I thought would never happen for one child, but today, I have five."

A troubled sleep at first, but the rest of the night, Sacora rested. The sun shining bright through her window, she awakened to a child crying. She came to her senses and realized it was Sadie. She went to her, and Sadie was sitting up in the crib.

Sadie said, "My wet the bed."

Aylassa said, "I didn't."

Sacora said, "I will change you, Sadie, and Aylassa, you can go potty."

Sacora took care of the girls and then carried them to her bedroom and sat them on the bed.

Sacora said, "I am going to my closet to change, and you sit here while I am getting dressed."

Sadie and Aylassa started jumping on the bed. Aylassa started a rhyme. Alisha came through the door and joined in with her.

Two little monkeys jumping on the bed, one fell off and the other one said, "Call the doctor," and the doctor said, "One more monkey jumping on the bed."

Sacora came from the closet dressed and started putting up her hair. Alisha jumped down from the bed and said, "Can I brush your hair and put it in a ponytail?"

Sacora smiled and said, "Yes, ma'am, you can."

Alisha put her hair in a very neat ponytail.

Sadie said, "My think you are georgous, Zora."

Aylassa asked Alisha, "Will you brush my hair?'

Alisha did and kissed her little cheek. Alisha said, looking at Aylassa, "My think you are georgous too."

Sacora said, "Thank you, my little ladies. Let's go see where the brothers are."

Chapter Twenty-Nine

S acora and the girls made it upstairs and found Jeremiah placing his clothes in the dresser as Sacora had requested him to. He smiled as she looked through the door. Jeremiah said, "I am almost finished finding a home for the things you bought me yesterday."

Sacora answered, "Great, we will think about breakfast."

Elijah came to them and said, "I have put my things in the dresser also. I'm hungry ready to eat breakfast."

Sacora asked, "What about pancakes? I have a variety of flavored syrups too."

The children all agreed to pancakes and went to the TV to watch the Disney station while Sacora cooked breakfast. Sacora opened the back door for Eeyore to go out, but this morning, Eeyore came back in instead of staying outside. After she had the table set and the platter of pancakes on the table, Sacora went to get Aylassa and Sadie to wash their hands and faces for breakfast. She instructed Alisha, Elijah, and Jeremiah to wash their hands and faces and sit at the table. Alisha was the first to take a seat and looked at the variety of syrups. When the toddlers were seated and the boys, Sacora asked, "What syrups would you like?"

Alisha decided on maple, and Sadie and Alyassa wanted Mrs. Butterworth's. Jeremiah's choice was strawberry, and Elijah wanted Log Cabin brand. The children's quietness while they were eating gave Sacora the idea of the manners they had been taught and was enjoying their company. Chocolate milk and orange juice were refilled a few times, and then the children's comments of wanting to go back to the TV gave Sacora the opportunity to clean the table. After the dishwasher was loaded and started, Sacora went to the laundry room and folded the children's clothes and put her clothes in the dryer. She started a load of towels and cloths and carried the children's clothes to them. Jeremiah and Elijah started up the stairs to put their clothes in their dressers, and Alisha said, "I will put mine in my backpack."

Sacora said, "Okay, here they are." Sacora and the children had started down the stairs when she heard loud Foo Fighters music. She went to the front door and unlocked it and waved at Joe McCarley. Behind his truck was another truck that Sacora did not recognize. The young man went to Joe's truck, and Sacora went also. Joe introduced him to her, "This is my longtime friend and football pal, Tyler Green."

Sacora said, "It's nice to meet you."

Tyler said, "I will be helping Joe today."

Sacora said, "Thank you, and this way." Sacora opened the door wider to the babies' room and pointed to where she wanted the rocker and the chests. Joe and Tyler had placed the rocker, and Tyler was programming the PlayStation to the TV. When he was finished, he handed Jeremiah and Elijah two bags of games. The thrift store had separated the games for ages, difficulty, and challenges. The children's reaction was, "WOW, look at all these games." Elijah, being the oldest, read each one's title. "*Little Big Planet 2, Skate 3, Ratchet and Clank, All 4 One, Kataman Forever, Eye Pet and Friends, Wonder Book*, and *Walking with Dinosaurs*."

Alisha said, "I like the *Eye Pet and Friends*. I would like to play that first."

Tyler put the game on program to start when Alisha started screaming, running up the stairs, "There is a squirrel in here!" Alisha started running, and so did the boys chasing it. Sacora was comforting Sadie and Aylassa from crying. Joe and Tyler were chasing the squirrel out the door. Sadie went to Joe and said, "My don't wike skuirrels."

Aylassa tugged at Joe's hand and said, "That skart me."

Joe picked up Aylassa and said, "That will be the last we will see of him. He didn't bring his toothbrush."

Sacora giggled and took Aylassa and Sadie to the kitchen for a snack while Alisha, Elijah, and Jeremiah were playing the PlayStation.

Joe and Tyler went outside to bring in the chests. Sacora showed them where she wanted the chests earlier. Sacora and Sadie were in the kitchen, and Aylassa carried Joe and Tyler a glass of lemonade. Alisha ran to them and said, "Aylassa, Sacora said to stop making lemonade until you can open the bottles of water and not get the water from the toilet."

Joe and Tyler immediately started spitting it out and poured it out on the grass. Joe picked up Aylassa and said, "Thank you, but I can wait until you can open bottled water."

Chapter Thirty

Sacora came outside to ask Joe and Tyler if they would like to stay for lunch. She was cooking hot dogs. Tyler said, "I have to get back to the hardware store, but thank you anyway."

Joe said, "I have another repair to do today, but I would have taken you up on your offer if I hadn't."

Sadie came to her room when Joe and Tyler had placed both chests, and Joe picked her up. Sadie said, "My wike it, Doe. My wike Zora rockin' too."

Joe said, "You have a rocker now. Rock on."

Joe put her down and went outside with Tyler. Sacora followed. Sacora told Tyler goodbye and thank you after Joe said goodbye and thank you.

Tyler was driving out of the driveway when Sacora asked Joe, "What do I owe you today?"

Joe said, "We are going to put it on your account on account you needed a truck and two men. My birthday is July thirtieth, and Tyler gave me two tickets for the Foo Fighters' concert in Mobile the second weekend of August. I would love for you to go."

Sacora said, "I would like that. I will need to plan a babysitter for the children's evening while we are gone."

Joe said, "I have the best ever. My Joy will be here this weekend, and she is the best with children."

Sacora said, "Sounds good. I will be in touch."

Joe said, "See you later."

Sacora watched Joe as he left and didn't go inside until she no longer could hear the music from his truck. Sacora was watching Sadie and Aylassa looking at the TV while Alisha and Jeremiah were playing *Eye Pet and Friends*. Elijah was patiently waiting a turn to play. Sacora said, "I am going to the kitchen to cook lunch, some hot dogs, and I will tell you when to wash your hands."

Alisha said, "Can I help? I will put things on the table when you tell me to."

Elijah said, "I will take your place with the game, Alisha, while you help Sacora."

Sacora and Alisha went to the kitchen, and cooking the hot dogs didn't take long. Alisha went to get Jeremiah and Elijah to wash their hands and be seated at the table. Sadie and Aylassa were seated, and Alisha said, "Can I say the blessing?" Sacora said, "Yes." Sacora was surprised and realized she should have been saying the blessing before the other meals.

Alisha started the prayer, and the boys joined in.

> *God is great, God is good, and we thank him for our food.*
> *By His hands, we all are fed. Give us, Lord, our daily bread.*
> *In Jesus's name, amen.*

Sacora asked Aylassa, Alisha, Elijah, and Jeremiah what they wanted on their hot dogs and handed it to them. When she asked Sadie what she wanted, she was surprised at her answer. Sadie said, "My wike the lellow and the red."

Sacora asked, "You want mustard and ketchup?"

Sadie said, "The lellow and red."

Sacora said, "Okay, here it is."

The children seemed to be enjoying the hot dogs, and Eeyore decided to join the meal with a hot dog or two. After lunch, Aylassa said, "I'm sleepy."

Sacora said, "Okay, we will take a nap after we finish cleaning the table."

Alisha said, "I can put things back in the refrigerator."

Sacora said, "Thank you, and I will help."

Jeremiah asked, "Can I be excused and go back to play the game?"

Sacora said, "Yes, when you finish."

Elijah asked, "Can I play the game while Aylassa is napping?"

Sacora said, "Yes, you can."

The boys went to the TV and continued to play the game. Alisha helped Sacora put things in the sink for the dishwasher. Sacora changed out the clothes in the laundry room and carried her things to her dresser. She stopped suddenly and realized she had not made the beds. This was unusual.

Sacora held Aylassa and Sadie in the rocking chair until they were asleep, singing "Grandma's Lullaby." She put them in their cribs and turned around to look at the peaceful sleeping babies. This was something she thought she would never have.

Chapter Thirty-One

S acora went to her bedroom and made the bed. When she passed through the living room, she told Alisha she was going upstairs to make beds. Alisha asked if she could help her, and Sacora was on her way up the stairs with Alisha following. Alisha's bed was made, and Sacora was impressed, giving her a smile. They made Elijah's and Jeremiah's beds and came back downstairs to where the boys were playing the game. Sacora's phone rang, and she went in the kitchen to talk to Julie.

"Hey, little Mommy, I'm on my way to see you. I'm bringing some gifts. You have two little girls and one little boy?"

Sacora said, "No, I have three little girls and two little boys. I will tell you about it the first chance I get. I won't know the details about Sadie and Jeremiah Walters until Tuesday when I go back to work. I will be happy to see you today."

Julie said, "I am on my way after I stop to get surprises. Bye."

Sacora said, "Bye, Julie."

Sacora went back to the living room, and Alisha had fallen asleep on the sofa. Sacora took a small soft blanket and covered her up. Eeyore was sitting in the floor with the boys and napping. Sacora took a break sitting in the recliner, looking at the sight of children in her home. Her silence was interrupted when Sadie woke up and hollered for her, "Zora, my finished with nap."

Sacora went to get her and changed her diaper, and then she was ready to go play.

Sadie went to Jeremiah's side. "My set with you, bubba?" Jeremiah reached out to help her sit down.

Elijah said, "She talks different."

Jeremiah said, "Yes, she does. She uses *my* for *I* and *mine* for *my*. After you listen for a while, you will understand what she is saying. Uncle Luke's favorite is *georgous* for *gorgeous*."

The next few minutes, Aylassa was coming to the living room. She said, "I gotta potty." Sacora took her to potty and was pleased her pull-up was dry. She asked the children what they wanted for dinner.

Sadie said, "My wants macaroni and cheese."

Aylassa said, "Pot pie."

Elijah said, "Fish sticks."

Jeremiah said, "Fish sticks."

Alisha woke up and said, "Pot pie too."

Sacora went to the kitchen and started the oven, putting pot pies and fish sticks on a cookie sheet to bake. Sadie's macaroni and cheese was starting to boil when the doorbell rang.

Sacora greeted Julie with a smile. "Come in and meet everyone. I'm going to let Eeyore out for a while."

Eeyore went out. Julie came in and opened Walmart bags. She had the boys some toy slingshots and the girls some nail polish. Sacora pointed to each child and introduced them. She said, "This is Elijah and his sisters, Alisha and Aylassa Malone. This is Jeremiah and his sister, Sadie Walters."

Julie spoke, "I'm Julie, Sacora's friend. I hope you enjoy what I brought for you."

Sacora said, "Julie, would you like to eat dinner with us? I can make your favorite salad."

Julie said, "I would love to."

While everyone was seated at the table and enjoying the food they had chosen, Julie looked at Sacora and said, "Congratulations on the family you always wanted."

Sacora said, "They have made me happy."

Julie said, "I can only stay for a while. I have got to get back home soon. I told Mom I would go to church with her tomorrow."

Sacora said, "I have enjoyed your visit. Thanks for all the surprises."

Julie got up and hugged Sacora and said, "Keep in touch. You will be busy, but find time for me, okay?"

Sacora said, "I will. By the way, I am going with Joe McCarley to a Foo Fighters concert the second weekend of August, Friday, I think. I told you, you would be the first to know."

Julie squealed quietly. "Have a great time, and let me know all about it."

Sacora said, "You know I will." She walked Julie to the door and watched her drive away.

The boys got her attention and asked, "Can we go to the barn and play with our slingshots and Eeyore?"

Sacora said, "Yes, it is cooler now. We will after I clean the table and dishes."

Chapter Thirty-Two

S acora finished the dishes, just a few she hand-washed and Alisha wanted to dry. Sacora put the dishes up after Alisha had dried them. Sacora asked, "Where did you learn to be such great help with housework?"

Alisha said, "I used to help my momma when she got sick. It always made her smile."

Sacora said, "It makes me smile too. I enjoy spending time with you. I am going to get the towels and cloths from the dryer and fold them and put them away before we go outside to play in the barn."

Alisha said, "My momma always played a game to teach Aylassa and me shapes and colors. I folded cloths in squares, rectangles, and triangles. Aylassa always separated the different colors."

Sacora said, "Okay, show me."

Alisha did, and Aylassa came to the sofa and started folding also. Sadie was still sitting by Jeremiah and watching the game they were playing on TV. Sadie said, "My wanna pay." Sacora gave her a cloth, and she folded it in a rectangle. When it was done, Sacora put it all away.

The boys turned off the TV after they paused the game and said, "We are ready to go outside."

Sacora said, "Put on your shoes. The ground is hot from the sun. Little ladies, what about polishing our nails while the boys are using their slingshots?"

Sacora put her shoes on, and Sadie and Aylassa had some help from her. Alisha put her shoes on and tied them in a neat bow. The boys were ready, and they all went to the door and called Eeyore. The walk to the barn was pleasant, and the boys picked up stones for their slingshots. The girls found a cool spot on the steps of the barn to polish their nails. Suddenly the sound of Foo Fighters music was heard. Sacora's heart skipped a few beats.

In the driveway parked Joe McCarley in his truck. A young girl came around the truck from the passenger side. Joe came toward Sacora and said, "This is my daughter, Joy. She is visiting for a while."

Sacora said, "It is nice to meet you. This is Sadie, Aylassa, Alisha, Elijah, and Jeremiah. Elijah and Jeremiah were wanting to learn to use their slingshots that Julie gave them. I know nothing about them but trying to figure it out. But the girls are polishing nails, and I know about that."

Joy said, "I would love to polish my nails with Alisha, Sadie, and Aylassa."

Sacora said, "Sure, what's your favorite color?"

Joe interrupted and said, "We need some stones. Round flat ones work the best."

The boys said, "Let's go look."

They went to look for stones, and Joe looked at Sacora and said, "I wanted you to meet Joy. I have just now picked her up from the airport. How has your first Saturday being a momma been?"

Sacora said, "It has been a different Saturday for sure. The children have been enjoying all the things you brought this morning. I'm getting the impression that outside playing at the barn is where their interests are."

Joe smiled and said, "Children need the sunshine and outside air to breathe. They can get it plenty here."

Sacora said, "We will be here for a while if you would like to visit."

Joe said, "No, thank you, Sacora. Joy has been traveling today, and I will get her home settled in for the night."

Sacora, disappointed, smiled and said, "I understand that and will see you later."

The children told them bye. Elijah and Jeremiah said, "Joe, thank you for teaching us how to use the slingshots."

Joy and Joe went to the truck, and Sacora waved quietly. The children stayed out playing. Aylassa, Sadie, and Alisha chased fireflies when their nails dried. Jeremiah and Elijah put their slingshots down and chased fireflies too. When the sun was completely gone, Sacora said, "Okay, it is time to go in and get baths and showers."

Eeyore was the first on the porch and ready to eat and drink water like Sacora had never seen her before. After Eeyore was finished, the children asked for chocolate milk and drank it with laughter. Sacora gave the girls a bath in her bathroom, and the boys showered upstairs to finish their first Saturday with Sacora.

Chapter Thirty-Three

S acora made it to her bed and felt such tiredness that she has never felt before. Sadie and Aylassa had enjoyed the rocker and "Grandma's Lullaby" before falling to sleep. Alisha was ready for her cozy bed and good-night wish. Jeremiah and Elijah were ready to dry their hair and sleep soundly too. Such happiness in her heart that she realized this was the dream she had months ago in her apartment. The large white house with children's laughter and her happy heart were in her dream. So many hours she had thought about her dream, but the vision of having a family had been for years. Five children had come in her life so quick, just fifteen minutes, not even hours. She fell asleep with a smile on her face.

The sun shining woke Sacora up before the children had begun their day. Eeyore was ready to go outside, and she decided to go to the front porch and drink coffee and be quiet so they could finish sleeping. Yesterday at the barn tired them; they all have slept soundly. On the porch she was thinking about her parents in Africa and wondering what they would think when she would tell them of the children's life with her. Her parents had always been supportive of her goals. The goal of a family had vanished with the diagnosis of endometriosis years ago.

Sacora's thoughts were interrupted with Eeyore coming to her, and she petted her quietly, speaking so softly, "Eeyore, you are enjoying your new family, aren't you? You are gaining weight and glowing with happiness."

After an hour or so, Sacora heard Alisha push through the door, and she came to sit by her. Alisha said, "Everyone else is still sleeping, but I am awake. I seen you through the window. Can I sit here with you? I will be quiet."

Sacora answered, "Yes, ma'am, I would love for you too. But you don't have to be quiet."

Alisha spoke quietly, "I will so Aylassa and Sadie can sleep a while longer."

Sacora smiled and said, "Okay. We will be quiet."

Alisha spotted a butterfly, and Sacora was impressed how she knew how to patiently catch it when it lighted on her knee.

After thirty minutes, Sacora heard Sadie and Aylassa. Alisha and Sacora went inside to get them, and Elijah and Jeremiah came down the stairs. Everyone was smiling, and Sacora asked them, "What do you want for breakfast?"

The children's choice was pancakes again with variety of syrups. Jeremiah asked Sacora, "What is your favorites? You are always asking about ours. What would you like for lunch?"

Sacora answered, "My favorite is sloppy joes. I have always liked sloppy joes."

Elijah asked, "Can you fix sloppy joes for lunch?"

Sacora said, "Yes, I can. I do have what we need."

After the children ate and Sacora was cleaning the table, Alisha and Aylassa helping with the syrups being put away, Alisha asked Sacora, "Today is Sunday, isn't it?"

Sacora said, "Yes, it is. What makes you ask?"

Alisha answered, "We go to church on Sunday."

Sacora said, "It is too late for us to go. I wasn't prepared to go and didn't know about your clothes."

Alisha said, "When my momma was sick, we would go to the living room and sit on the couch and have church. Seth would be at work and couldn't take us. We will show you after we get dressed, okay?"

Sacora said, "Sure."

After everyone was dressed and seated on the couch, Alisha started singing "Amazing Grace." Then the other children joined in and sang with her until she had finished. Alisha started singing "Jesus Loves Me" and then "Jesus Loves the Little Children." Aylassa sang loudly with her sister, and Sadie made an attempt to sing. Jeremiah and Elijah sang the loudest on "Jesus Loves Me."

When Alisha stopped singing, she asked Elijah, "Are you ready for a Bible story?"

Elijah said, "I sure am, and I have a great one for today."

Elijah started with the story of Adam and Eve and their sons Cain and Abel. How the jealous heart of a brother could destroy another brother. Elijah finished his story with, "I never had a brother, but I have one now and it is such a wonderful thing."

Chapter Thirty-Four

Sacora being the daughter of a Christian couple and their dedication to be missionaries had always loved the God Almighty and his Son, Jesus Christ. But she had never felt the presence of the spirit before like today in the living room of her home. How the children have sang and Elijah's Bible story touched her in so many ways. After the children announced, "Church is over," Jeremiah asked Sacora, "Are you still going to make sloppy joes for lunch?"

Sacora said, "I am."

Elijah asked, "Can we play the game until you have it ready?"

Sacora said, "Yes, you can."

Sacora finished lunch, and everyone was seated. Jeremiah asked, "Can I say the blessing for lunch?"

Sacora said, "Yes." All the children joined in with him.

The children agreed that the sloppy joes were awesome and found Sadie's messy face to be funny. Sadie said, "My wike woppy doe too."

While Sacora cleaned Sadie's and Aylassa's faces, the boys went to the living room to play *Skate 3*. Alisha started cleaning the table. Sacora said, "What about we go back to the barn this afternoon and play?"

Alisha was the first to answer, "Yes."

After everything was finished, the children put their shoes on and went happily to the barn to play. Eeyore even seemed to have a pep in her walk. Elijah and Jeremiah decided to play cowboys and Indians with their slingshots, and the girls played tag. Sadie started crying when Alisha said, "You are it."

Sacora explained to her, "This means you run after them."

Sadie did, and with all the laughter of the children playing, time got away. The fireflies began to spin around, and the children were chasing them. Sacora finally asked them to go inside for supper and "What would you like?" It was agreed pizza for everyone. The boys went upstairs to wash their hands and faces, and the girls went to Sacora's bathroom. After the blessing, the pizza tasted the best ever. The children were happy with one another.

Sacora decided to give Sadie and Aylassa a bath, while Alisha, Elijah, and Jeremiah played *Skate 3*. Alisha went to get her bath after Sacora had the babies ready for bed. Alisha could hear Sacora singing "Grandma's Lullaby" while she rocked them. Sacora had put Sadie and Aylassa in their cribs and slightly left the door open. Alisha's hair was wet, and Sacora dried it. Alisha was ready for her bed, and Sacora walked upstairs with her and told the boys, "It is time for showers and bed."

The boys went to their rooms and got clothes for showers, and Alisha went on to bed. Sacora told her "Good night and sleep tight." The boys were drying their hair, and then they went to their rooms, Sacora telling them good night. Sacora gathered all the laundry and started the washing machine before she settled in her hot bath. She went to the laundry room and put their clothes in the dryer for tomorrow after her bath. Sacora settled in her bed tonight with tears falling from her eyes. Her tears were for Autumn Malone, the mother of three children. How much attention and affection she gave her children that she had to leave behind. Autumn had given her heart and so much devotion to their behavior and love for the Lord.

Sacora had left her door slightly open, and for the first time since Eeyore had been with her, Eeyore came to lay on the bed beside her and licked her tears. Sacora didn't mind Eeyore's actions and was comforted for a while. Eeyore did go back to her blanket, and Sacora slept. First Sunday of being a momma would be one to remember for sure.

Chapter Thirty-Five

Monday morning came early. Sacora was awaken at five o'clock without the alarm, just excited about starting the day. She decided to shower and get dressed before the children had awakened. Sacora had opened the door for Eeyore and made her bed. She was turning on the coffee maker when she heard Alisha coming down the stairs already dressed.

Alisha said, "I have made my bed and ready to start my day."

Sacora asked, "Do you want to eat breakfast now?"

Alisha said, "No, ma'am. I would like to sit with you on the porch while you drink your coffee and wait to eat."

Sacora said, "Let's go to the porch."

Eeyore came to Alisha, and she petted her quietly, and it was an hour before they went inside to make breakfast. Sacora made grilled cheese toast and was setting the table before the first sound of Sadie and Aylassa came. Sacora went to get Aylassa, and she went to potty. Sadie was ready for a diaper change and said to Sacora, "<y wanna potty wike wlassa."

Sacora said, "Okay, let's go."

Sacora was surprised that Sadie pottied, and she changed her into her clothes. Aylassa said, "I am ready to eat."

Sacora was washing Aylassa's hands and Sadie's when Jeremiah and Elijah came downstairs with their hands washed, dressed, and ready to eat. Alisha was the first at the table, and she handed the cheese toast to the boys. Orange juice was already in their cups. Sacora was pleased with the smoothness of this morning.

After Sacora had cleaned the table and put dishes in the dishwasher, her cell phone rang, and it was Mr. Hamilton. Sacora answered with a cheerful hello.

Mr. Hamilton said, "I have received confirmation on a day care for the children until school starts, and the location is on your way here to the office."

Sacora said, "That is great. Can I go introduce the children to them today?"

Mr. Hamilton said, "Yes, I thought you could around noon. The director will be looking for you then. She will go over with you paperwork. The human resources of Baldwin County have submitted their documents."

Sacora said, "Okay then, and I will be back to work in the morning."

Mr. Hamilton said, "Sounds good. Hope you have a good day with the children."

Sacora said, "Thank you and goodbye."

Sacora decided and to take the children to McDonald's for lunch and go to the day care after they had eaten. Aylassa and Sadie were playing in the living room watching the game of Skate 3, Alisha, Elijah and Jeremiah were playing. Sacora went upstairs to make beds and clean the bathroom. She gathered some dirty laundry and carried it to the laundry room. Taking care of this business was going to be difficult when she returned to work, but it was something she would figure out.

Sacora was ready to go to the van and had the children neatly dressed by eleven o'clock. She still had a busy six hours, and she was feeling anxiety of the new schedule she would have to have for work and day care. Putting thoughts and anxiety aside she called to the children to buckle up and put Sadie and Aylassa in their seats.

At McDonald's, Alisha decided she wanted chicken nuggets and Sadie and Aylassa did also. Jeremiah and Elijah wanted cheeseburgers, and Sacora had her usual meal of burgers and fries. Sacora looking at the children's faces how they always had such happy expressions gave her more confidence to keep on pursuing her dream of being a momma.

Twelve o'clock, Sacora parked at the day care, and the children were mannerly entering the door when a woman introduced herself, Jeannie Koch. Ms. Koch instructed Sacora what she would need for each child and showed so much kindness that Sacora was pleased to leave the children with her. After the meeting, the children went back to the van buckling up, Sadie and Aylassa were buckled in their seats, and Sacora looked in the review mirror and took a deep breath. "It is here, my dream is here."

Parking in her driveway and the children going to the porch, Sacora opened the front door, and Eeyore was the first to make it through the door to the kitchen. Sacora fed her some more Pedigree and water. Eeyore was eating more and playing with the children. She was finally looking like a family pet.

Chapter Thirty-Six

The children came in hot from the sun and drank some more orange juice. Sadie and Aylassa went down for a nap, and Elijah and Jeremiah wanted to play the PlayStation. Elijah asked Jeremiah, "Do you mind if we play *Eye Pets and Friends*? That is Alisha's favorite."

Jeremiah said, "Sure, that is okay."

Jeremiah asked Sacora, "Can we play at the barn again today after supper? It should be cooler then."

Sacora said, "Yes, that will be good. I am cooking spaghetti for supper tonight, and we will go after I clean the dishes." Sacora sat down in her chair and watched the children play quietly for the babies to nap. Eeyore sat down beside Jeremiah watching the game and dozing occasionally. This afternoon had gone by, and Sacora started to cook supper when she heard Sadie say, "My finished, Zora. My weady to pay."

Aylassa got down from her crib and went to the bathroom. Sacora was surprised how independent she had become today. Sadie went to the bathroom after Aylassa, and Sacora was surprised that her diaper was dry and she was showing independence too.

Sacora boiled some carrots to put in the spaghetti sauce, and the tossed salad had a mixture of vegetables. She decided to watch what vegetables the children would eat, getting an idea of what their favorite was. Sacora had ranch dressing and Thousand Island. She asked the children if they were ready to eat. The boys went upstairs to wash their hands and faces, and Sacora washed Sadie's and Aylassa's hands and faces when Alisha went to her bathroom.

Once again the blessing was said, even Aylassa was saying what words she knew. The spaghetti was eaten like a treat, and the idea of vegetables in the salad worked for Sacora. She soon figured out that Jeremiah liked broccoli with ranch, Elijah's favorite was tomatoes, and Alisha liked the carrots in the spaghetti and everything in the salad.

It was nice moments at the table, and Sacora cleaned faces and hands again of Sadie and Aylassa. Sacora said, "While I put dishes in the dishwasher, will you please put your shoes on and get ready to go outside to the barn?"

Jeremiah said, "Yes, ma'am, and I will pause the game and turn off the TV."

Elijah, Alisha, and Jeremiah were ready when Sacora had Sadie and Aylassa dressed for the hot sun and temperature. At the barn, Jeremiah and Elijah found their slingshots and stones, and the girls played tag. Sadie understood more of the game today and laughed when it was her turn to be it.

When Sacora was tying Aylassa's shoes, she noticed a thin jacket setting on the rail of the barn stairs. She thought, "This must be Joy's. I will text Joe to tell him it is here." Fireflies came out, and Sacora decided she would chase them too tonight.

The sun had gone down, and it was time to start it all over again with baths and showers. Today had gone so fast, and so many memories already had found a home in Sacora's heart. The walk back to the front porch was joyful, and Eeyore was ready to eat again and drink with the children. Upstairs went Jeremiah and Elijah, and Sacora bathed the babies while Alisha brushed her teeth and gathered her clean clothes. Sadie and Aylassa were ready for bed, while Alisha got in the bathtub. Alisha could hear Sacora singing "Grandma's Lullaby," and she knew the babies were going to sleep. She was quiet, as she knew to be, and Sacora came to dry her hair.

The boys upstairs were almost finished, and Sacora went upstairs with Alisha and tucked her in her bed. The boys dried their hair, and Sacora said good night to Jeremiah and Elijah, leaving their doors open slightly.

Sacora put the laundry in the washing machine and started her bath. Sacora took out her cell phone and texted Joe about Joy's jacket. She even asked him and Joy to have supper with them tomorrow night. Her plans were to put a pot roast in the Crock-Pot before she left for work in the morning.

She was pleased when he accepted her invitation. Joe asked if he needed to bring something. Sacora added, "*All I have for beverages are chocolate milk and orange juice and bottle water. You might want to bring a soda, lol.*"

Joe answered with, "*Yes, ma'am, see you soon.*"

Sacora, in her bed after another day of happiness, slept with a smile on her face. Her first day of a working single mom was tomorrow. All she can do was plan and enjoy everything that came with it.

Chapter Thirty-Seven

Sacora woke up before the clock again this morning. She decided to shower quickly before the children were up and drink coffee on the front porch. She made her bed and opened the door for Eeyore. Eeyore was outside and ate Pedigree and drank water on the porch. The sun was shining for another hot day in Alabama. Alisha came to the front porch and sat with her for a few minutes and then went inside to start the first day of a single working mom.

Alisha said, "I have already made my bed, and I'm dressed for day care."

Sacora said, "Yes, ma'am, I see, and thank you."

The cheese toast were finished and being set on the table when Sadie and Aylassa had awakened and Jeremiah and Elijah came downstairs dressed to eat. Sacora sat the children down with orange juice and cheese toast before she went to dress Sadie and Aylassa. Sadie wanted to potty like Aylassa, and Sacora dressed them after changing pull-ups. They washed their hands and were ready to eat. Sacora ate with them and cleaned the table while they played TV PlayStation. Sacora put the pot roast in the Crock-Pot with potatoes, carrots, green pepper, and mushroom soup. One less thing to do before Joe and Joy came for dinner.

Sacora packed bags for Sadie and Aylassa, and Alisha, Elijah, and Jeremiah were ready for the day. Sacora dressed in cool khakis and denim blouse for the hot day and was ready for work. She buckled the children in the van and was heading out the driveway. Sacora looked at the clock on the van, and she decided she was making good time. When she pulled in the parking lot of the day care, Sacora said, "Here we are. Let's get started on our good day."

Sacora put Sadie on her hip and held Aylassa's hand. Alisha, Elijah, and Jeremiah followed and went inside. Ms. Koch was ready to greet each child and show them where to place their bags. She took the bags of Sadie and Aylassa, and an assistant took Aylassa showed her to the table of three-year-olds. Sadie went with another assistant, and Alisha, Elijah, and Jeremiah went to the school-age stations. Sacora had told them bye and started out to the van. She took a minute just to take in the moment of leaving the children for the first time.

On to work at the office, she would focus on the situations she needed to finish before lunch. At her desk for a few minutes, Mr. Hamilton came to her and said, "We are having a conference call with Baldwin County Department of Human Resources' Ms. Hines at nine o'clock concerning Sadie and Jeremiah Walters. We will get you information with the children if you still want to foster them as you have this weekend."

Sacora smiled and said, "Yes, I do and would love to keep them with me. I have grown attached to them already."

Mr. Hamilton said, "I will be prepared by the conference call."

Sacora went on with her work, not paying attention to her coworkers. Nine o'clock had come so soon, and Mr. Hamilton came to her and said, "Are you ready for the conference call?"

Sacora got up for the conference call, still not paying attention to her coworkers. She went in Mr. Hamilton's office and sat down. He made the call, and Ms. Hines answered the call. "Baldwin County Department of Human Resources, Ms. Hines speaking."

Mr. Hamilton's voice was stern and professional when he answered, "This is Mr. Hamilton of Mobile County Department of Human Resources with Ms. Sacora Hill."

Ms. Hines asked Sacora, "How are things going with the children? Have we set everything up for your fostering?"

Sacora answered, "Yes, ma'am. I have enjoyed them, and the day care has them today."

Ms. Hines asked, "Are you wanting to continue to foster the Walters children as well as the Malone children?"

Sacora answered, "Yes, ma'am. I think they are adjusting to me and I have adjusted to them."

Ms. Hines said, "We are ready to make them permanent with you as their foster parent."

Sacora said, "I was informed that today I would have some information on them. I would like to know as much as allowed to be able to interact with any behavior they may have."

Ms. Hines said, "What I will tell you is that last May, the children were taken to your Department of Human Resources Mobile County for removal of their parents' care."

Sacora broke in the conversation and spoke, "I remember them. Sadie had a broken arm, and Jeremiah had a broken nose."

Ms. Hines said, "Yes. When their uncle Luke was granted custody, he had a home in Baldwin County, and we were given this case. Luke is in college and no longer could provide for them. The children's parents still reside in Mobile County, but we are still in authority for the foster care of them. This gives us privilege to allow the children's foster care be with you."

Sacora asked, "Have I been given all the required information as far as school starting with immunization records and etc.? I would love to have them enrolled and be with me until further notice."

Ms. Hines answered, "Yes, we will have all that ready for you in a few weeks. Also you will be given an allowance for them with Medicaid. If you have any questions later, just give me a call. I'm certain the children will be just fine with you."

Sacora said, "Thank you, and I will do what I can to give them a good school year and a steady, structured home. Bye, Ms. Hines."

Ms. Hines said, "Goodbye, Ms. Hill, and we are here when or if you need us."

Chapter Thirty-Eight

Sacora left Mr. Hamilton's office with Luke on her mind. The college days for her were so carefree days with Julie and such pleasant memories. Luke must have been so dedicated to his niece and nephew to even attempt to be responsible for them. Her heart was full of emotion when she heard her coworkers scream, "Surprise!" Sacora noticed a banner that said, "*Congratulations, Little Momma.*"

Cam said, "We have decided to give you a children's shower. You have become a momma of five children at one time."

Shamilha said, "This weekend is tax-free weekend, and we have you a Walmart gift card for school clothes and etc."

Dillon added, "We have brought you lunch and goodies to celebrate, and here is another surprise."

Julie came out from the front entrance and hugged her friend. Sacora was thrilled but should have known Julie had something to do with the shower when she read *Little Momma.* Julie smiled and enjoyed the celebration with Sacora, and then it was time for her to return to the courtroom.

After everyone had eaten and cleaned up the break room, Sacora went back to her desk feeling so uplifted with support, and their encouragement was appreciated. She finished her assignments and told everyone thanks again before leaving. In her van, she took a deep breath, still taking in the moments of being a single working mom.

She arrived at the day care and went inside. She was greeted again by Ms. Koch, and the children were instructed to gather their things to leave. Sacora picked up Sadie and Aylassa first, and then Alisha, Jeremiah, and Elijah came to the door ready to leave. Ms.

Koch announced that they had a pleasant day and would be ready for tomorrow.

Sacora put the children in the van and headed home. Joe and Joy were coming for supper, and she would be ready. The pot roast had been cooking all day. The additional vegetables would not take long. Her plan was to add cream potatoes, broccoli, and dinner rolls.

Sacora was driving up to the house when Aylassa said, "Aylassa's house."

Sadie said, "Mine house too. My happy to be at mine house."

Alisha said, "I am ready to be out of my shoes."

Elijah and Jeremiah hurriedly ran to the porch looking for Eeyore. Sacora opened the door, and everyone ran in, Eeyore the last. Sacora fed Eeyore food and told Sadie and Aylassa to go to potty, and Alisha asked, "Can we turn the TV and game on while you cook?"

Sacora said, "Yes, you can."

The children carried their bags to the living room and started playing the game while Sacora cooked. Sadie and Aylassa ate a snack with chocolate milk. Sacora was getting ready to set the table when she got a text from Joe, "*We're on our way.*" Her heart skipped a few beats, and she finished setting the table, placing the children's cups at their place. Sacora called to the children that supper was ready for them to wash up. Sadie and Aylassa wiped their faces and hands with an antibacterial wipe and waited on Sacora to put them at the table.

Joe and Joy pulled into the driveway and stopped at the barn. Sacora could see Joy had gotten out and found her jacket. When the doorbell rang, Sacora went to open the door and was still smiling when she showed Joe and Joy to the table. Joe and Joy washed their hands at the kitchen sink and sat down where Sacora asked them to. Joe had brought Coca-Cola for their drinks. Sacora placed glasses with ice on the table, and Alisha said the blessing, with the children joining in.

Sacora was nervous and decided to focus on the children's day. She asked them, "What did you do today?"

Sadie answered, "My wearned to tweet obers wike mine wanna be tweeted."

Aylassa said, "I learned 'bout dinosaurs and how they lived on the earth many millions of years ago, in the 1990s."

Alisha said, "We watched *Cinderella* today, and I will tell you one thing. If I had mean stepsisters like Cinderella's, I would kick them in the nuts."

Sacora and Joe looked at each other smiling, but Joy busted out in loud laughter. Joe said, "Joy and I went to the beach for a while and had lunch. What about your day, Sacora?"

Sacora answered, "I have had the best day ever, full of surprises and love."

Chapter Thirty-Nine

Jeremiah said, "Asher talked to us today about his sheep and wanted us to come on Saturday to play at his house."

Elijah asked, "Can we go, Sacora?"

Sacora answered, "No, I'm sorry, buddy. We have to go school shopping Saturday. It's tax-free weekend."

Sadie said, "My don't wanna go chopping. My wanna pay with cheep."

Joy broke in the conversation and said, "I will stay with Sadie and Aylassa while you take Alisha, Elijah, and Jeremiah school shopping, if you would like me to? I will be able to stay here with them."

Sacora said, "That sounds like a good idea. I will let you know what time."

Joe said, "The meal was good, Sacora. Thanks for inviting us."

Sacora asked, "Who is in for some ice cream sundaes?"

The children were all excited, and Sacora went to the kitchen to get it. After a few minutes, she returned with eight sundaes and spoons. Everyone started eating when Joy spoke to Sacora, "The supper was great, and the sundae was delicious."

Joe decided it was time to go and told Sacora and the children goodbye. Joy also said thank you again before leaving. In the truck, Joy looked at Joe for a few minutes and then she spoke, "You know, Dad, it would be all right if you loved the children at Sacora's house. It would be all right too if you loved Sacora."

Joe asked, "What makes you say that?"

Joy answered, "I'm going on sixteen, and I will be leaving for college and won't have the time to spend with you like I have. Maybe you need another companion."

Joe said, "Thanks, sweetie. I do think Sacora is a great companion, and I get laughs out of what the children are thinking and saying. Do you think you would mind watching the children while I take Sacora to the Foo Fighters concert for my birthday?"

Joy said, "I would be just fine with that. I have been to so many Foo Fighters concerts that I would not mind at all. I hope you have fun."

After a few minutes, Joy looked at Joe and said, "Do you ever think you would pursue your career as a high school history teacher and football coach? You always said that spending time with me is the reason you didn't choose an occupation using your degree. That the job you have of repairman gave you the flexibility to be with me when I came from Miami."

Joe asked, "Why are you asking, Joy? What is on your mind?"

Joy answered, "I am looking at a school here that I can finish high school and start college at the same time. I would like to live with you and go to this school."

Joe asked, "Have you talked to your mom about it?"

Joy said, "No, sir. I always talk to you first."

Joe said, "I don't think Brandie will go for that."

Joy answered, "Dad, I am going to be sixteen, and I don't think she has a choice."

Joe was quiet for a few seconds and then spoke, "Joy, I have always cooperated and made decisions to make you happy. If you think this is what you want, we can try it. But don't burn bridges in Miami. Keep things so you can return if it does not work out for you."

Joy said, "Yes, sir, Dad. I have thought about it for two years and done the research on the school."

Joe said, "We will look into it soon."

Joy said, "Thank you, Sad. Are we still going to Granny and Poppy's on Sunday for lunch?"

Joe answered, "Yes, we are."

Joy asked, "Are you inviting Sacora and the children?"

Joe said, "No. I can't get Granny all excited. You know she has always wanted me to start over, marry again, and have a family. I won't get her excited again, okay?"

Joy said, "I understand, Dad. Sacora is just the person to get Granny excited. She is an awesome person."

Joe smiled and said, "Yes, she is. Well, here is home, and I am ready. What about you?"

Joy answered, "Yes, I am. We have a had a big day."

Chapter Forty

Sacora was cleaning the table and the children went to the living room to play the game on PlayStation. Aylassa and Sadie were in the kitchen playing with Eeyore until Sacora had started the dishwasher. Alisha came in and asked, "Can we go to the barn to chase fireflies?"

Sacora answered, "No, baby, it's late. Almost time for baths and showers, and I have to start the washer and dryer, getting ready for another day. What about chasing fireflies in the front yard for a while?"

Alisha said, "That is a great idea. I'm getting my shoes on."

Sacora started the washing machine, and then everyone went outside to chase fireflies. Sacora sat on the front porch watching the smiles and hearing the laughter of all five children having a good time until time to go in and shower. Elijah and Jeremiah went upstairs to their bathroom, and Sacora put Sadie and Aylassa in the tub. Alisha went upstairs to gather her pajamas and came back downstairs to Sacora's bathroom. Sacora finished dressing Sadie and Aylassa. She rocked them singing "Grandma's Lullaby" while Alisha was in the bathtub.

Sacora put the babies in the cribs and came to dry Alisha's hair. Alisha was very tired and went upstairs after her hair was dry. Sacora went to check on Jeremiah and Elijah. They were ready to dry their hair, so Sacora went to tuck in Alisha.

Sacora said, "Good night, little lady. We have had a big day. Sleep well so we can do it again tomorrow."

Alisha said, "Good night, Sacora, and may you have sweet dreams."

Sacora whispered, "Same to you." Sacora kissed her forehead and left the door opened some. She had planned on returning to her room with clean clothes to put in her backpack and did not want to disturb her sleeping.

The boys were finished in the bathroom, and Sacora gathered their dirty clothes. She tucked in Jeremiah first and told him, "Can you be thinking of what you would like to buy on Saturday for school? I think I have arranged for you to be with me for this coming school year."

Jeremiah answered, "Yes, I will. I am thinking about what backpack I want and shoes."

Sacora said, "Okay, good night, and tomorrow will be full of surprises."

Sacora left the door opened some and went to Elijah's room and turned back the bed and told him good night.

Elijah said, "Sacora, thank you for all you do for us. I have not seen Alisha and Aylassa this happy in a long time."

Sacora said, "You are welcome. Now it is time for you to call it a day. Good night, buddy, and sweet dreams."

Elijah said, "Good night, Sacora, and may you have sweet dreams of Joe."

Sacora asked, "What makes you say that?"

Elijah said, "I see the way he looks at you. The way Seth looked at my momma. Seth loved my momma and us. You need to have love like that."

Sacora answered, "Thank you very much. Good night."

Sacora went through the door puzzled about what this child had seen about the way Joe looked at her. She left the door opened some and picked up the dirty laundry and went to the washing machine to put the laundry in the dryer. As she was putting the clothes in the washing machine, she heard her phone and went to check it after she started the washing machine.

It was a text from Joe. "*Thank you for supper tonight, and Joy and I had a pleasant evening with you and the children. They just crack me up. I discovered I am older than dinosaurs and Cinderella's stepsisters have nuts. Lol. Good night.*"

Sacora giggled to herself and finished putting her clothes out for tomorrow and packing the children's bags. She went upstairs to place Alisha's clothes in her backpack and Jeremiah and Elijah's clothes in their dressers.

She went to her long, hot bath sighing, "So this is a single working mom's life." But to Sacora, it had been to live an impossible dream. Eeyore had gone back to the kitchen to drink, and Sacora opened the front door for her. Eeyore went to potty and came back in ready for her blanket. Sacora was in bed by nine forty-five, exhausted and ready for sleep.

Chapter Forty-One

Sacora made it through the rest of the week with the same schedule of work and day care. Saturday morning, the sun was shining bright when she woke at seven thirty. The children were still sleeping. The week of day care and the Friday evening before of chasing fireflies, playing late, had them extremely tired. She opened the door for Eeyore and changed the sheets on her bed and showered before she started the washing machine.

Sacora went to the front porch to sit with her coffee and enjoy the July weather. Eeyore ate her dog food and drank water on the front porch by Sacora. Alisha came to the porch after an hour or so and spent time being quiet and enjoying the weather too. Sadie and Aylassa slept the longest. Elijah and Jeremiah came to the front porch and were excited about the day of not going to day care. They had brought their slingshots outside and were going to play for a while before going school shopping. Sacora went inside to start breakfast, and Elijah and Jeremiah stayed outside in the front yard playing. Alisha decided to sit on the front porch with Eeyore.

Sacora had the biscuits, bacon, and eggs finished and on the table when Sadie said, "My finished, Zora." She went to see if Sadie and Aylassa had awakened. She carried them to potty and told Alisha, Elijah, and Jeremiah to come wash their hands. The children sat at the table ready to eat, said the blessing, and started talking about what they wanted for school.

After breakfast, Sacora told Alisha, Elijah, and Jeremiah to get ready to go shopping. She carried Sadie and Aylassa to change into their clothes. Joe called. Sacora's voice sounded with happiness when she answered.

She said, "Good morning, Joe. What is going on with you this Saturday morning?"

Joe answered her question, "I have some repair work to do, and Joy had mentioned to you she would come to sit with Sadie and Aylassa while you went school shopping. I will bring her when you are ready to leave."

Sacora said, "Yes, that's great. What about an hour from now?"

Joe said, "That will be fine. I will see you then. Bye."

Sacora said, "Goodbye, Joe."

Sacora started with getting Alisha's bedsheets changed and then Elijah's and Jeremiah's. She noticed how the boys were keeping their clothes in the dressers and Alisha was still wanting her clothes in her backpack. Sacora came downstairs to put sheets in the washing machine, and Sadie was watching the PlayStation. It would be a few more weeks, and she would try to play with Alisha.

Aylassa was asking Alisha what would she buy school shopping. Alisha was thinking and not answering. Sacora had the children ready when she heard the loud Foo Fighters music coming toward the front porch. The children were ready, and Joy came in smiling at the living room. Aylassa and Sadie were ready to play with Joy.

Sacora showed her where their clothes were in case of accidents and in the kitchen where she kept their snacks and macaroni and cheese. Joy looked in the refrigerator for their chocolate milk. Joy assured Sacora that she could handle them for a few hours. Joe left first after telling Joy bye and then Sacora. He told Elijah, Jeremiah, and Alisha bye when they were getting in the van. Sacora gave hugs to Aylassa and Sadie and went to the van, getting ready for her first school shopping day as a mom.

The shoe store was first on Sacora's list. The boys were trying on shoes, immediately selecting what they liked. Alisha was not selecting shoes to try on at first. She looked at Sacora and said, "I like these. Do we have enough money for these?"

Sacora said, "Yes, ma'am, we do. Would you like to have shoes for church also?"

Alisha did try on Nike and shoes for dresses and asked for what she liked. Elijah decided on New Balance, and Jeremiah wanted a pair of Reebok with dress shoes for church. Sacora paid, and the children carried out the bags. All three were thrilled and grateful for their shoes.

Chapter Forty-Two

Walmart was next on her list. Sacora decided it would be awhile before all the school supplies would be found. She handed Elijah his list and started with what he needed. Elijah chose a backpack after he had found all the items on his list for fourth grade.

Jeremiah's list for third grade was similar to Elijah's, a few more hand sanitizer supplies in form of liquid and wipes. Jeremiah's paper was to be in loose leaf with folders, and his art supplies were in a variety pack.

Alisha had been looking at the supplies but could not read her list for first grade. She handed her list to Sacora and then asked, "Do you mind if I get some things for Aylassa? I would like for her to have a box with scissors, glue, crayons, and pencils. I think she would like a coloring book and a sketch pad to draw on."

Sacora said, "Sure. We will get your things first, and then we will get hers."

After all the lists were rechecked, Sacora asked Alisha, "Have you seen what you want for Aylassa?"

Alisha said, "Yes, I have. I want this yellow box. Aylassa loves yellow."

Sacora said, "We will get the red box for Sadie, and will you pick out a coloring book for her also?"

Alisha said, "Yes, I think this one will be good. We all love Winnie the Pooh."

Sacora asked, "Would you like to get three, one for each of you?"

Alisha said, "Yes, ma'am, I would." Alisha chose three Winnie the Pooh coloring books and put them in the cart.

Sacora asked Jeremiah and Elijah, "Is there something you would like to have before we go to the clothes section?"

Jeremiah's answer was, "I would like to have a haircut."

Elijah asked, "Yes, Sacora. I would love to have a haircut. Can we go to the barbershop today?"

Sacora answered, "I think I will call Ginger and Sandy after we get finished shopping. They might be able to cut your hair this afternoon at their salon."

Elijah said, "I'm ready to go look at shirts and shorts if you are ready."

Sacora said, "Let's go."

The tables of matching shirts and shorts caught the eye of Jeremiah. He stopped and picked up a couple of sets. He asked Sacora, "I like these. Can I have it?"

Sacora said, "Yes, and you need to choose three more. This will do until it is time to buy jeans. You will be growing before then."

Elijah saw shorts on hangers and asked for Sacora to find matching shirts. Sacora did and decided on five sets. Sacora asked about underwear and socks. Elijah found what he wanted, and Jeremiah's selection was not as well stocked with variety. He took a few seconds before he asked for what he wanted.

Alisha was ready for her moments in finding outfits for school. She liked the matching shorts and shirts on the table. Sacora was surprised as Alisha did the coordination of the clothes. Alisha assembled her five outfits and put them in the cart. She had seen underclothes and socks that she liked and asked Sacora about them.

Sacora said, "We will go to the checkout if everyone has what they want."

The children agreed and started toward the checkout. Sacora decided to call Sandy and Ginger for the boys' haircuts while they waited in line. Ginger said, "Be here as soon as you can, and we will work them in. We are ready to meet them."

Sacora paid for the school supplies with the Walmart gift card her coworkers gave her. She had a few dollars left and decided to use it for groceries or lunches. The bags were put in the cart, and out the door they went. Elijah was the one who said thank you first, and Alisha's and Jeremiah's thank you was just as sincere.

Sacora looked in the review mirror at the smiles on the children and decided she had a pleasant day of shopping as a mom's first school shopping too. She started out of the parking lot, and on the way to Ginger's and Sandy's salon, she said, "You need to be thinking about how you want your haircut."

Elijah and Jeremiah's response were, "Yes, ma'am."

Chapter Forty-Three

S acora pulled up to the parking lot of the salon. The children got out and went inside. Ginger was at the door and introduced herself to the children. Sandy came to Sacora, hugged her, and introduced herself to the children.

Sandy said, "Elijah, come with me and tell me how your hair needs to be cut. Jeremiah, you can go with Ginger."

Ginger asked, "How do you want your hair cut?"

Jeremiah's choice was to be short, and Elijah's choice was to be shorter, almost a buzz cut. Alisha decided to sit down and wait. She thought her hair was just fine like it was.

Sacora was sitting with Alisha when an older woman under the hairdryer asked Sandy and Ginger, "Did you know Mrs. Taylor has passed this week? She was a school friend, lifetime friend of Samantha Hill's mother, Mrs. Baker. She had went to the nursing home some months back. I will remember the last few years she had a dog, Lab mix with husky, one blue eye and one brown eye that she carried everywhere she went. I wonder where the dog is now."

Sacora knew she was talking about Eeyore and decided not to respond with any comment. This lady did have answers to her questions about Eeyore how she knew the way around her home and being well behaved in the house, not ever bothering the children either.

Sandy finished with Elijah's hair, and he went to sit by Alisha and Sacora. Ginger was finishing Jeremiah's hair when Ginger asked Sacora, "Have you called Joe McCarley yet?"

Sacora answered, "Yes, I have. He does a good job."

Elijah spoke, "Yes, ma'am, we like him too. He comes around some and has dinner with us. Sacora is going to a Foo Fighters concert with him for his birthday."

Sandy and Ginger stopped what they were doing and looked at Sacora with large smiles. Sacora rebutted, "It is not what you think. I'm going to have a good time, and his daughter will be with the children. His daughter, Joy, has Sadie and Aylassa now."

Sandy said, "Okay, whatever you say. Hope you have a good time."

Ginger said, "Tell us all about it when you can."

Sacora said, "Yes, I will. It will be another few weekends."

Ginger was finished with Jeremiah's hair, and Sacora went to pay at the register. Ginger met her there and smiled when she spoke, "Sacora, you have what you have wanted for a while, and we could not be any happier for you. You know we are here if you need us. We love you, girl."

Sacora answered, "Yes, I know you are my support team while my mom is in Africa and always before then. And yes, I am happy to be a momma, even if it is only for a while."

Sandy said, "Baby, it might not be for a while. These children look happy with you as much as you look happy with them."

Sacora answered, "I have loved this week with them. I would like to have more. All right, let's go home."

Sacora hugged Sandy and Ginger bye, and the children buckled up in the van. Elijah spoke first, "Sacora, thank you for making this school shopping and haircut possible today."

Jeremiah's comments about how much he liked Sandy and Ginger was in his gratefulness of her day with them too. Sacora was quiet on the way home wondering how Joy handled Aylassa and Sadie. At home, she found Joy in the kitchen and Sadie and Aylassa sleeping. She had cooked macaroni and cheese for their lunch with hot dogs. The children started bringing their bags into the living room and sorting out of what belonged to whom.

Joy asked Sacora, "Would you like to ask Alisha, Jeremiah, and Elijah if they would like to eat lunch now?"

Elijah's and Jeremiah's answer was yes. Alisha went to wash her hands and was ready to eat too. Elijah said the blessing, and the hot dogs were such a great lunch after a day of school shopping. Sacora was very pleased with Joy's efforts of sitting with Sadie and Aylassa and lunch for them all. It was now almost three o'clock, and Sacora was waiting to hear from Joe.

Chapter Forty-Four

Three fifteen, Joe texted, "*I am almost finished. Are you back from shopping?*"

Sacora text back, "*Yes, we are. Joy has fixed lunch, and we are finished. She has done a great job today. Would you like to eat lunch when you get here?*"

Joe replied with, "*No, thank you. I have already had lunch. See you around four o'clock.*"

Sacora helped the children carry their things to their rooms upstairs and helped Jeremiah and Elijah put their new clothes in their dressers and shoes in the closest. Alisha was trying to put her new clothes in her backpack, but it all would not fit. Sacora showed her to put her shoes in the closet and the rest of her things on hangers. Sacora asked, "Do you not want to put your clothes in the dresser?"

Alisha answered, "No, ma'am, I won't be here that long."

Alisha asked, "Sacora, are we going to church tomorrow?"

Sacora answered, "Sweet baby, I forgot about buying church clothes today. I will go tomorrow night and buy some for next Sunday when we go buy groceries."

Alisha said, "Yes, ma'am. I would love to have some new dresses."

Sacora said, "We will look for summer and winter dresses. Let's go downstairs and visit with Joy before she leaves with Joe."

In the living room, everyone was enjoying the PlayStation. Aylassa was watching Elijah, and Sadie was watching Jeremiah. At four o'clock, Sacora heard the Foo Fighters loud, and Joe parked in the driveway. He came to the door, greeted by Sacora smiling.

Joe said hello to everyone and kissed his daughter, Joy, and asked, "Have you had a pleasant first impression of babysitting for Sacora? Sacora said you had done a good job today."

Joy said, "Yes, I have, Dad. I have enjoyed the time with Sadie and Aylassa."

Elijah broke in their conversation and asked Sacora, "Are we going to church tomorrow?"

Sacora said, "No, buddy. I forgot to buy you church clothes, and we will get some tomorrow night when we buy groceries."

Joe looked at Sacora and said, "You and the children are invited to go with me and Joy. We go to a local cowboy church, come as you are. After church, we are going to my parents for lunch, and you are invited to meet my parents."

Joy looked at Joe with a large smile. Sacora was hesitating, and Elijah spoke, "Sacora, can we go, please? I would love to go."

Sacora said, "I guess we can. What time, Joe, and where is it?"

Joe answered, "The church is by Dairy Queen and across from the car lot where you bought your van, and the time is eleven o'clock. I will meet you there. You will see my truck."

Sacora said, "Yes, that sounds great."

Joe, Joy, Sacora, and the children exchanged goodbyes and see-you-laters. In the truck, Joy looked at Joe for a long time before she spoke. She finally asked, "So, Dad, when did you change your mind about asking Sacora to meet Granny and Poppy?"

Joe answered, "I changed my mind this morning and called Granny, and she is excited, but I still repeatedly spoke of Sacora as a friend."

Joy said, "Sacora is a lady to take home to Momma. Just saying, Granny is going to be excited to get to know her."

Joe replied, "I have not invited a lady for a family lunch since Brandie. I guess that Sacora being the first in so many years is enough to get Granny excited."

Joy nodded and spoke, looking at Joe, "The children are so blessed to have her too. I can see the sparkle in Sacora's eyes when she looks at them. It is such a magical feeling in her home. It's full of welcoming love and pleasantness. I enjoy being there too."

Joe said, "Joy, I am grateful you have a place to be feeling loved but hope you have the most loved feeling with me, right?"

Joy giggled and said, "Yes, Dad, you are my number one."

Joe shook his head and said, "You are my number one, and here we are at last, home."

Chapter Forty-Five

S acora thought that she had not driven the Bug any in a few days and decided she might need to let it run for a while. She asked the children if they would like to go to the barn in the Bug. They were excited and put their shoes on. Sacora was putting Sadie's shoes on when Aylassa was trying to tie her shoes. Alisha came to help, and this surprised Sacora at Alisha's instructions to teach a three-year-old to tie shoes.

When everyone was ready, Sacora buckled up Sadie and Aylassa together in the middle of the back seat, and Elijah and Jeremiah wanted to be in the back seat on each side of Sadie and Aylassa. Alisha rode in the front seat with Sacora. Sacora started the Bug and turned the air-conditioning on full blast and got the Bug cooled before she started toward the barn. At the barn, Alisha was out first and then Jeremiah. Elijah got out after Sacora, and Sadie and Aylassa were unbuckled and ready to play tag. Sacora went to sit on the steps of the barn, thinking about Joe's invitation to his parents after church. She decided yes, she was ready for taking five children to church and lunch with Joe and Joy at his parents'.

It was a beautiful night in Alabama, fireflies and cooler temperatures, Sacora hated when it was time to go inside. She remembered her nights on the beach with Barton, but she could not remember the peace of happiness she felt with the children and Joe. She called the children to get back in the Bug, and Sadie and Aylassa went to the middle of the back seat to be buckled up. Elijah and Jeremiah buckled up in their seats and then Alisha. Sacora turned the air-conditioning on and looked in the review mirror. It was just months ago she bought this Bug being all alone and heartbroken after Barton decided to end their marriage to be with Rachel. She looked at the giggling little girls by their brothers, how this was just a fairy tale. She looked at Alisha cooling her face with the air-conditioning vent and started toward home.

Sacora got out, and the children followed after she unbuckled Sadie and Aylassa. On the front porch, Sacora saw Eeyore and wondered where she had been. When they went inside, Sacora told the children to wash their hands and faces while she fed Eeyore and put their snacks on the table before baths and showers. Elijah and Jeremiah were first to be finished and headed upstairs. Sadie and Aylassa had their baths downstairs, and Alisha went to the bathroom with her clothes after Sacora went to dress them. Alisha was in the bathtub when she heard Sacora singing "Grandma's Lullaby" and stopped to listen. Alisha washed her hair when she heard Sacora put the babies in their cribs. Sacora came to help Alisha with the hair dryer, and Alisha was nodding some.

Sacora asked, "Are you tired from today? We have had a big day."

Alisha said, "Yes, I am. I am ready for a fluffy pillow and sleep."

Sacora said, "We are finished. I will go tuck you in."

Upstairs they started when Alisha grabbed Sacora's hand into hers. She tugged a little and said, "Thank you so much for today. It has made me happy."

Sacora turned back the covers on her bed and kissed her forehead. She said, "Good night, my sweet Alisha. You are so welcome for everything. You make me happy too."

Alisha asked, "What was Ginger and Sandy talking about when they said you looked happy today? Were there days when you were not happy?"

Sacora answered, "Yes, sweet baby, it was. Just months ago my heart was broken, and it showed to the people who loved me the most."

Alisha said, "Maybe you won't ever be unhappy again. Good night, Sacora."

Sacora said, "Good night." She left the door opened some and heard the hair dryer with Elijah and Jeremiah talking about their day but mostly talking about their ride in the Bug to the barn. Sacora went downstairs to the laundry room with the girls' dirty laundry and saw where Joy had folded the sheets that she had washed and dried this morning. It was such a big help with what Joy had done for her today. She started the washing machine and went upstairs to say good night to Jeremiah. She turned back the covers and said, "Good night. We have another big day tomorrow."

Jeremiah said, "I am ready. The days I have been with you have all been big days. I think Sadie is happy too. Good night, Sacora."

Sacora went to check on Elijah, and he was ready for his bed. Sacora tucked him in and said, "Good night, buddy. We are planning on a big day tomorrow too."

Elijah said, "Yes, we are. I'm going to have a good time with Joe. Good night, Sacora."

Chapter Forty-Six

Sacora finished her long, hot bath with Eeyore laying on the floor resting. She made it to her bed tired from the big day she had with the children. Eeyore was extremely tired and went to her blanket ready for the night of quiet and sleep. Sacora was thinking about the next morning of church with Joe and Joy and meeting his parents and finally fell asleep.

The sun woke Sacora at seven forty-five. All the children were still asleep, and Sacora took the minutes to shower and plan on everyone's clothes for their big day. Eeyore was ready to go outside, and then Sacora fed her, filling her water bowl. In the kitchen, she decided on cheese toast and cereal for breakfast and started putting it on the table. Alisha was the first up, and Sacora asked if she wanted to choose her clothes for church.

Alisha said, "Yes, ma'am. I know what I want to wear. I will put it on after my bath. Momma always gave us a bath before church."

Sacora said, "Okay, and I will finish breakfast. It will be on the table when you are ready."

Alisha went to the bathroom and came back to the table dressed. She wanted cheese toast so she would not get anything on her clothes. Sacora went to get Sadie and Aylassa, and they ate cereal and drank orange juice. Elijah and Jeremiah came downstairs to eat and then went upstairs to get ready for church. Sacora carried Sadie and Aylassa to get them ready, and she put them on her bed while she changed into a cotton skirt and shirt with matching sandals. Everyone was ready for church by ten twenty. Sacora put bags of extra clothes and pull-ups in the van for their lunch with Joe's parents. Everyone buckled up and was ready for another big day. Sacora made it to church and saw Joe's truck.

She parked close to his truck, and he came to help with Sadie and Aylassa. Aylassa went to him, and Sadie went with Sacora. Alisha, Elijah, and Jeremiah went with Joy. As they entered the church building, everyone's welcoming greetings made the morning go smooth. Sacora was pleased at the children's behavior and their participation when they were asked to go to the front and sing "Jesus Loves Me." After the services, Joe introduced Sacora and the children one by one. They were asked to come back to church for every service. Joe helped Sacora put Sadie and Aylassa in the van and buckled them up, and Elijah and Jeremiah asked to ride in the back seat of Joe's truck.

Joe said, "Yes, that is good with me. Ask Sacora. She will have to follow me to my parents' home anyway."

Sacora said, "Okay. In what way are we headed?"

Joe said, "We are going back towards your home and keep going straight until the first red light and take a right. It will be the sixth house on the right."

Sacora said, "Sure, see you there."

Alisha, Sadie, and Aylassa were very quiet as they were following Joe. As they parked into the driveway of the sixth house, Sacora took a long, deep breath. Alisha was the first out, and Joe came to help with Sadie and Aylassa. Everyone went to the front door, and Joe rang the doorbell. His mother opened the door and introduced herself, Wendy McCarley.

Wendy said, "Come on in. Lunch is on the table."

Wendy hugged Joy, and Joe's dad came to meet everyone and introduced himself, Zac McCarley. Everyone went to wash hands, and Sacora used wipes on Sadie and Aylassa. At the lunch table, the children's manners were pleasant. Sacora was pleased with the meal, pot roast, potatoes, green beans, broccoli and cheese, salad, and dinner rolls. This was what she had for Joe and Joy their first dinner with her. The children's appetites were good, and they enjoyed the vegetables. Wendy McCarley brought out hot fudge cake for dessert, and the children ate giving compliments to the McCarleys' choice of food. It was not long until lunch was over and they were ready to play in the front yard.

Sacora helped Wendy clean the table and wash dishes. Joy carried Alisha, Aylassa, and Sadie to the front porch with her. Joe went to get a football, and Elijah and Jeremiah were introduced to throwing and catching a football. Three o'clock came so suddenly. Sacora announced to everyone it was time to go.

Zac and Wendy McCarley said goodbye. Joe helped Sacora put Sadie and Aylassa in the van. He told Alisha, Elijah, and Jeremiah he had a good day with them when he said goodbye. Sacora left with a pleasant sigh. It all seemed to go well.

Chapter Forty-Seven

Sacora took advantage of the children's tiredness of being quiet to concentrate on the way back home. It wasn't far from her home, and Sadie and Aylassa were almost asleep when she parked into her driveway. Elijah and Jeremiah were on the front porch looking for Eeyore. After calling a few times, Eeyore came to the porch. Alisha slowly petted Eeyore, asking her, "Where have you been?" Sadie and Aylassa decided they were ready for their cribs and a nap.

Sacora asked Alisha, Elijah, and Jeremiah if they would like to watch a Disney movie while Sadie and Aylassa napped. They decided on a movie, and Alisha fell asleep on the couch while watching it. Eeyore napped on the floor by her. Five o'clock had come, and Sadie and Aylassa had not awakened. Sacora decided to make a list for groceries and be ready when they woke up. Alisha woke up at five thirty and went to change her clothes for their shopping at Walmart. Elijah and Jeremiah went upstairs to change and were talking about what they wanted for suppers the following week.

Sadie and Aylassa made a noise of being awake around six o'clock, and Sacora changed their clothes and packed the bag for shopping. In the van, all the children were buckled up and ready for another big shopping trip. Sacora asked Alisha to be thinking about what she wanted to look for in dresses and groceries.

Sadie said, "My want mac and cheese."

Aylassa said, "I want everything."

Sacora laughed and nodded. In Walmart parking lot, Sacora got the children out, and together they went toward the carts. Sacora suggested to Alisha, Elijah, and Jeremiah to get a cart for their selections, and she would put some things in hers. Sadie sat in the front of Sacora's cart, and Aylassa wanted to sit in Alisha's. Their first stop was in clothes for church. Jeremiah seen pants and shirts that he liked that would be for summer and winter. Elijah selected pants from the clearance rack and some shirts that he liked in the Polo style. Sacora assisted in finding at least four combinations for each of them.

Alisha decided on some dresses that she could wear this summer and also in the winter with a denim jacket. Sacora found a denim jacket that she could wear hopefully for two seasons. Sacora's surprise was in the children's attitude to help with Sadie's and Aylassa's dresses and shoes. They had a big laugh with Sadie saying, "My wike everything."

After Sacora had put the dresses in the cart and a pack of pullups, she motioned toward the grocery section. Elijah had suggested what he wanted in vegetables and snacks. Jeremiah also had his suggestions ready. Alisha was happy with hot dogs, pizza, and macaroni and cheese with the others. At the checkout line, Sacora asked, "Do you want a candy bar for after we eat supper?"

They each chose a candy bar. When the total was announced, Sacora used the remaining amount of the gift card and her debit card. She was content on how she used the benefits of tax-free weekend and the gift card. In the van, all the bags were put carefully assorted of groceries and clothes. Sacora watched Elijah and Jeremiah put the carts in the outside cart bin by her parked van. Sacora decided she needed to go to the local meat market to buy meats for their suppers. At the meat market, she found in the deli plate lunches at a discounted price for the time of it closing. She asked the children to look for what they wanted and took the plates first. She saw a bundle of meat for a price of one hundred dollars and took it. Ground beef, pot roast, chicken tenders and breasts, with sausage and bacon was a great buy.

Sacora put all their purchases in the van and headed home. Elijah and Jeremiah suggested to put all the bags on the front porch and Alisha and Sacora could put the bags in the kitchen. Alisha put their church clothes in the living room for sorting later after the groceries were in their proper place and after supper. After the groceries were finished, Sacora called them to wash their hands and placed the plates from the deli on the table with chocolate milk. Alisha had put the candy bars in the refrigerator, and Sacora gave the children their bars. It was time for baths and showers, and this weekend was gone.

Alisha, Elijah, and Jeremiah sorted out the church clothes while Sacora gave Sadie and Aylassa a bath. Alisha was going upstairs when she heard Sacora singing "Grandma's Lullaby." She knew another big day had ended.

Chapter Forty-Eight

Sacora came from the babies' room and asked Elijah and Jeremiah if they needed help with hanging their church clothes in their closets. Alisha had already gathered her dresses and put them in her closet, still wanting most of her clothes in her backpack thinking she was not going to be with Sacora long.

After Sacora had finished, Elijah and Jeremiah went to shower, and Alisha had finished her bath. Sacora dried her hair. She had washed it before church too but let it dry in curls. Sacora tucked in each one, telling each one good night. Alisha, Elijah, and Jeremiah were grateful for what she had bought them today.

Sacora settled down in a long, hot bath thinking about today. All the minutes of today seemed to go so fast. After her bath, she fed and watered Eeyore again, noticing how tired she seemed to be just since she had left for grocery shopping. Sacora was getting ready for Monday morning, packing bags and putting her clothes out for work, when her phone rang. It was her mom.

Sacora answered, "Hello, mom. I am so glad to hear from you."

Samantha said, "We have finished the church and left it in good hands of a young man named Kwenda Madu [Quinnday Madew]. We are coming home a month earlier than expected. Me and the captain are ready to see you."

Sacora said, "I am ready to see you."

Samantha asked, "How are things going? Have you settled into your new home and job?"

Sacora said, "Yes, I have. I have been fostering five children for a few days now and have enjoyed them so much. I can't wait for you to meet them."

Samantha said, "That is great. I know how much you wanted to have a family. It's been your impossible dream. What are their names and ages?"

Sacora answered, "Elijah Malone is the oldest. He is nine years old and will be in the fourth grade this school year. Jeremiah Walters is eight years old and will be in the third grade this school year. Alisha Malone is six years old and will be in the first grade. I have made arrangements to have them with me all school year. Aylassa Malone is three, and Sadie Walters is two. The Malone children's mom died with cancer, and I am not sure about the next steps with them. Jeremiah and Sadie's arrangements are only temporary, and I have no certainty of how long I will be with them."

Samantha said, "This sounds great. I will bring two boy's gifts and three girl's gifts when we come home. Captain has come in and wants to talk to you. Love you, my baby."

Sacora said, "I love you, Mom, and ready to see you too."

Corey said, "Hello, my treasure. I am ready to be home. We will be leaving in a few weeks. Is everything good with you?"

Sacora said, "Yes, Dad, it is. I have adjusted to a life in Grandma's house with fostering five children, two boys and three girls. I have been happy with them, and seems like they are happy with me."

Corey said, "We are wrapping everything up here and might even be home earlier. We have been assisted by responsible people, and they are taking over with a positive transition."

Sacora said, "Okay, Dad, I will be looking forward to seeing you both soon. Goodbye, Dad."

Corey said, "Goodbye, my treasure."

Sacora put her phone on charge when she got a text from Joe. "*Can I call you?*"

"*Yes, you can*" was the text Sacora sent. Joe called.

Sacora answered smiling, "Hello, Joe."

Joe said, "Hello, Sacora. I don't mean to interrupt you this late at night. I wanted to tell you thank you for today. My parents enjoyed your and the children's visit for lunch today. My mom and dad have been talking about the cute things the children said and did at lunch. Elijah and Jeremiah seemed to like football too."

Sacora said, "I think they all had a great time, and lunch was very good. We all liked church too."

Joe said, "Well, maybe Sunday we can have another great day of church and lunch. Goodbye and good night, Sacora."

Sacora said, "Yes, Joe, that sounds great, and I will be looking forward to it. Goodbye, Joe."

Chapter Forty-Nine

E eyore was already on her blanket sleeping soundly. Sacora put her phone back on the charger and went to bed for the night. This weekend had been amazing hours of her living an impossible dream. School shopping with the children and tonight's shopping had been part of a dream she had for a while. Sacora knowing her parents were coming home earlier than planned gave her some sense of peace. The day with Joe and meeting his parents today was the most thing on her mind as she fell asleep. Sacora fell asleep ready for another week.

The week had flown by with the children in day care and her work of assignments, eating supper with the children and talking about their days at day care with the new friends they had made. Elijah and Jeremiah had made plans to go to Asher's house to play with the sheep on Saturday morning.

Sacora woke on Saturday morning to a cloudy day. The temperature was cooler, and she had opened the door for Eeyore. Sacora drank coffee on the front porch before the children had awakened. Eeyore sat outside with her. Alisha was the first one up and sat with Sacora and Eeyore on the porch. After thirty minutes or so, they went in to cook breakfast. The bacon was fried and the eggs scrambled and the biscuits baked and sitting on the table when Elijah and Jeremiah came downstairs. Sadie and Aylassa had awakened, and Sacora went to get them.

Ready to eat, the blessing was said, and the children talked about their day off from day care. Jeremiah was dressed in play clothes, and Elijah changed after breakfast to play with the sheep at Asher's. Sacora cleaned the table and dishes and changed Sadie and Aylassa into play clothes too. Alisha was ready and put pull-ups in the bag for Sacora, while Sacora was putting in a change of clothes for Sadie and Aylassa.

In the van, everyone was buckled up and was ready for another big day with Sacora. Asher's mom had given her directions to their home yesterday at day care. When they started up the driveway, the children were in awe of the animals they saw. Goats, chickens, and puppies with the sheep caught the eyes of Jeremiah. Elijah was impressed with the ponies. Sacora parked the van and gave advice of staying with her or with Asher's mom, Lynette.

Asher's mom, Lynette, came to greet them. Sacora was smiling when she said, "I see the children have noticed our animals. What would you like to visit first?"

Elijah said, "I like the ponies."

Lynette said, "Let's go see them this way."

Sacora and the children followed her to the ponies. Elijah started petting a pony and asked to ride. Lynette agreed, and Jeremiah choose a pony to ride. Alisha took a turn and enjoyed the pony. Lynette picked up Aylassa to sit on one of the small ones and led her around for a minute. Aylassa giggled, enjoying the ride. Sadie cried and did not take a ride.

Lynette said, "This way to the sheep. We have lambs that are very adorable and friendly. The white ewe and the black ram are for sale to a good home."

Elijah and Jeremiah went straight to them and petted and looked at Sacora. Elijah asked, "Please let us take them home for the barn. We all love the barn, and I'm sure the sheep will."

Sacora asked Lynette, "How much are for both lambs? I do have a barn ready for them, and the children seem to love them."

Lynette said, "One hundred fifty dollars for the pair or one hundred for one. I would like to keep them together."

Sacora said, "I will have to ask Joe with his truck to take them home. I can get them and pay you today, this afternoon, if that will be okay?"

Lynette said, "Yes, that will be just fine."

Sacora asked the children, "Are you ready to go and to make arrangements for the sheep to come home with us?"

Chapter Fifty

E veryone was excited and ready to buckle up in the van. Elijah said he wanted the black ram and named him Diesel. Jeremiah said he wanted the white ewe and named her Clover 'cause she was white like a field of white clover. When they reached the barn, everyone was out and looking for a place to put the sheep. Sacora called Joe.

Joe answered quickly, "Hello, Sacora. I was getting ready to call you. I am at your next-door neighbor's home for a repair call when I noticed Eeyore playing with some rabbits. I did not know if you knew she was gone."

Sacora said, "No, I did not. I have been with the children at Lynette's. What is Eeyore doing there?"

Joe said, "She has made friends with some bunnies the past few days. Mr. Holden said she has been coming every day for a while to play with them. He said they belong to his daughter, who has gone to college, and would like to know if you would like to have them. I know I can fix a place in the barn for them."

Sacora said, "Yes, sure. I can put them in the barn. Sounds like Eeyore has already made a decision to bring them home. I wondered where she had been going and coming home so tired. If you bring home the rabbits, maybe she will stay home with them and not wander to their home again."

Joe said, "I lack just a few more things, and then I will bring them to you. Joy is with me, and she will help with the children while we make them a home."

Sacora said, "Joe, there is a reason I was calling you. I have bought two lambs from Lynette and would like to know if you could bring them to us in your truck this afternoon. I will fix us some lunch before we go."

Joe said, "Yes, sure, that sounds great. Joy and I will be there just as soon as I get finished. I will put Eeyore and the rabbits in the truck and be right there."

Sacora said, "Goodbye, Joe, and thanks."

Joe said, "See you soon, goodbye."

Sacora looked at the children and said, "Guess what? Joe and Joy are bringing you a surprise."

Jeremiah asked, "What is it?"

Sacora said, "If I tell you, it won't be a surprise. Let's go inside and wash up and get ready for lunch. I think I will make sloppy joes for lunch and celebrate Joe's surprise and the two lambs coming home with us."

The children were ready and buckled up quickly in the van, and Sacora parked in the driveway. Sadie and Aylassa cooperated getting out the van. Alisha grabbed the bag, and Elijah and Jeremiah waited on the front porch for Sacora to open the door. Inside, Sacora put her purse down and put her phone in her pocket as she headed toward the kitchen. She told the children they could play games on the PlayStation while she cooked sloppy joes.

Jeremiah looked at Elijah and said, "We have already had a big day with Sacora, and it is not but half over. I am wondering what Joe and Joy have us."

Alisha said, "I like the sheep, and I like their names. I can't wait to see what Joe and Joy are bringing us too."

Sacora had put the plates and sloppy joes on the table when she heard a loud Foo Fighters sound coming toward the house. Joe was here, and she told the children to wash up and get ready for lunch. Joe would give them the surprise after they ate. Joe put Eeyore on the ground but left the rabbits in his truck.

At the lunch table, the children ate eagerly but asked over and over about the surprise Joe and Joy had. Joe insisted that a full stomach would make it even a better surprise to eat all their lunch. The children did, and Sacora started to clean the dishes when Joe asked her to wait and go with him to give the surprise.

At Joe's truck, he told the children, "Close your eyes 'cause I have you a surprise." After they closed their eyes, Joe handed Sacora a rabbit and Joy the other one. Joe let them know when to open their eyes, and Aylassa and Alisha was the first to show excitement.

Jeremiah said, "Sacora, since Elijah and I named the sheep, do you think Sadie, Alisha, and Aylassa should name the rabbits?"

Sacora said, "I think that is a great idea. What about it? What are their names?"

Alisha said, "I like Hugs and Kisses."

Aylassa and Sadie agreed, and so the rabbits were named Hugs and Kisses.

Chapter Fifty-One

Joe broke up the giggling and excitement of the children when he asked Sacora if she was ready for him to bring home the sheep. Sacora was going to the house for her purse when Joy suggested she stay with the children while Sacora went with Joe to Lynette's and she would finish cleaning the table from lunch. Sacora thought it was a good idea and was very appreciative of Joy as the children could play with the rabbits while they were gone.

Sacora told the children, "Bye, be good for Joy," and they all waved from the front porch when Joe and Sacora were leaving. In the truck, Sacora had an opportunity to talk to Joe, and she took it.

Sacora said, "Thank you, Joe, for making us all happy. I agree with you, the children need sunshine, outdoor activities, and I think the rabbits and sheep are such a great idea."

Joe said, "I have noticed the children are very happy with you, Sacora. Joy is always ready to visit you. She has always loved children, and she looks forward to be able to spend time at your home."

Sacora said, "Three weekends so far just seems so magical. I have had many memories in just such a few days. It has made me enjoy life like I had always dreamed. I have enjoyed you and Joy also. Thank goodness for a broken water faucet."

Joe replied, "Yes, that is how it all started. Would you like to go the feed store to buy rabbit food and food for the sheep first?"

Sacora said, "Yes, that is a good idea. I will need your opinion on what to buy. I have never had rabbits or sheep before. I have not had a chance to google what we will need. What about bedding for the rabbits? Will we need to have pine chips or straw to keep them from the ground?"

Joe said, "Yes, I'm sure the feed store will have a variety to choose from. They might even have a kennel or cage that would work."

Sacora said, "That sounds good. Here we are, and let the shopping begin."

In the store, Joe walked with Sacora and suggested what would be the best for what Sacora would need for the animals. The bedding for the rabbits were pine-scented chips, and the kennel was sized for approximately four rabbits. The food was suggested by the clerk, so this was what Sacora selected. The sheep would need a water container and salt. The type of grain was young cut brome hay, and grazing on the grass would be okay also. The clerk suggested one handful of Grower Lamb food twice a day until five or six months of age. Purina brand was in stock. Dewormer and vaccines would come from the veterinarian. Hoof trimming could be done by the local horse shoe stable, and the clerk gave them the number. The clerk also suggested collars and leash for the children to continue to maintain ability to interact every day. The clerk also informed Joe and Sacora that Ole English Southdown miniature baby doll sheep were submitted into a register and should have a tag on their ears. The clerk also suggested a pair of cutters to cut the wool from their eyes to keep vision from being impaired. Sacora and Joe took all the information the clerk gave and the products that were suggested. All the items were put in Joe's truck, and they were to Lynette's ready for the sheep.

Lynette greeted them and showed them to where she had the sheep. She had given them a bath in dog shampoo but told Sacora she could use Dawn dish detergent also. She informed them that the male had been castrated and given five hundred units of tetanus antitoxin at three days old. The lambs had been weaned for a while. They were three months old. Both lambs had been docked. They have been dewormed and would need to be dewormed again in a month. The lambs had been registered in the log and were ready for their new home.

Sacora took the money from her purse and looked at Joe and asked, "Did you get all of that? I will be a novice at this for a while, but I will get it."

Lynette said, "I am just a phone call away. When you get all of the information formed into a habit, you will be just fine. The miniature baby doll sheep are such a joy for family pets."

Joe picked up Diesel and put him in the truck and then Clover. He looked at Sacora and asked, "Are you ready to be a lamb momma?"

Sacora answered, "Yes, I will give it a try. What about you, are you ready?"

Joe said, "Yes, ma'am, let's go get started."

Chapter Fifty-Two

Joe started the truck and drove slow showing consideration to the lambs in the back. They did ride well and seemed to be pleasant on the way home. Sacora sat in quietness thinking about the information that she had been given on the sheep. Her first attempt at being a momma with pets for the children was going to be trying at first with work and day care. When they pulled into the driveway, the children ran out to meet them.

Sacora opened the bag with the collars and leashes and handed them to Joe. He put one on Diesel first and then sat him on the ground. Elijah took the leash from Joe and started petting Diesel right away. Joe put the other collar and leash on Clover and handed it to Jeremiah when she was on the ground. He was petting her and saying her name. Clover would respond occasionally with "Baaaaa." Alisha, Sadie, and Aylassa came to pet Diesel and Clover and were excited.

Joe asked Sacora, "Where do you want the rabbits' kennel?"

Sacora said, "Let's try to put them by Eeyore's doghouse on the back porch. Maybe Eeyore will stay home now while we are gone through the week."

Joe carried the kennel to the back porch beside Eeyore's doghouse and set it up with bedding. Sacora put Hugs and Kisses in their kennel for the night. She made sure their water and food were secure on one end of the kennel and they could sleep on the other side. Joe and Sacora asked the children to walk Diesel and Clover to the barn. The lambs at first seemed to be confused and then seemed to cooperate, walking toward the barn. Elijah and Jeremiah were smiling, walking to the barn, that Sacora thought, "Yes, this is good." Joe was waiting at the truck for everyone to be at the barn before he moved the truck. Sacora motioned for him to bring the food and supplies to the barn. The children were waiting inside the barn with Diesel and Clover.

Joe stopped and started to bring the food first. Elijah and Jeremiah gave the leashes to Sacora and Joy while they helped Joe with the supplies. After everything was unloaded, Elijah and Jeremiah took the leashed lambs and began to pet and talk to them again. Joe showed Sacora where the cut on and off valve to the water was at. He had a water hose that he put on the faucet. Sacora started filling the container with water, and Joe put a handful of feed in his hand and started feeding Diesel. Elijah said, "Can I give him some more?"

Joe said, "Yes, and Jeremiah, here is some for Clover."

Sacora smiled the biggest smile Joe had ever seen. Alisha took a handful of feed and offered it to Diesel, and Aylassa offered a handful of feed to Clover. All the children were feeding the lambs but Sadie. Joe picked her up and gave her a few pieces and then lowered her toward Clover, and she gave it to the lamb.

Joe asked Joy if she was ready to go, and she told everyone bye. Sacora gave appreciation to both Joe and Joy before they left. Sacora sat down on the steps and watched the children play with Diesel and Clover. Aylassa was laughing the loudest and squealing trying to get them to run with her. Sadie stayed close to Jeremiah, imitating what he did petting Clover. It was beginning to be late. The fireflies had started glowing. Sacora announced to the children that it was time for baths and showers. The children helped her put the lambs in their place for sleeping, placing the water container where it would be available, but not turned over.

Sacora walking down the driveway to the house felt content with the new additions to their family. Eeyore was still on the back porch with the rabbits, and Sacora called her for her food and water. Jeremiah was the first upstairs, and Alisha and Elijah went to gather their clothes. Sacora took Sadie and Aylassa to her bathroom, and the girls were giggling about the animals.

Alisha went to the bathtub and heard Sacora singing "Grandma's Lullaby" and knew another day was gone. After Sacora put Sadie and

Aylassa down in their cribs, Joe texted, "*Hey, I forgot to ask you if you wanted to come to church in the morning. I will be looking for you if you are. We can go somewhere after church for lunch before you are home and taking care of the animals.*" Sacora texted back, "*Yes, that sounds great. See you then. Good night, Joe, and thank you for today.*"

Chapter Fifty-Three

Sacora went to Alisha and dried her hair and went with her upstairs to tuck her in. Alisha asked if they were going to church in the morning, and Sacora made her happy with yes. Alisha told Sacora which dress she wanted to wear and shoes she had bought for church. Elijah was finished with his shower and was drying his hair, and Sacora tucked him in. Elijah's comments of today were thank you and how much he enjoyed Joe and Joy being with them today. Jeremiah was grateful, and his comments at good night were how he was going to enjoy Hugs, Kisses, Diesel, and Clover.

Sacora gathered all the dirty laundry and started the washing machine. Looking at the dining room empty where a late lunch with so many smiling faces had been, she found it be so comforting. Sacora went to her bathtub, and Eeyore followed her, laying on the floor beside the tub. She rested some and then decided to finish the laundry before going to bed. Just one more hour or so, she finally found Eeyore on her blanket, and Sacora fell asleep into a peaceful sleep.

Sunday morning found her rested and the sun shining another summer day in Alabama. She made her bed, opened the door for Eeyore, showered, and went outside to the front porch for coffee. There for only minutes, she heard Elijah and Jeremiah coming down the stairs with Alisha. Elijah and Jeremiah wanted to go to the barn to visit the lambs for a few minutes to feed them. Sacora agreed, and when she went to cook breakfast, Alisha went to the back porch to open the kennel for the rabbits. The rabbits were out, and Eeyore was all over the yard with them. Sacora had started putting breakfast on the table when Sadie and Aylassa woke up. Aylassa had figured out how to get out of her crib and meet Sacora at the door. She went to potty by herself, and Sacora carried Sadie. After Elijah and Jeremiah came to the kitchen, hands and faces washed, Sacora asked them about Diesel and Clover. Sadie was eating breakfast, and Aylassa was listening to the stories of the lambs. Alisha finished eating and went to get ready for church.

Elijah finished breakfast first and went upstairs to shower and get dressed. Jeremiah took some time with Sadie, talking to her that he would help her feed the lambs this evening. Sacora took Sadie and Aylassa to the bathroom and bathed and got them dressed in their room. Sacora put them on her bed while she got dressed into a cotton cool summer dress with sandals. Jeremiah had gone upstairs to shower and dress for church.

Alisha came in while Sacora was applying makeup and said, "Sacora, you are not old enough to wear lipstick. You need to wear lip gloss."

Sacora said, "Yes, ma'am, I will." She handed Alisha the gloss to choose which color. Alisha handed her the red tube. Sacora said, "Red it is."

Sadie said, "Zora, you are georgous."

Aylassa said, "Zora, you are beautiful."

Sacora said, "Okay, let's go see your brothers and head to the van."

The girls were ready. Alisha had the bag for church and lunch with Joe and Joy. Elijah and Jeremiah were dressed in the new clothes and shoes, smiling and ready for their day, all buckled up and leaving the driveway at ten fifteen. Sacora thought this was good timing.

At church, Sacora found Joe's truck and parked close. He came to the van with Joy. Aylassa went to Joy, and Sadie went to Joe. Sacora grabbed the bag, and Alisha, Elijah, and Jeremiah followed them in. Everyone was again very welcoming, and church service was over with the children singing "Jesus Loves Me." After dismissing from service, Joe asked Sacora where would she like to go for lunch. It was decided Olive Garden for lunch, and the children were buckled up in the van. Sacora insisted that she buy for her and the children and Joe could buy for Joy.

The children ate very well and had some leftovers for tonight. Sacora and Joe paid, and Sacora and the children exchanged goodbyes. On the way home, Sacora was relieved how today had been. Through the front door, Elijah and Jeremiah ran upstairs to change into their play clothes. Excited, they asked to go to the barn, while Sadie and Aylassa napped. Alisha wanted to play with Hugs and Kisses. Sacora agreed, figuring how she would watch Alisha and Eeyore with the rabbits. Elijah and Jeremiah said they would be only thirty minutes or so and then go back when everyone went.

Sadie and Aylassa slept, and Sacora sat with Alisha, Elijah, and Jeremiah playing with the rabbits. Five o'clock, everyone was ready to eat supper.

Chapter Fifty-Four

Sacora washed the hands and faces of Sadie and Aylassa. Alisha, Elijah, and Jeremiah came to the table with hands and faces washed and ready to eat. Sacora had made some macaroni and cheese for Sadie's request, and most of the Olive Garden was eaten. Aylassa ate and let Sacora know she was ready to see the lambs. Sacora cleaned up and got Aylassa and Sadie ready for the barn. Alisha, Elijah, and Jeremiah went to put the rabbits up for the night. They made sure they had carried enough water and food to the kennel. Eeyore went inside after the rabbits were up for the night.

At the barn, Diesel seemed ready to eat, greeting Elijah. Elijah put some food in his hand, and he ate aggressively. Jeremiah got a handful of food for Clover, and she ate it slowly. Jeremiah handed Sadie some food and helped her feed Clover. She giggled at the tickling of Clover's mouth and tongue.

Aylassa's handful of food to Diesel was gone quickly. Alisha gave each lamb a handful of feed. Sacora changed their water and put out some food for the night. She sat on the steps watching the children giggle and entertain the lambs. Sacora put the leashes on, and Diesel and Clover walked some on the driveway and around the barn. They were friendlier today. Fireflies began to glow, and Sacora decided to call it bath time and start another ending to the weekend.

As the children were leaving the barn, Elijah and Jeremiah asked if they could come back in the morning before day care, and Sacora agreed. On the walk to the house, Alisha caught some fireflies, and Aylassa started to catch some. Sadie just enjoyed the chasing of the girls catching fireflies. Jeremiah was walking behind Sadie and pretending to catch her. She giggled when he did catch her and picked her up, swinging her around. In the house, Sacora was surprised everyone went about the business of baths and showers without any instructions from her.

After Alisha was in the tub, Sacora had Sadie and Aylassa ready for the rocking chair and with "Grandma's Lullaby." Alisha listened very quietly until she heard Sacora put the babies in their cribs. Sacora came to dry Alisha's hair and tucked her in upstairs. She told her good night and went to check on Elijah. Jeremiah was drying his hair first tonight, and she tucked him in, leaving the door opened some. Elijah came to his room, and Sacora tucked him in. All the children and Eeyore were sound asleep. In Sacora's bathtub of rest, she thought about Joe's birthday coming up on Tuesday. She decided she would ask if he wanted to come to supper for hamburgers and hot dogs. She texted him before going to sleep.

"*Hey, would you like to come on Tuesday night for hamburgers and hot dogs for your birthday? I can have it ready around six o'clock.*"

Joe texted back "*No, I can't. I'm going to my parents for supper, and I was hoping you and the children would come. I need help blowing out so many candles and eating a large cake that can hold it all, lol.*"

Sacora texted in response, "*Yes, that sounds great. I will meet you there. See you then.*"

Joe answered, "*Good night, and I will be looking for you.*"

Sacora fell asleep ready to tackle another week of work, day care, animals, and Joe. The house was so quiet of sleeping children, tired from their big weekend.

Chapter Fifty-Five

Sacora was ready for Monday morning. Waking up by five o'clock and showering, she got ready for another day. Coffee on the front porch, Eeyore was out eating and drinking before the rabbits were out for the day. Her quiet moments were almost for an hour when Alisha came outside to sit. She petted Eeyore for a while, and then it was time to get ready for breakfast and day care. Sacora was surprised that Elijah and Jeremiah were up and dressed, ready to eat and go to the barn to feed the lambs. Sadie was up first. Aylassa slept in for thirty minutes, and then it was time to make final moves for the day. Alisha went to set the rabbits out, and Eeyore followed her. In the van, everyone buckled up and headed out the driveway.

At the day care, Sacora had a few words with Lynette, and she was supportive to Sacora with the lambs. The children were ready to start their week, and Sadie kissed Sacora and said, "My wuv you, Zora." Sacora's heart just melted. Aylassa kissed her and said, "I love you, Zora, and I will be ready to go to Aylassa's house with you."

Alisha, Elijah, and Jeremiah had gone to their part of the day care for school children with a wave and "Have a good day." At the office, Sacora took her assignments from Mr. Hamilton, who was always smiling and could tell she was being happy with fostering the children. This day was over in a hurry, and at the day care Aylassa was ready to go to Aylassa's house. The evening of feeding animals, petting, walking lambs on leashes, and putting the rabbits in their kennel for the night and baths and showers were so pleasant that it seemed like Sacora did not remember a month ago when she was all alone. In her hot bath, with Eeyore laying on the floor, she thought about tomorrow night at Joe's parents and how she needed to handle the feeding of the lambs before she went. Eeyore and the rabbits could wait until bedtime for their food. Another day of her impossible dream, she slept soundly.

Tuesday morning July 30, she decided to text Joe "*Happy birthday*" before she started her day. He texted a few minutes later with "*Thank you, looking for you tonight.*" Sacora smiled and made her bed, let Eeyore out, showered, and went to the front porch for coffee. Six o'clock, and Alisha was not up. Sacora started breakfast, and then Elijah and Jeremiah came downstairs with Alisha. They ate breakfast and asked to go to the barn to feed Diesel and Clover after they opened the kennel for the rabbits to play with Eeyore all day. Eeyore ate dog food quickly and was ready to play with the rabbits. Alisha went to the barn with Elijah and Jeremiah for a quick visit. Diesel was ready to eat some food out of Elijah's hand. Clover ate from Jeremiah and Alisha's hands. The walk back to the house was quick to be ready for day care. Sacora was dressing Sadie and Aylassa when they made it back. She had already cleaned the table. Alisha put clothes and pull-ups in the bag for Sacora. Out to the van to start another day, buckled up, and leaving the driveway in plenty of time. Sacora told the children bye, and again Sadie and Aylassa had such a sweet goodbye. Alisha took time to give her a kiss on the cheek, and Elijah and Jeremiah were longer with a wave and "Have a good day."

At work, Sacora couldn't keep her thoughts off tonight with Joe and his parents. Lunchtime came, and she went to get a burger, just to rest and to indulge in plans for tonight. Five o'clock came, and Sacora made it to the day care. Making it home to the barn, she opened the van door for Elijah, Jeremiah, and Alisha to feed and water Diesel and Clover. When she parked the van in the driveway, Aylassa said, "Aylassa's house."

Sacora opened the door, and Sadie and Aylassa went with Sacora to get ready for Joe's birthday at his parents. Alisha, Elijah, and Jeremiah came in to wash up and change clothes after petting and feeding the lambs. Eeyore was in the backyard with the rabbits. Sacora put some dry dog food in her bowl. Out the door, in the van again, buckled up, and headed to Joe's parents, first red light, right turn, sixth house on the right.

Chapter Fifty-Six

Sacora parked by Joe's truck. Joy was sitting on the front porch. Zac and Wendy McCarley came to greet Sacora and the children. Elijah was first to Joe. "Happy birthday, Joe" came from Elijah, and then Jeremiah said, "Happy birthday." Alisha did not wait. She started singing "Happy Birthday," and Sadie and Aylassa joined in. Joe was smiling and looking so pleased with his company of Sacora. Wendy invited everyone in. Supper was on the table getting cold. Barbecued chicken breast, baked potatoes, tossed salad, garlic bread, baked beans, corn on the cob, and birthday cake were waiting on them. After the blessing, everyone started eating. Sadie started eating the corn on the cob and was having a difficult time. Alisha showed her how to hold it, and Sacora helped her out some. Aylassa finished eating and was ready for birthday cake first. Sacora watched her impatiently wait on time for the birthday cake. Finally Wendy brought the cake with candles. Zac lit the candles, and "Happy birthday" was sung again.

Joe made a wish and blew out the candles. Aylassa was first to get her cake. So much laughter and happiness, Sacora was at ease with the visit. Joe went to get the football, for Jeremiah and Elijah wanted to play. Joy went to the porch with Alisha, Sadie, and Aylassa. Before Sacora could think of what to say to Wendy while cleaning the table and dishes, Wendy broke the silence.

Wendy said, "I have not seen Joe this happy in a long time. He is my only child, and Joy, my only grandchild. It has been a pleasure having you and the children around. I hope you come around more often. Joe has not brought anyone to lunch or supper in years, and it has been nice."

Sacora was hesitant in replying, "I have enjoyed being here. Joe has assisted me in adjusting from being alone to a parent of children and animals. He seems so dedicated to being Joy's dad. I have needed the support he gives from his experience. I don't know how long I will have the children with me, but I have enjoyed every minute of it. Joe has been the reason it has gone so beautifully."

Wendy added, "Joe is in consideration of your feelings, I can tell, and the way he looks at you adds hope for me that one day he will love again. I wanted him to have a large family so that I could have numerous grandchildren. That might be selfish of me, but that is what I wanted for us all."

Sacora said, "My parents wanted me not to be an only child, but that is the way it worked out. My mom being an only child knew how it felt even though she had Ginger and Sandy. The way they have loved children is the reason missionary work was started."

Wendy asked, "When are they coming home? Joe mentioned they were in Africa."

Sacora answered, "They will be coming home earlier than planned. My dad is an engineer, and his company sponsored my parents' expense and some other employees and families to construct and establish churches in rural Africa. My mom being a schoolteacher was an additional needed skill. Another employee was an architect sent for buildings that were needed for churches and schools."

Wendy said, "Sounds like your parents will have a good bit in common with Joe and Zac. You know they did all the renovation and remodeling on your grandmother's house and barn?"

Sacora was stunned. Before she could respond, Joy came in with Aylassa, Sadie, and Alisha. Sadie said, "My fristy, Zora."

Aylassa asked for more birthday cake, and Alisha wanted a drink. Wendy very enthusiastically gave each one what was asked for. After the children had finished, Sacora helped clean up and decided to end the visit. She told the girls to tell Wendy, Zac, Joe, and Joy bye and go to the van. Elijah and Jeremiah said goodbye and went to the van.

Joe came to Sacora to buckle up Sadie and Aylassa in their car seats and told the children thanks for the nice birthday. He looked at Sacora and told her thanks for the evening.

Sacora looked at Joe with some anger and said, "Wendy says you knew my grandmother and all the renovations and remodeling on the house and barn were done by you and Zac. Why did you not tell me you knew my grandmother?"

Joe answered softly, "Sacora, you never asked. Have dinner with me Saturday night, and I will tell you everything and anything you want to know about Mrs. Baker."

Chapter Fifty-Seven

Sacora looked at Joe for seconds and never responded, still in a daze. Wendy McCarley did not know that she did not know her grandmother apparently. Joe broke the silence, still speaking softly.

Joe said, "My mom would love to have the children Saturday night, and you meet me here around five o'clock. We will have a long evening, nice meal, and I will answer any and all your questions. What about it?"

Sacora took a minute and said, "Yes, sure, and I will see you then."

Everyone exchanged goodbyes again, and Sacora was leaving the driveway still angry. She turned on the country music station for comfort, and Trisha Yearwood's song was playing, "There Goes My Baby." This was what made her realize that her grandmother rejected her all her life and this young man not only accepted her but had made life so much easier for her living her impossible dream.

Sacora stopped at the barn to take one more check on the lambs. Aylassa was almost asleep but woke up to feed some food to Clover with Jeremiah. Sadie just watched Alisha and Elijah give a handful of food to Diesel. Sacora filled fresh water in the container, and as she touched the water hose, her heart melted. Joe knew where the cut off and on valves were 'cause he put them there. And yes, she never asked him.

Sacora put everyone back in the van and headed up the driveway. Elijah and Jeremiah were on the porch, and Eeyore came to them. Sacora opened the door, and without any instructions, Alisha went to check on Hugs and Kisses, and Elijah and Jeremiah went upstairs for their showers. Sacora put Eeyore's food in her bowl and filled her water bowl. Alisha had carried the rabbits more water and food and put them in the kennel for the night. Aylassa was ready for her bath, removing her clothes by herself. Sadie watching started to taking off her shirt and said, "Zora, my stuck." Sacora gave the babies a bath and dressed for bed. She sat in the rocking chair with them, singing "Grandma's Lullaby." When she put the babies in their cribs, she looked in their room and decided everything in here was Joe. Everything had been touched by Joe McCarley, even her heart. Sacora left the door open some and could hear Alisha in the bathroom ready to dry her hair. Sacora finished drying her hair, tucked her in, and said, "Good night, sweet baby."

Sacora gathered the dirty laundry and put it in the washing machine. She went back upstairs to Elijah and Jeremiah, tucking them in, saying good night. She gathered up their dirty laundry and started the washing machine. Eeyore was already on her blanket but joined Sacora in her bathroom, laying on the floor dozing while Sacora enjoyed her long, hot bath. Nine o'clock, Sacora charged her phone and fell exhausted into her bed. She had let her anger go because she knew Joe was right and started to look forward to seeing him again. She knew that Wendy would enjoy the children being with her while she would be with Joe. Another day of happiness had ended.

The next following days of work, day care, and the animals just flew by. Saturday morning found Sacora with tiredness like she had never felt before. She knew the housework needed to be done of vacuuming and dusting, in addition to sheets being changed. Sacora had gotten up to open the door for Eeyore and drank her coffee on the front porch. Eeyore ate dog food and drank her water resting by Sacora. The children were tired and slept till nine thirty.

Elijah and Jeremiah wanted to go the barn right after breakfast. Eeyore and Alisha went to the rabbits. Sadie and Aylassa stayed with Sacora while she changed sheets and started the washing machine. Sacora put Alisha's clean clothes in her backpack, still not putting them in the dresser. Most of the housework was finished by eleven o'clock, and Sacora started cleaning the bathtub in her bathroom. Sadie and Aylassa thought it was a good idea for them to help her but actually played in the water.

Sacora called to the children for lunch at twelve thirty. After they had washed up and said the blessing, their appetites were stimulated by playing with the animals. Sacora was impressed with the happiness the animals had brought within just a week. The children wanted to go outside to play again. Sacora suggested to Elijah and Jeremiah to bring Diesel and Clover on their leashes to the front yard while she finished the kitchen. Sacora watched the lambs being difficult at first but made it to the front yard and started to graze some. At three o'clock, they all walked to the barn to put the lambs up for the night. Sacora filled fresh water in the container and removed their leashes, hanging them on a nail. It was time to be ready for her night with Joe.

Chapter Fifty-Eight

Sacora started back to the house from the barn and just took a long look. Joe had made this house that her mother grew up into a home for her. It had become Aylassa's house and home to the other children. Not even a month yet, and it was like this was the way life had always been. Sacora told the children to wash up, change clothes, and play the games on the PlayStation while she got ready for her night with Joe. Alisha watched Sadie and Aylassa coloring in their Winnie the Pooh coloring books while Sacora was in the shower.

When Sacora came out dressed, Alisha wanted to help with her hair and makeup. Aylassa and Sadie came too, jumping on the bed before they sat down. Sacora watched in the mirror Aylassa and Sadie watching Alisha brush out her hair. Sacora decided to put it up in a ponytail and started her makeup. Alisha reminded her that she was not old enough to wear lipstick and she needed to wear lip gloss. Alisha chose pink tonight to coordinate with Sacora's clothes.

When Sacora went to the bed to help Sadie and Aylassa down, Sadie looked at Sacora and said, "My think you are georgous, Zora."

Aylassa said, "You are the beautifulist, Zora, eber."

Alisha handed the bag to Sacora to put the babies' things in for their visit at Wendy McCarley's. Elijah and Jeremiah turned off their game and TV, ready to be in the van. Sacora looked at the Bug and decided she needed to drive it tomorrow, maybe again to the barn. Everyone buckled in, Sacora started down the driveway. First red light, right turn, and sixth house on the right. Joe was there four fifty, and Sacora parked by his truck. Joy came out of the house with Wendy, and Sacora handed her the bag and informed her they had not eaten supper and appreciated her invitation for supper with them. Sacora said goodbye to everyone, and Joe opened the door of his truck for Sacora. She was quiet for a while when Joe asked, "Anywhere particular you would like to eat?"

Sacora answered, "What about LongHorn Steak House? I think that we should have privacy there and not be rushed out the door."

Joe said, "Yes, that sounds great."

The drive was pleasant, Sacora not saying much, not wanting to say the wrong thing, and decided not to say anything about her grandmother. She would let it go for now and maybe forever. Joe had done an outstanding job on the renovations and remodeling that she found that to be the most important thing. It also gave her the impression that Joe was dedicated to his parents, and she was thankful for that quality. At the LongHorn Steak House, Joe came around and helped her out of the truck. The wait was only a few minutes, being ten minutes after five o'clock.

At the table, Joe asked, "What are you having?"

Sacora said, "I think a hamburger steak with a baked potato and salad. I think I will even have a Coca-Cola."

When the waiter took their order and left, Joe said, "I was not sure you would come tonight."

Sacora asked, "What made you think that?"

Joe answered, "I could tell you were angry with me not telling you Dad and I did the renovations and remodeling at your home. And I did not give you any indications that I knew Mrs. Baker. So what are your questions? What would you like to know?"

Sacora said, "I have not any questions, Joe, about my grandmother. All I want to know is about you. I look around the home that makes me so happy living my impossible dream, and all I see is you. Even in the barn with the lambs, all I see is you."

Joe smiled and said, "I worked many days with my dad there, and it has great memories for me too. I learned everything I know about carpentry, plumbing, and electrical from my dad. I have a college degree in education, history major, and football coaching and never spent one day using it. When Brandie and I divorced, Joy was my everything, and I could schedule work around her visits. My mom worked, and Joy was with her some. I wanted her with me as much as I could schedule it."

Sacora said, "You being a devoted dad has helped me with my adventure in parenthood and animals. I have never and will ever be able to say thank you enough."

The waiter brought their orders, and Sacora took a break from conversation and looked up at Joe, occasionally smiling. The evening was going so well that they sat in the LongHorn Steak House for an hour and a half.

Chapter Fifty-Nine

Sacora asked Joe, "You think your mom is okay with all of the children? I hope they are good for her and she does not regret entertaining them tonight."

Joe said, "I don't think that will happen. My mom has always loved children, like you."

The waiter offered to-go cups, and Sacora accepted with Coca-Cola refill. Joe declined and paid the ticket and out the door to his truck. He opened the door for her and asked if she would like a walk on the beach. Orange Beach was where they walked. It was a warm night and quiet on the beach for some reason. The night ended with Joe taking Sacora's hand while they walked back to the truck. Eight o'clock, and Sacora and Joe were headed back to the McCarleys' to say goodbye.

Joe asked, "Can I expect to see you at church in the morning?"

Sacora said, "Yes, I think so, Joe. I have had a rememberable night. Thanks."

Joe said, "You are welcome. Here we are. Let's go see if Dad has on nail polish and his hair in a ponytail."

Sacora giggled but did burst out laughing when she saw Zac McCarley's face covered in makeup. Wendy McCarley's was makeup scattered on the floor. How did Alisha, Aylassa, and Sadie talk him into that?

Wendy was the first to speak. She said, "Did y'all have as much fun as we have? The girls have enjoyed my makeup and Zac's face. Jeremiah and Elijah threw and caught Joe's football till dark. Everyone ate a healthy supper and with dessert."

Aylassa said, "We watched the pretty man on TV. I like the pretty man."

Sadie said, "My wike the pretty man when he dances."

Sacora looked at Wendy and asked, "Who are they calling the pretty man?"

Wendy laughed and said, "I have some revised DVD's of Elvis Presley. They have watched one of him over and over. Joy has always enjoyed watching Elvis, so they watched it with her."

Sacora said, "Okay, now I know about the pretty man too. Everyone in the van and let's get buckled up."

Zac and Wendy told everyone goodbye and they enjoyed their visit. Joe walked Sacora out, helping buckle up Sadie and Aylassa in their car seats. He told Sacora it had been an awesome night for them all and he would look for her in the morning at church. On the way home, Sacora noticed that the children were tired. She parked in the driveway and did not stop at the barn. Elijah and Jeremiah wanted to go to the barn after breakfast in the morning before church. Sacora agreed. She opened the front door, and Eeyore came in with them and was ready to eat. Sacora went to the kitchen, Alisha, Eeyore, and Aylassa following her. Sadie went with Jeremiah to the kitchen asking for chocolate milk. Elijah went upstairs to shower, ready to call it a day.

Alisha found the rabbits' food and carried it out with water and put them in the kennel for the night. Sacora put the babies in the bathtub and was sitting in the rocker when Alisha came to her.

Alisha asked, "Sacora, can I shower tonight in your bathroom? I think I can get all the shampoo out of my hair."

Sacora answered, "Yes, sweet baby, you can. If you need me, let me know."

Sacora started singing "Grandma's Lullaby," and Alisha started the shower. Jeremiah had gone upstairs to shower. Elijah had finished and was drying his hair and ready for bed first.

Sacora had put the babies in their cribs and went to check on Alisha. Sacora dried her hair, and Alisha was nodding, being so tired. Sacora walked upstairs with Alisha and tucked her in. She went to Elijah's room and told him good night. Jeremiah was last to his bed.

Jeremiah asked Sacora, "Did you have a good night with Joe? We had a blast at the McCarleys'. It has been another big day with you, Sacora."

Sacora said, "Yes, it has, sweetheart. I did have a good time with Joe, and I'm content with you having a good time at the McCarleys'."

Jeremiah said, "Yes, we did. I love throwing the football with Elijah like Joe taught us. Good night."

Chapter Sixty

Sacora made it to her bathtub looking at its cleanness. Touching the sides of the tub, remembering Sadie and Aylassa's help, playing in the water while she cleaned. Today had been another big day, as Jeremiah called it. She thought about her minutes with Joe on the beach, how different it was from being with Barton. Joe was a very different man than Barton, and it would be in her best interest if she would not doubt Joe's integrity again or compare him to Barton Haynes.

Sacora thought about what she and the children would be wearing tomorrow with Joe going to church. She finally made it to her bed with tired, sleeping children beside her and above her. She fell asleep tired from another day of living her impossible dream.

Sacora woke around eight o'clock, with the children still sleeping. She made her bed, opened the door for Eeyore, showered, and drank coffee on the front porch. Eeyore came to her for a minute and then went to the back porch, where the rabbits were. Alisha came to the front porch and sat quietly for a few minutes and then asked to open the kennel for Hugs and Kisses.

Sacora went inside to start breakfast. Elijah and Jeremiah came downstairs, dressed in their play clothes and shoes. Sacora agreed they could go check on the lambs after eating breakfast. Alisha had the rabbits playing with Eeyore and came in to wash up to eat breakfast. Sadie and Aylassa were up by eight fifty and ready to eat. After the blessing, Sacora gave orange juice and chocolate milk with bacon, scrambled eggs, and biscuits. The children ate well, and Elijah and Jeremiah went to fed and water the lambs.

Alisha went to shower and dress for church. Sacora put Sadie and Aylassa on her bed after she had them ready for church. Alisha came to her room dressed for church and sat with Sadie and Aylassa while Sacora brushed her hair and put on makeup. Sacora and Alisha packed the bag for church and lunch. Elijah and Jeremiah came in after thirty minutes or so and went upstairs to shower and dressed for church.

Everyone was ready in the van ten fifteen and out the driveway to church. Sacora parked by Joe's truck and was surprised as Zac and Wendy McCarley were with him and Joy. Elijah and Jeremiah were out first and ran to Joe. Alisha went to Joy and then Wendy McCarley. Joe helped Sadie out, and she went to Sacora. Sadie patted Sacora's hip and said, "My wanna be here."

After Aylassa was out of the van and going to Joe, Sacora picked up Sadie and put her on her hip and grabbed the bag, entering the church. Everyone was friendly, and Zac and Wendy McCarley sat on one side of the pew and Joe and Sacora on the other side with the children between them. The children sang "Jesus Loves Me" again so cooperatively and smiling. Services were over, and in the parking lot, Zac asked if everyone wanted to go to eat at McDonald's. Sacora smiled. It had been awhile since she has been there. Everyone agreed. Elijah and Jeremiah wanted to ride in Joe's truck with Joy, and Sacora was okay with it.

At McDonald's, the children ate very well, interacting with Zac and Wendy, and Sacora was thinking that it was like they had known them forever. Sadie ate chicken nuggets and asked for more. Joe went to order, and Alisha, Elijah, and Jeremiah followed him to bring back ice cream cones for them all.

Lunch was over, the children told everyone goodbye, buckled up, and headed back home. Sacora thought that went very well. The morning had been very pleasant, and now the afternoon was full of things to do with the animals. Sacora parked into the driveway, and Aylassa again said, "Aylassa's house." Sacora opened the van door, and Aylassa had learned to unbuckle herself, and Elijah helped her out. Sadie was unbuckled and ready to be in her crib for a nap. Aylassa went to sleep in her crib also.

Elijah, Jeremiah, and Alisha changed clothes to play with the rabbits and lambs but played games while the babies took a nap. Sacora took the time to just think about this morning with Joe McCarley and his family. Zac and Wendy were genuine in caring for the children and good company for her.

Four o'clock, and Sadie and Aylassa were up. Sacora asked if they would like to ride in the Bug to the barn. Jeremiah was excited and was out the door first. Alisha waited until Elijah and Aylassa were in buckled up, and she got in the front seat. Sadie and Jeremiah were buckled up and then Sacora started the Bug, cooling it off before heading to the barn.

Chapter Sixty-One

Sacora made it to the barn, and the children wanted to sit under the air-conditioning for a few minutes longer. The first weekend of August, another hot day in Alabama, air-conditioning was needed. When Alisha got out of the Bug, Elijah jumped out and was the first to Diesel. He started feeding Diesel, and then Alisha, Jeremiah, and Aylassa went to Clover. Sadie stayed with Sacora.

Sadie said, "My don't want to get dat on mine zoes."

Sacora looked at the feces and realized she did not buy shovels to clean out the stalls of where Diesel and Clover spent their nights. She looked at the salt, and it was almost gone. Still plenty of food, she would have to go tomorrow after work to the feed store. She remembered seeing shovels hanging on the wall of different sizes and thought she would buy two of the short ones for Elijah and Jeremiah and a regular-sized one for her. Sacora took the leashes from the nail and handed them to Elijah and Jeremiah. The lambs seemed to be grateful for the walk around the driveway and barn. Aylassa wanted to try to lead Diesel with Elijah and he showed her what he would do to get Diesel to corporate.

Seven o'clock, Sacora motioned to prepare the lambs for bed-time. Sacora filled the water container with fresh water and the amount of food by their remaining salt. In the Bug, everyone buckled up and ready for the air-conditioning. Sacora parked, and everyone was out. Sacora went to cook some supper, and Alisha, Elijah, and Jeremiah went to play with Eeyore, Hugs, and Kisses. Sacora had Aylassa and Sadie cleaned up and ready to eat when she told the others to put the rabbits in their kennel for the night and wash up for supper. Eeyore was first through the door, and Sacora fed her with dog food and water. Alisha was sitting at the table with Sadie and Aylassa and said the blessing when Elijah and Jeremiah sat down.

Jeremiah said, "Sacora, we have had another big day. I have liked being with Joe and his family too. Will we be with them again?"

Sacora said, "Yes, sweetheart. Saturday night, I go with Joe to the Foo Fighters' concert, and you will be with Joy."

Elijah said, "Cool, that is something I will look forward to this week. Can we go to Zac and Wendy McCarley's with Joy?"

Sacora answered, "I don't know. I think Joy will be here with you, buddy."

Sacora noticed everyone had finished eating and told Sadie and Aylassa bath time. She picked up Sadie, and Aylassa followed her to the bathroom. Jeremiah went upstairs, and Alisha went to gather her clothes. Elijah went upstairs, and he was ready for the shower. Sacora had finished dressing the babies and started rocking, singing "Grandma's Lullaby" when Alisha decided to take a bath instead of a shower. Alisha was quiet and listened to Sacora sing. After Sacora put the babies in their cribs, Alisha finished her bath and was ready for Sacora to dry her hair. Alisha was tired but not nodding tonight.

Sacora went upstairs to tuck Alisha in and checked on the brothers. Sacora turned back the bed for Alisha, noticing how she learned to make up this large bed immaculately. Alisha jumped in, ready for her pillow and snugging the quilts.

Alisha asked, "Is this my last week of day care? Will I be starting school next Monday?"

Sacora stopped to think and answered, "Yes, it is, my sweet baby. You will have your first day of first grade on Monday."

Alisha said, "Good night, Sacora. I love you, and sweet dreams."

Sacora said, "Good night, my sweet baby, I love you too, and sweet dreams to you."

Elijah was finished drying his hair and met Sacora in the hall toward his room. She followed him, and he did not give her a chance to turn back the covers. He was in his bed quickly, yawning, and ready to say good night. Sacora returned good night and left the door opened some. Elijah was so tired he had nothing to say about today or Monday morning being the first day of school.

Jeremiah was finished with his shower and drying his hair. Sacora turned back his covers, and he suddenly jumped into his bed. Jeremiah was tired too, and after good night, Sacora left the door opened some and went downstairs. She gathered dirty laundry, cleaned the table, and then started the washing machine. After a long, hot bath, Sacora was ready for her night of sleep too.

Chapter Sixty-Two

Sacora was up around five thirty and opened the door for Eeyore, showered, and then had coffee on the front porch. Eeyore finished some dry dog food on the front porch and sat laying on the porch by her. Alisha came and sat quietly, and then after an hour, it was time for breakfast and to start the week.

At breakfast on Monday morning, Sacora was more into a habit of getting everyone ready for out the door. Sacora enjoyed a relaxed breakfast with the children. Jeremiah had heard Alisha's questions about school starting next Monday last night and decided to ask more questions at breakfast.

Jeremiah asked, "Sacora, am I going to be here when school starts? Are you going with me the first day like my mom? Will the school allow you to complete my registration and sign it, or will I have to wait for my mom?"

Sacora answered, "Yes, sweetheart, I am going with you on the first day of school and will sign your registration. No, you will not have to wait on your mom."

Jeremiah asked, "So this is our last week at day care? I have really like spending my days with Asher."

Sacora said, "I am not sure where Asher will be going to school, but we do know where he lives, and we can visit. It is time for us to start our day. Are you and Elijah going to the barn to check on the sheep?"

Jeremiah and Elijah did go to the barn and feed the sheep. They put more food out by the salt, filled the water container with fresh water, and took a few minutes to pet them, talking to them about what they would be doing today in day care. All the way to the front porch, Elijah and Jeremiah were running and laughing. They needed to get ready for day care.

Alisha had went to the back porch and opened the rabbits' kennel. Eeyore was ready to play all day with Hugs and Kisses. The children went upstairs to dress, and Sacora dressed Sadie and Aylassa. Sacora went to her room to dress, putting Sadie and Aylassa on her bed. Sacora and Alisha packed the bag for them. It was time to buckle up in the van and start another week.

Sacora left the children with Ms. Koch with sweet goodbyes and left for work. It was the last week for Alisha, Elijah, and Jeremiah to be here, and it would be an adjustment to add school to her schedule. She needed to remember to make arrangements with Mr. Hamilton for Monday morning taking the children to school for the first day. She should only be a couple hours late, not even a half day until she made it to work.

At work, around ten o'clock, Sacora got a text message from Julie. "*Will you please call me on lunch break. I have some GOOD news on Barton's motion. I will need to fill you in on the judge's decision, and I will send it to you through the mail.*"

Sacora did take a moment to discuss her Monday morning taking the children to school with Mr. Hamilton. He would work out the time with her as he did the other parents that worked in the office and would be absent for the first day of school. At lunch, Sacora did call Julie.

Julie said, "Hello, little momma. I have great news for you."

Sacora said, "I am always ready for great news."

Julie said, "The judge has denied the motion for Barton. The technicality I rebutted on was the wording of the trust fund. The wording is, "This trust fund is to Barton Haynes and Sacora Hill Haynes. It is not or/either or to wife of Barton Haynes." It is to you, Sacora Hill Haynes. The judge's order will let them know the only way you will not receive your part is by your signature, which you said you would not sign. The other thing is that I am sure Barton will be in touch after he is notified that you will be receiving your amount due. You know, Sacora, this amount would ensure you that you could stop working and be a full-time mom. You could actually retire on this amount. I am estimating the amount of two point five million dollars after I am paid. The amount of the trust fund in full is almost six million dollars."

Sacora said, "Thank you, Julie. You have always done a great job for me. I will be in touch if Barton has any more trouble for me."

Julie said, "Okay. I will talk to you later. Is this Saturday when you go with Joe McCarley to Foo Fighters' concert?"

Sacora said, "Yes, and I will talk to you about it on Sunday night."

Julie said, "All right. Talk to you then."

Sacora said, "Bye, Julie."

Chapter Sixty-Three

Sacora went back to her desk and finished the assignments that Mr. Hamilton had given her. Her thoughts were going back and forth about the money she was entitled to. Sacora needed the job with the Department of Human Resources for the insurance, other benefits, and steady income. Also, the certainty of the children's custody, residing with her was slim to none in percentage.

Five o'clock came, and all her coworkers said goodbye for the day. Sacora went to the feed store before going to day care for the children. She found the shovels she had seen and thought about buying and salt for the lambs. She paid for the items, and the clerk carried them out to her van. Sacora was still in deep thought about Barton on her way to day care. She went into the marriage for love and gave him ten years of her life, the best ten years. She had so many disappointments in her marriage to him, mostly wanting a family. Through the divorce, he took 95 percent of everything, and she didn't have any regrets. The life of the house, children, and Eeyore was so much more than a fair exchange. And yes, Joe was such a joyful addition.

At the day care, Ms. Koch greeted her and informed her, "Friday, there will be a party for the children going back to school." Ms. Koch said she had loved Alisha, Elijah, and Jeremiah and would miss them every day. There was a program that she had for after school. A van would pick up the children at school and bring them to the day care, and Sacora could pick them up with Sadie and Aylassa. The foster program of the State of Alabama would still be responsible for the payment. Sacora agreed to this program and enrolled them to start on Monday. She would go the first day, and the van would bring them to Ms. Koch.

Aylassa was the first one to Sacora and said, "Is it time to go to Aylassa's house?"

Sacora said, "Yes, it is, baby. Sadie, are you ready to go?"

Sadie and Aylassa were with Sacora when Alisha, Elijah, and Jeremiah came to say goodbye to Ms. Koch. Sacora buckled up Sadie, and Aylassa buckled up herself. Alisha, Elijah, and Jeremiah buckled up and asked Sacora, "Are these shovels for us?"

Sacora said, "Yes, they are. I also got some salt for the lambs."

Aylassa asked, "What are the shovels for?"

Elijah answered her, "The shovels are for us to clean up feces from Diesel and Clover. Would you like to help?"

Aylassa said, "No, thank you. I will jest feed and pet Clover."

Sacora pulled up to the barn and opened the doors for everyone to go to Diesel and Clover. Aylassa unbuckled herself, and Sacora helped Sadie. Sacora put the salt out for the lambs, combining the remaining salt. Jeremiah was trying out the shovel and asked Sacora, "Where do we need to pile the feces up?" Sacora designated a place, and Elijah followed Jeremiah with his shovel full. The sheep's manure was dry and stayed in the shovel until it was thrown into place. Alisha petted and fed clover, and Sacora with Aylassa's help fed and petted Diesel. When Elijah and Jeremiah were finished with the cleaning of the feces, Sacora handed the leashes to them. They walked the lambs around the barn and driveway. Jeremiah asked Sacora, "Can we walk them to the front yard?"

Sacora agreed. She told them to wait at the barn while she drove the girls in the van before they started toward the house. Sacora buckled Sadie up, and Aylassa buckled herself again. Alisha got in the front and buckled up. Sacora headed toward the house looking in the review mirror to make sure of the safety of everyone, even the lambs. When she parked, the lambs gave a fuss at first but then followed Elijah and Jeremiah to the house. They proudly walked the lambs around the front yard. Sacora suggested not to worry about the feces. It would be a fertilizer on the grass. Sacora opened the door, and Sadie and Aylassa went to potty. Alisha was ready to feed and water the rabbits.

Alisha opened the back door, and Eeyore came in to be fed and watered, mostly loved on. After all the animals were taken care of, Sacora started to cook spaghetti for supper. Aylassa and Sadie sat down with Eeyore while Sacora made the salad. To keep their attention, Sacora was asking, "Now what vegetable to we need to add with the lettuce? Sadie, would you like tomatoes? Aylassa, would you like to add cucumbers?"

Sadie answered, "Yes, my wike cheese too."

Sacora said, "Yes, ma'am, a little or a lot?"

Sadie and Aylassa both answered, "A lot."

Sacora called to Jeremiah and Elijah to walk the sheep to the barn and put them up for the night. It was suppertime.

Chapter Sixty-Four

Sacora watched the handwashing and face cleaning of Alisha before she cleaned up Sadie and Aylassa. Alisha helped to put the salad dressings on the table and garlic bread. Sacora put the spaghetti and salad on the table and then plates and silverware.

Sadie said, "My do it." She climbed in her chair. Aylassa helped herself too. Jeremiah and Elijah came in and washed up. When they sat down at the table, everyone said the blessing. Sacora was enjoying the minutes with the children's appetites indulging in the spaghetti and salad. After everyone was finished, Alisha started helping Sacora clean the table. Aylassa said, "Can I help?"

Alisha said, "Sure. Take these to the refrigerator, and I will put them up."

Sacora cleaned Sadie's face and hands. She looked up at Sacora and said, "My wuv you, Zora." Sacora's heart melted, and she kissed Sadie's cheek and said, "My wuv you too, Sadie."

Aylassa and Sadie went to the living room with Alisha, Elijah, and Jeremiah to play games on the PlayStation. Aylassa was sitting with Elijah and Eeyore came to sit by them. Aylassa was watching every move Elijah was making. Sadie and Jeremiah was sitting on the other side and Sadie was just watching the TV.

After the dishwasher had started, Sacora was sitting down when her phone showed an incoming call from her mom. She answered, but the call was dropped. Sacora called back, and her mom answered. "Hello, my sweetie," Samantha Hill's voice sounded so enthusiastic. "Guess what? We are coming home, leaving out in the morning. We should see you in a few days."

Sacora said, "That is so great. I am ready to see you. It seems like forever since I have seen you. Are you going to notify me when you land at the Mobile airport? I will meet you."

Samantha said, "Yes, we will. We are packing up after we leave Kwenda Madu all the information he will need for the churches and schools. Captain wants to talk to you."

Sacora said, "Hello, Dad. I am ready to see you."

Corey Hill's voice was anxious. "I am ready to be home. Our work here went fast and thorough with good people to leave it with. How are things going? Speak loud because your mom is listening."

Sacora giggled and spoke loudly, "Everything is great. The children's first day of school is on Monday, and we are getting ready for that. Sadie and Aylassa are going to potty and doing well in day care. And for me, it's going good. I have a young man I would like for you and Mom to meet. His name is Joe McCarley."

Corey said, "Great. Will we meet him soon or just whenever?"

Sacora said, "I think you will meet him soon."

Samantha broke in the conversation and said, "We have a lot to do, Sacora. We will be in touch about our travel plans. Sounds like you have done well putting your life on a different path after your heartbreak with Barton. I can't wait to meet the children and Joe."

Corey said, "Goodbye, my sweetie. I am bringing the children's gifts too."

Sacora said, "Bye. I am ready for you to be home too."

Sacora put the phone down with a smile. Elijah turned around and asked, "Who was that, Sacora? I can see the call made you smile."

Sacora said, still smiling, "My parents are coming home from Africa. I am ready to see them."

Jeremiah said, "Sacora, I like being here with you. Will I have to go back to my parents one day?"

Sacora looked at him and spoke softly, "Jeremiah, I would like for you and Sadie to be with me forever. I am doing all I can to make it happen. Okay, everybody, time for showers and baths. We got to get ready for another day."

The TV was turned off, and Alisha went outside to put Hugs and Kisses up for the night. Eeyore followed her. Sacora went to bathe Sadie and Aylassa. Up the stairs went Jeremiah and Elijah. Another day was over.

Chapter Sixty-Five

Sacora made it through the week of day care, work, suppers, baths, laundry, making beds, and loving every minute of it. Saturday morning found her suddenly with the thought of being with Joe tonight at the Foo Fighters' concert. She thought she would deep condition her hair in the sun on the front porch when she drank her coffee, in the quietness of waiting on the children to wake. Eeyore went outside and waited patiently on her food and water. Alisha was the first to the front porch, sitting quietly with Sacora. After an hour or so, Elijah and Jeremiah came downstairs ready to play with Diesel and Clover.

Sacora said, "After an hour, I will have breakfast on the table. Will you please look for us to motion you when it is ready?"

Elijah said, "Yes, ma'am. We might not be that long. We will wait until after breakfast to shovel the barn out."

Sacora heard Sadie and Aylassa getting down from their cribs. Sacora met them at the door and carried them to potty. Sacora washed their faces and hands and put them in the kitchen. Alisha went outside the back door and put Hugs and Kisses out with food and water. Eeyore went with her.

Sacora cooked a large breakfast this morning, biscuits, scrambled eggs, sausage, with the addition of some pancakes. Alisha came in and went to the front porch to motion for Elijah and Jeremiah to come in to eat. They were already coming down the driveway. Alisha went in to wash up and told Sacora they are coming. Sadie and Aylassa climbed into their chairs ready to eat. After Elijah and Jeremiah sat down, the blessing was said, and the children giggled and had such a large appetite that Sacora was content with the choice of cooking extra. It was all eaten.

Elijah and Jeremiah went back to the barn to shovel the stall in the barn. Alisha and Eeyore went outside to play with Hugs and Kisses. Sacora, Sadie, and Aylassa went to the front porch. Sadie and Aylassa decided to play tag in the front yard while Sacora sat in the sun deep conditioning her hair more. It had been a pleasant Saturday morning. Sacora was also pleased of the housework she had completed last night. Changing sheets and laundry was a mark off her list.

Sadie ran and enjoyed the sunshine for a while and then sat by Sacora. She said, "Zora, my firtsy and hot. My don't wana pay."

Sacora called to Aylassa to come to the kitchen with her and Sadie while she got their cups of orange juice. Sacora went to the back porch for Alisha to come in and drink. Eeyore was ready for drinking in her bowl. Sacora told them to sit in the living room with the TV and their drinks while she washed out her hair. The girls went and were cooling off watching TV. Elijah and Jeremiah came in too, ready to drink some chocolate milk. They had put Clover and Diesel up for the night.

After nap time for Sadie and Aylassa, Sacora prepared for Joy what she would need for supper and went to get ready for her night with Joe. She showered, putting another conditioning product on her hair. She decided she would flat iron her hair straight. Alisha came in to her room while she was putting on her makeup and selected another lip gloss. Sacora giggled when Alisha told her again she was not old enough to wear lipstick.

Sadie and Aylassa woke up and came into Sacora's room. Aylassa said, "Zora, wear lellow for me, peaze."

Sadie said, "My wike wed, Zora."

Sacora went into her closet and changed into a yellow-and-red-rose cotton shirt with khakis, matching sandals, and a denim jacket for when it cooled off. She came out dressed, and the girls made a wow sound together.

Sadie said, "My think Zora is georgous."

Aylassa said, "I like the lellow."

Alisha said, "And I helped with her hair and makeup. You are beautiful, Sacora."

Sacora went to the living room and told Elijah and Jeremiah it was time for her to go. Sacora said, "Joy will have your supper, and you know about showers, baths, and bedtime. Be good for Joy, and I will see you after a while."

Sacora heard loud Foo Fighters music and went to the front door. She stepped out on the porch with butterflies in her stomach. Joe and Joy McCarley were here.

Chapter Sixty-Six

Sacora waited on Joe and Joy to come to the door. She gave Joy a run-down of what she had prepared for her to have for supper and Sadie's and Aylassa's clothes after their baths. Alisha would put Hugs and Kisses in their kennel for tonight with food and water. Sacora kissed each child good night and then looked at Joe with "I am ready."

Joe said, "We will be back late. Joy, I know you have everything in control."

Sacora looked at Joy and said, "Make yourself at home. You can sleep on the sofa when the children go to sleep or you can go to my bed. Eeyore will go outside one more time and should go to her blanket."

Out the door for the first night out of Foo Fighters with Joe. Sacora was shocked when she walked out and did not see Joe's truck. He opened the door to a Red Dodge Charger. Sacora thought it was nice and spoke, "When did you get this car?"

Joe answered, "Today. I thought it would make an easier ride to the concert for you."

Sacora said, "Yes, it will be." She buckled up smiling. He had bought this today for her. Wow!

The drive to the concert was very pleasant with small talk, and Sacora, again not wanting to say the wrong thing, was mostly quiet.

Joy told the children, "I have a surprise for you. I have a DVD of my dad playing football."

Jeremiah was excited and asked, "Can we see it now?"

Joy said, "Yes. I will turn it on."

Joy started the DVD, and the children's attention focused on every football play. The music Joy put with it was Foo Fighters' "My Hero." Joy watched Jeremiah's eyes glowing with what he saw.

High school played with Tyler Green blocking for Joe catching passes, running hundreds of yards for touchdowns. Joe running with Tyler Green blocking, catching passes for touchdowns. Joe breaking tackles, picking up blitzing line backers in pass protection, and surprising fans with open field speed.

College was the same amazing catches and Tyler Green being Joe's blocker and most inspiration for successful games. Many of the most mesmerizing moments/highlights came from basic I-formation lead plays with Tyler clearing the way with a block on the linebacker. Joe making a move on the safety out running him for a big play for six points. College was different formations than high school, mainly shotgun but the basic blocking concept the same. Tyler Green always making the key block sometimes on a filling linebacker and other times on the edge.

In the NFL highlights, Joe still had the speed, strength, and intelligence but did not have the blocking or support of Tyler Green. His caught passes for touchdowns were repeated in the video. The celebrating of football players at Miami and fans were also included. And there was one or two of Joe celebrating holding Joy as an infant.

Elijah asked, "Joy, why did Tyler not go to the NFL with Joe?"

Joy said, "Sometimes life is just that way. Tyler's position was phased out that year, but the most thing was Tyler's dad being diagnosed with cancer. He went home to be with him and keep the hardware store open for income. His college degree was in business, so he is using it. His dad passed within six months of diagnosis, and Tyler has never regretted it."

Jeremiah asked, "When did Joe stop playing football?"

Joy answered, "I was young, but I do remember, and this is what I think. The chemistry that dad had with Tyler, he did not have in Miami. Tyler not only blocked for dad to make touchdowns. He blocked to keep him safe. Dad had a rough tackle that left him permanently injured. Even after a complete knee replacement, his knee did not heal and left him with a limp. He was never able to return to football. My mom divorced him to marry the general manager of the football team, and he came to Mobile to work with my grandfather in home repair. He spent every minute he could with me for the past years. This DVD is such a precious thing for me. I thought you would like it."

Jeremiah's reaction was, "Can we watch it again?"

Joy played the video over and over until it was time for supper and bedtime.

Chapter Sixty-Seven

Sacora and Joe decided on going to the Olive Garden to eat before the concert. Sacora indulged in the salad and chicken alfredo. Joe enjoyed his Tour of Italy. They had plenty of time before the concert to take minutes of relaxed atmosphere and some conversation. Joe was unaware of Sacora's intentions of him meeting her parents and showed it when she spoke.

Sacora said, "My parents are coming home early from Africa, and I would like for you to meet them. I thought you would go with me to the airport to pick them up when they arrive in Mobile. It should be next weekend."

Joe stumbled over the words, "Yes, I will. Have they given you any schedule of a flight yet?"

Sacora said, "No. The schedule when they left wasn't a for sure plan, and I suspect the schedule coming home will be the same. Mom will let me know just hours in advance of their landing in Mobile."

Joe said, "Okay, that will be good."

The waiter came with another salad and drinks. Sacora was beginning to ask Joe about his marriage to Joy's mother when he started the conversation about her first. He spoke of Brandie, a love of his through college and married before he went to the NFL, Miami, Florida.

Sacora asked, "Why did you break up?"

Joe said, "After I was injured permanently, couldn't go back to playing football, she decided to marry the general manager of the football team and stay in Miami, Florida. I said okay and returned to home Mobile, Alabama, and worked with my dad in his home repair business. I was spending all my time with Joy when she came to visit. She was around three years old when everything was settled."

Sacora said, "I know the heartache of being deceived. I thought things were great between me and Barton. I wasn't happy with not having a family, but I still thought we were great. The day he brought it to my attention that we were no longer going to be married was a crushing day for me. I look at where I am now from May till August, and I am pleased to be here. I hope you find happiness also."

Joe said, "I have found the check, and we need to be on our way."

Sacora gathered her leftovers in a carryout plate and put them in a bag and started out after Joe paid. Joe opened the door for her in the Dodge, and she buckled up. Joe took the leftovers and put them in a cooler he had brought with some drinks. Sacora asked, "How much further to the concert?"

Joe said, "It is almost six miles, but the traffic will make it almost an hour, I think."

Sacora was enjoying the ride in the Dodge and looked at the congested traffic before them and behind them. It was going to be a traffic jam for a while. Sacora settled in for a comfortable ride to the stadium, where the concert seemed to be expecting a large audience. She was watching as Joe followed the parking attendant's motion to park. Sacora, looking around, thought the walk to their seats would be a while to reach. Joe opened the door for her and asked, "Are you ready to walk a ways?"

Sacora said, "Yes, I am."

Joe took her hand, and they headed toward the stadium. Tyler had done well in buying the tickets for seats in the front portion were difficult to buy. After thirty minutes, they found their seats and were content of the location. Their seats were close enough for good pictures on their phones and further away from the standing fans at the bottom of the stage. Sacora took Joe's hand and said, "Thank you. This is the first Foo Fighters concert for me."

Joe said, "Thank you for coming. I hope you enjoy their music."

Chapter Sixty-Eight

Sacora watched the band enter with the fans screaming and welcoming each member as they took their place on stage. Joe screamed, applauded, and whistled, having a good time. Sacora listened to every introduction of the songs that the lead singer Dave Grohl would give before playing. She decided by the time the concert was over that her favorite Foo Fighters songs were, "The Sky Is a Neighborhood," "Walk," and "My Hero." The lead singer's daughters, Violet and Harper, came on stage to sing "The Sky Is a Neighborhood" with their dad, and Sacora was touched as this loving father was having moments with his daughters.

The walk back to the Dodge was longer than she had thought it would be. When they made it to the parking lot, Joe pressed the panic button for the Dodge to show the direction in which they needed to go. At the Dodge before Joe opened the door for her, he stopped for a minute and kissed her passionately. He said, "I have wanted to do that for a while."

He opened the door, and Sacora buckled up. A long wait in line leaving the concert, Sacora took his hand and said, "Thank you. It was a great time."

Joe said, "What about a walk on the beach and eating the leftovers in the cooler with the drinks I brought?"

Sacora said, "Sure, I am ready to eat again."

The traffic started going smooth. Sacora and Joe made it to Orange Beach with the cooler on the sand. They sat down and ate the leftovers from Olive Garden and enjoyed the sound of the waves hitting close to them. After the leftovers were gone, Joe put the cooler back into the Dodge, and they walked down the beach for a while.

Sacora looked at her phone and said, "I need to get back home. It is almost three thirty a.m."

Joe said, "Yes, ma'am, it will be almost four thirty when Joy and I make it home. Am I to expect you at church later this morning?"

Sacora said, "I am not sure. I have not been home getting ready for today."

Joe said, "Okay, I have kept you out all night. But if you do, I will look for you."

On the way to Sacora's home, Joe could tell she was tired and talked very little. When Joe parked in the driveway, Sacora asked if he would like to come in for Joy. He declined, and Sacora went in to wake her on the couch. Joy went out to Joe after telling Sacora the children were good and she had a great time. The video of Joe playing football, she left for Elijah and Jeremiah to watch as she had another copy.

Joe left the driveway quietly without music playing. Sacora checked on the sleeping children. She went to bed tired and happy. It had been an amazing night with Joe. Even the Foo Fighters concert was such an awesome event she would remember. The kiss at the car, eating leftovers, and walking on the beach were still on her mind and how she looked forward to seeing him hours later at church.

At eight o'clock, Sacora woke up to Elijah, Jeremiah, and Alisha coming down the stairs. Sacora went to the bathroom and heard Sadie and Aylassa climbing down from their cribs. Alisha went to the kitchen, and Elijah and Jeremiah went to the TV. Sadie and Aylassa went to the potty and were ready for breakfast. Alisha went out the back door, and Eeyore went with her to put Hugs and Kisses out for the day.

Jeremiah and Elijah asked Sacora, "Can we watch Joe's football video that Joy made us before breakfast and play with Diesel and Clover?"

Sacora said, "Yes, you can, and I will start breakfast. What about cereal since we are later and going to church?"

Everyone washed their hands, sat at the table, said blessings, and enjoyed their cereal with milk. Sadie wanted orange juice, and Aylassa wanted chocolate milk after eating cereal. Elijah and Jeremiah went to the barn to feed and water Diesel and Clover. Alisha went to get ready for church. Sacora showered while Alisha watched the video of Joe playing football with Sadie and Aylassa. When Sacora was dressed, she carried Sadie and Aylassa to be ready for church. Elijah and Jeremiah came in to shower and put their church clothes on. Ten o'clock, everyone was ready. Sacora and Alisha put pull-ups and clothes in the bag for church and lunch. Ten forty-five, Sacora parked close to Joe's car. He came to help her with Sadie and Aylassa. Alisha, Elijah, and Jeremiah noticed Wendy and Zac McCarley with Joy. Everyone went in for service smiling and being welcomed.

Chapter Sixty-Nine

Sacora and Joe sat through service with his parents and the children sang "Amazing Grace" after Jesus Loves Me. After services were over, Sacora and Joe made plans to take lunch to Gulf Shores beach with Joy and the children. Wendy and Zac had other plans and told everyone goodbye at the van. Aylassa buckled herself, and Joe buckled up Sadie. Joe and Joy went to his home to get his truck to tailgate at the beach. Kentucky Fried Chicken was the lunch chosen for today. Sacora went to Kentucky Fried Chicken with orders from everybody. At the beach, Joe and Sacora placed the children with their orders and drinks and made a great tailgate lunch. Around three o'clock, it was time to leave, and Sadie was ready for a nap. Sacora reminded the children first day of school is tomorrow. After cleaning everything up and putting the children in the van, Sacora told Joy "Thank you for the great job you did last night" and goodbye to Joe.

Sacora parked in the driveway and asked Elijah and Jeremiah if they would like to put Diesel and Clover on a leash to walk around the driveway and front yard. Elijah said, "Yes, ma'am, I think I can reach the nail and put the leashes on them."

Sacora said, "After Sadie and Aylassa nap, we will all go to the barn in the Bug to water and feed the lambs. Would you like to?"

Elijah and Jeremiah decided to shovel the feces out of the barn before they walked them around. When the shovels were put on the post, Diesel was ready to walk with the leash. Clover was hesitate for a few minutes but then decided to follow Jeremiah as he walked toward the house. The lambs grazed on the grass close to the front porch.

Sadie and Aylassa took a nap and Alisha sat on the back porch with Hugs and Kisses. Being so tired, Sacora decided to wait after work and school to buy groceries tomorrow. She thought about supper and started cooking a pizza. When it was done and on the table, she called Alisha, Elijah, and Jeremiah to wash their hands and sit at the table. Sadie and Aylassa went to potty and washed their hands. All the children said the blessing and started talking about this weekend with Joy, Joe McCarley, and his parents. Jeremiah talked about Joe playing football and how anxious he was to play. They mentioned the first day of school tomorrow, and Sacora assured them she would be taking them and everything would be fine.

After eating and cleaning the kitchen, Sacora said, "Elijah and Jeremiah, if you would like to take Diesel and Clover to the barn, I will wait and bring the Bug when you are safely in the barn."

Elijah said, "That will be good, and we will start their fresh water."

Jeremiah said, "I would love to ride in the Bug."

Alisha carried Hugs and Kisses's food and water and put them in their kennel for the night. Eeyore came in to eat and drank all the water from her bowl. After Elijah and Jeremiah were safely in the barn, Sacora buckled up Sadie, and Aylassa buckled herself. Alisha buckled in the front seat, and the air-conditioning blowing on her face cooled her before they made it to the barn. Sadie was ready to be out to play, and Aylassa went with Alisha. Clover ate a handful of feed from Alisha, and Diesel ate a handful from Aylassa. Sadie wanted to run playing tag. After Sacora made a thorough look for the lambs' night, she watched Sadie running with Aylassa playing tag. Within just days, these two little girls have bonded and learned so much.

Sacora said, "All right, everything is good. It is time to go and get ready for school tomorrow."

Everyone buckled up, and Sacora started the Bug and parked in the driveway. Elijah and Jeremiah went upstairs to shower, and Sacora started the bathtub for Sadie and Aylassa, while Alisha went upstairs to gather her clean clothes. After Sadie and Aylassa were dressed in their pajamas, Sacora started singing "Grandma's Lullaby" in the rocking chair. Asleep in their cribs, Alisha was ready for her hair to be dried, and Sacora gave her some help.

Sacora gathered all the dirty laundry and carried it to the washing machine. She went upstairs to tuck in Alisha. Sacora noticed how neat she kept her room. Her clothes were still in her backpack; she did not think she would be here long.

Sacora tucked in Elijah and Jeremiah and put their dirty laundry in the washing machine and turned it on. Sacora started her long bath. Eeyore was already on her blanket for the night. Through the quietness of the house, Sacora started thinking about her night with Joe and how nice it was. She fell asleep, determined to be great tomorrow for the children's first day of school.

Chapter Seventy

Sacora slept soundly and was awakened at five o'clock. She opened the door for Eeyore and took a quick shower after making her bed. She dressed for work and took her coffee to the front porch, not to wake the children. Watching the sun rise, she thought about today with the children not being with their parents for the first day of school and how insecure they must feel.

Alisha came to sit with her after six o'clock and read a small book of Winnie the Pooh that she read last night. Sacora asked her, "Are you ready to start your big day?"

Alisha said, "Yes, ma'am. I will put Hugs and Kisses out for the day when you cook breakfast. I will go upstairs and get dressed before I eat breakfast."

Sacora went in to cook cheese toast and was finished when Sadie and Aylassa awakened. Elijah and Jeremiah came downstairs to eat breakfast and go to the barn before they left. Sacora gave cups of orange juice and chocolate milk. Jeremiah was going to the barn and told Sacora he would need to shower before school from petting Clover. Elijah said that they would hurry and be in the van ready for school. Alisha was ready.

As they had promised, Elijah and Jeremiah were showered and dressed in their school clothes and buckled in the van by seven fifteen. Sacora carried Sadie and Aylassa to Ms. Koch'a day care first. Ms. Koch reminded Alisha, Elijah, and Jeremiah that the van would be picking them up from school and bringing them to the day care.

The elementary school was organized with traffic, and Sacora did not have any trouble finding a parking place. She walked inside with the children and asked for the directions of first grade, third grade, and fourth grade. The assistant principal, Zaden Hall, gave her a list of the teachers she needed to find for each child. Elijah stopped when he found Ms. Meagan Dunn's fourth0grade classroom and told Sacora goodbye. Ms. Dunn informed Sacora she would send all his information and forms home for her to complete and sign and to return them through Elijah.

Jeremiah's teacher, Ms. Amy Freed in the third-grade section, was very friendly and gave Sacora a packet of forms for registration and would be all right to return with Jeremiah tomorrow. Jeremiah's face was smiling as he spotted Asher in the classroom. Sacora had a feeling of happiness and relief for Jeremiah. He had been concerned about friends and a new school.

Alisha was in Ms. Joni Staggs's first-grade classroom. Ms. Staggs invited Sacora to stay for a while with Alisha. Sacora sat down by her, and Ms. Staggs started her speech.

"Boys and girls, we are now in the first grade. We are going to learn how to speak like adults." Ms. Staggs asked a student, "What did you do this weekend?"

The student replied, "I rode a choo choo with my pops."

Ms. Staggs said, "No, sweetheart. You rode a train with your grandfather." Ms. Staggs asked another student, "What did you do this weekend?"

The student replied, "I made cookies with my nana."

Ms. Staggs said, "No. sweetheart. You baked cookies with your grandmother." Ms. Staggs asked Alisha, "What did you do this weekend?"

Alisha replied, "I read a book."

Ms. Staggs asked, "What book did you read?"

Alisha thought for a few seconds and then proudly looked at Ms. Staggs with her answer of "Winnie the Shit."

Ms. Staggs looked at Sacora and said, "Can't get more adult than that, and I asked for it."

Smiling, Sacora kissed Alisha on the forehead and said, "You got this. I am going to work, sweet baby."

Sacora giggled on her way to the van, and as Ms. Staggs had said, she had asked for an adult answer, and Alisha gave her one. Sacora made it to work, and Mr. Hamilton gave her the assignments that would most likely take her all week to finish.

Chapter Seventy-One

S acora worked on the assignments until lunchtime and went out to eat lunch at McDonald's. She had finished lunch when Julie called.

Sacora answered, "Hello, Julie. What is going on with you today?"

Julie said, "I had to leave yesterday for court out of town this morning and did not have a chance to call you about your night out with Joe. How was it at your rock music concert?"

Sacora said, "I actually had a great time. I have been educated in why Joe loves this group so much. The lead singer is such a devoted dad to his daughters, and they were on stage singing with him. I have some new favorite songs too."

Julie said, "Yeah, and what about Joe?"

Sacora said, "Julie, you knew before me that I was infatuated. It has been changed from short-term infatuation into more for me. I am beginning to think more than just companionship for Joe also. I have been going to church with him and his family, and I am constantly thinking about the next minutes to spend with him. He is so much different from anyone I have ever known, especially Barton."

Julie giggled and said, "Well, I never liked the way Barton treated you, but you were so in love. I have a different opinion of Joe. I think what you see is what he is. I think he will treat you with consideration, devotion, and as the treasure that you are."

Sacora said, "Julie, I have discovered that Joe and his dad, Zac McCarley, made all the renovations and remodeling on my grandmother's house and barn. When I asked Joe about it, he said he would tell me anything and everything I wanted to know about my grandmother. I had a chance to have so many questions answered, but I just wanted to focus all my attention on Joe. My grandmother had always rejected time with me, and Joe seems as he is always there for whatever the situation is. I am holding on to this realization, and I have decided to let it go asking about my grandmother. I have gone to being alone in this large house to having children and Joe with his daughter, Joy, and this is what has made me happy. My parents are coming home from Africa early and should be here next weekend, and I have asked Joe to go with me to the airport and meet them."

Julie said, "If you have met his parents, I think he is interested in a relationship with you, Sacora. I have always heard about him when he was in the celebrity circle of being a down-to-earth person of integrity. I hope you the best, and keep in touch. Goodbye for now."

Sacora said, "Goodbye, Julie."

Sacora was little earlier returning to the office but would be taking shorter lunches until she had compensated the time she missed this morning taking the children to school. She was working on her documents for Mr. Hamilton when her phone showed a missed call from Barton. She decided that she would not handle his situation today and be in a good mood for the children's first day of school.

Five o'clock had come so quick that she worked a few minutes longer to find a stopping place. Sacora had told her coworkers goodbye and left out toward the day care. Another call from Barton, she ignored and parked the van. Sacora was relieved inside when Ms. Koch had greeted her and informed her everything went smooth with the transition of school, the van, and Alisha, Elijah, and Jeremiah's arriving at the day care. Sadie was first to her and hugged her so tight. Aylassa came running and asked, "Is it time to go to Aylassa's house?"

Sacora hugged her and said, "Yes, it is."

All the children came to Sacora and told Ms. Koch goodbye. Sacora buckled up Sadie, but Aylassa, Alisha, Elijah, and Jeremiah buckled themselves. Sacora asked, "How was your first day of school?"

Jeremiah answered first, "I had a great day. My teacher is so nice even though she is disciplinary. My favorite thing is I sit by Asher in the classroom. I have finished all my homework and ready to see Clover."

Alisha said, "I do like my teacher also. I am speaking like an adult, and she has noticed."

Elijah said, "Ms. Dunn has said that I am some advanced for the fourth grade and would like for you to review the paperwork she sent home for me to go to an advance class. I have finished my homework too, and Ms. Dunn has a form for you to sign after you have approved it."

Chapter Seventy-Two

S adie said, "My ain't got homework. Do my need dat?"
Sacora said, "No, you don't, sweetie. All your and Aylassa's work is finished at day care with Ms. Koch. What about going out for supper, something special to celebrate the first day of school?"

Alisha said, "What about Golden Corral. where we can have different things?"

Sacora said, "That will be perfect. Everyone else okay with Golden Corral?"

Sacora drove to the local Golden Corral and parked the van close to the door as she could get. Everyone unbuckled their seat belts, and Sadie said, "My do it," and she did. Sacora smiled and said, "You are getting to be a big girl."

Aylassa and Sadie held Sacora's hand through the door, and Alisha, Elijah, and Jeremiah followed. Inside, Sacora put Sadie and Aylassa in a high chair. She opened the antibacterial wipes and handed each one a wipe, and then to the bar of food Alisha and Elijah went. Jeremiah asked Sacora, "Would you like me to sit with Aylassa and Sadie while you go to the bar for a plate?"

Sacora answered, "I will after you have your plate, and I have Sadie's and Aylassa's plates on the table. Thank you so much for consideration."

Jeremiah's answer was, "Yes, ma'am. You are welcome."

Elijah, Alisha, and Jeremiah were seated at the table, and Sacora went to the bar for Sadie and Aylassa. All Sadie wanted was macaroni and cheese, but Sacora added chicken nuggets and potatoes. Aylassa wanted pizza and french fries, Sacora added some chicken nuggets and okra on her plate. Sacora sat the plates on the table, and Sadie and Aylassa started to eat. Sacora went to the bar for her plate, and from the distance, she was watching the children's expressions and laughter. She thought, "Yes, this is good."

Sacora sat down at the table and started to eat when her phone showed Barton calling. Sacora, enjoying her evening, pressed ignore again. She asked the children about their day and if they were ready to go back to school tomorrow. Alisha talked about her new friend Eemonie and how she played with her at recess and sat by her in the classroom. Elijah was entertaining Aylassa with different voices, and she was giggling at each one. Jeremiah was quiet, and he finally spoke about what was on his mind.

He asked Sacora, "Will I ever have to go back to my parents? Will Sadie and me be with you for all school year?"

Sacora said, "Sweetheart, as far as I know, you and Sadie will be with me. Do you want to go back with your parents?"

Jeremiah's answer broke Sacora's heart. He said, "I don't want to go back to my parents ever. Sadie and me are happy with you and not afraid at your house."

Sacora said, "Well, that is that, you are with me. It is time to go and check on our fur babies. Is everyone ready?"

Sacora gathered up her purse and phone after she cleaned Sadie's and Aylassa's face and hands. Her phone rang again, and she pressed the ignore option for Barton's call.

When she had all the children's seat belts buckled, she buckled up with her phone buzzing a text. She thought it might be Joe but was disappointed. An unknown number showed, and she read the text, "*I know you have been ignoring Barton's phone calls. You WILL endorse the paper for the full amount of the trust fund to go to Barton. I am Mrs. Barton Haynes now, and the money will go to me.*"

Sacora thought "I don't think so" and forwarded the text to Julie. Sacora thought this must be Rachel's text and she did not have to deal with her. Julie would handle it perfectly. Sacora started toward home, and her phone buzzed another text message. She waited until she parked in the driveway to look at it. It was from Julie. "*I will make a motion for them to stop harassing you. This text message is admit-*"

ting harassing phone calls and text. Communications are not to be to you but through me."

Sacora answered, *"Yes, thank you, and I will continue to ignore all communications."*

Sacora's thoughts were changed when Aylassa said, "Aylassa's house."

Sacora said, "Yes, ma'am, we are at Aylassa's house."

Chapter Seventy-Three

Sacora opened the door, and everyone was in. Eeyore came in, and Sacora fed her first. Alisha went out to water and fed the rabbits, putting them in their kennel for the night. Jeremiah and Elijah went upstairs to change into play clothes to walk and fed the lambs. Sacora asked Sadie and Aylassa if they would like to ride in the Bug to the barn. When Alisha, Elijah, and Jeremiah were ready to go the barn, Sacora had Sadie and Aylassa ready to go. In the Bug, everyone was buckled, and the air-conditioning felt very cool. In the barn, the lambs were ready for attention. Aylassa fed a handful of feed to Clover, and Elijah fed Diesel. Sacora changed their water and added some salt. Jeremiah took the shovel and shoveled out the feces. Elijah got the leashes and attached the collars and started walking around with Diesel. Alisha was with Elijah petting Diesel. Jeremiah was finished with the shovel, hung it on the nail, and took the leash of Clover with Aylassa walking Clover in the driveway and back to the barn.

Sacora said, "It is seven thirty. Time to go for showers and baths. Let's put everything in its place."

Elijah took the leashes and hung them on the nail. Jeremiah petted Diesel and Clover and said, "I will see you in the morning."

Everyone was in the Bug and to the house for bedtime.

Sacora gave Sadie and Aylassa their bath and dressed them in pajamas, rocked them, and sang "Grandma's Lullaby." Alisha went to the bathtub and listened to Sacora singing before she started her bath. Elijah and Jeremiah showered, dried their hair, and were in their beds before Sacora walked upstairs to tuck in Alisha. With Alisha's hair dried and she was dressed for bed, Sacora tucked her in. Alisha was tired but said "Good night, Sacora. You have given us another big day."

Sacora said, "Good night, sweet baby. You have given me a big day."

Sacora knocked on Jeremiah's door and said, "Good night, sweetheart. Tomorrow is another big day."

Jeremiah said, "Good night, Sacora."

Sacora closed the door leaving a crack for light and went to Elijah's room. Elijah said, "Good night, Sacora."

Sacora said, "Good night, buddy, and I will look at the forms and paper you brought home, sign, and will put back in your backpack."

Downstairs, Sacora took time reading all the information and completing forms and putting them in their backpacks. That was the moment Sacora found a picture in Alisha's backpack. It was a drawn picture of her family. It was a man (Joe), a woman (Sacora), children tall to short (Joy, Elijah, Jeremiah, Alisha, Aylassa, and Sadie), a dog (Eeyore), rabbits (Hugs and Kisses), and lambs (Diesel and Clover). Sacora whispered, "Yes, sweet baby, this is your family."

Sacora started the washing machine, folded the laundry in the dryer, and enjoyed her long, hot bath. Eeyore went out one more time and then to her blanket after drinking water. Nine o'clock in her bed exhausted from such a busy day. Her thoughts were on Jeremiah's statements of not wanting to go home because of happiness and safety. Before she fell asleep, her thoughts were on Barton's and Rachel's communications wanting her to endorse the document for the trust fund to be waived or forfeited. Most of all, Joe and Joy being part of her newfound family was such a pleasant thought.

Chapter Seventy-Four

S acora was up at five o'clock ready to start another busy day. Eeyore went out, and then she made her bed and had a quick shower, dressed for the day. Out on the front porch drinking her coffee was when she had started thinking about Alisha's drawn picture of her family. Aylassa stating "This is Aylassa's house." Elijah wanting her to be loved by Joe in comparison of Seth Bishop and Autumn Malone. With their mom, Autumn Malone, deceased, Sacora was thinking about adoption and how she would go about it.

Alisha was up ready to go to school after six o'clock sitting on the porch with Sacora and Eeyore. This sweet baby had touched Sacora so much during the time of just one month that it would be nice to make it permanent. Alisha interrupted her thoughts with permission to put Hugs and Kisses out for the day.

Sacora said, "Yes, sweet baby. I know you won't get dirty in your school clothes, and I will start breakfast."

Sacora watching Alisha out the kitchen window melted her heart thinking that someday this child would have to leave. Alisha still thought she would. All her clothes that would fit in her backpack and the others in the closet were an indication that she was not secure in residing with Sacora for a long period of time. Sacora's attention went to Aylassa coming into the kitchen. Sacora carried her to potty, and Sadie awakened. Sacora took care of their hands and faces for breakfast.

Elijah and Jeremiah went to the barn dressed in play clothes and shoes to fed and water Diesel and Clover. Within minutes, they had returned and showered and changed into school clothes, ready for breakfast. All the children ate well this morning, two bowls of cereal and milk with juice. Sacora finished packing the bags for Sadie and Aylassa, dressing them for day care and gathering backpacks for school.

Sacora reminded Alisha, Elijah, and Jeremiah to return the forms she had endorsed to their teachers. Elijah's form of request for the advanced classes was to be returned today, also with his journal of homework she approved. The children told Sacora goodbye and waved at her going down the sidewalk. How her heart was melting with every little motion of affection.

At the day care, Ms. Koch greeted her at the door for Sadie and Aylassa. Sadie hugged her so tight, and Aylassa kissed her check and said, "I will see you when it's time for Aylassa's house."

Sacora left feeling so loved and having love for these children. On her way to work, she thought about Ms. Angela Faith Mays, attorney at law. On her information with the summons of her grandmother's will, she remembered seeing adoption as one of the legal services that she specialized in. All morning at her desk, this situation tugged at her thoughts. On her lunch break, she went by Ms. Mays's office and set an appointment with consultation for what she would need to pursue the adoption of Alisha, Aylassa, and Elijah Malone.

When she returned to her office, she asked Mr. Hamilton the status of the Malone children and if adoption was in their future. What would need to be clarified for her to adopt them now?

Mr. Hamilton said, "What we need to do is to contact Ms. Hines at Baldwin County Department of Human Resources. She will give you all the information you will need."

Sacora said, "Can we make a conference call tomorrow?"

Mr. Hamilton said, "I will make arrangements and will inform you in the morning."

Sacora said, "Yes, that will be great."

Five o'clock came quickly again today, and Sacora left the office with her coworkers showing her support with her intentions of adopting the Malone children, whom she had loved and cared for this past month. Sacora went to the grocery store before the day care to have some more moments of thought on the next step of capturing the permanent status of Alisha, Elijah, and Aylassa Malone. She bought what was on her list of the children's ideas for breakfast and suppers. Their snacks were the usual requested and Sadie's macaroni and cheese.

Chapter Seventy-Five

After the day care, Sacora parked in the driveway and Aylassa said, "Aylassa's house." Elijah and Jeremiah brought the groceries in, and Sacora and Alisha put them away, with Aylassa helping. Sacora cooked supper and put it on the table. Elijah and Jeremiah had finished their homework at day care, and Alisha was almost finished. Sacora helped Alisha finish her homework, and it was time to put the rabbits up for the night. Alisha fed and watered Hugs and Kisses, putting them in their kennel for the night. Eeyore came in to be fed, and then they all went to the barn. Diesel and Clover enjoyed their walking, feeding, and petting of the little hands of all the children. Sacora filled the container with fresh water. When she turned off the water hose, she was reminded of Joe and his assistance in the transition of her days with the children. The leashes for Diesel and Clover were hung back on the nail. Elijah and Jeremiah shoveled out the feces and Sacora added more salt.

Sacora said, "It is time for showers and baths. Bedtime."

The children's energy was enough to run back to the house. Sacora was impressed that no instructions were given for bedtime. Alisha, Elijah and Jeremiah went upstairs, and Sadie and Aylassa were in the bathroom. After Sacora rocked and sang "Grandma's Lullaby" to Sadie and Aylassa, Alisha finished her bath and dried her hair. Sacora tucked in Alisha, Elijah, and Jeremiah, leaving their doors cracked for light. Eeyore went outside and came in to her blanket. In her long, hot bath, Sacora's thoughts were still on adoption and what she would say to Ms. Hines tomorrow. What information she would need to complete the documents to permanently have custody of the Malone children.

Sacora thought about Julie and how she always talked to Julie and her parents about what she worried about. These conversations would be soon. She fell asleep with a quiet little prayer of saying the right thing tomorrow and finding out what she needed before her consultation with Ms. Mays.

Sacora was up at four thirty, made her bed, showered, and dressed for the day. Eeyore went out with her for coffee on the front porch. Another hot day, Sacora had chosen cool clothes for everyone. On the porch with Eeyore, Sacora was thinking about her conversation with Ms. Hines. She had fears of what the result might be of the children's custody being given to someone else.

Her thoughts were interrupted with Alisha coming out on the front porch. Sacora showed enthusiasm for her sitting down beside her. Eeyore was finished eating and drinking, ready for Alisha to open the kennel of Hugs and Kisses. Sacora went with Alisha, starting breakfast and watching her again with the animals she loved. Elijah and Jeremiah came downstairs and headed out to the barn for the morning visit of Diesel and Clover. Sacora was putting breakfast on the table when Sadie and Aylassa came to the kitchen. This morning, everything went so well. Elijah and Jeremiah showered, dressed for school, ate breakfast, grabbed their backpacks, and were in the van ready for school.

Sacora dressed Sadie and Aylassa for day care and packed their bags. Alisha had her backpack and buckled in the van. When Sacora was in line of the school traffic, the children's laughter was loud because of Elijah making different voices saying nursery rhymes to Sadie and Aylassa. Sacora parked at the entrance, and with goodbyes, see-you-laters, and the waves on the sidewalk, she drove away to the day care.

Ms. Koch took the bags, and Sacora kissed Sadie and Aylassa bye. Aylassa held on a little longer than usual. Sacora waited a few more minutes and then left when she decided to play. Sacora whispered, "Sweetie, it won't be long until time for Aylassa's house. Bye, Aylassa. Bye, Sadie."

Sacora sat at her desk, and Mr. Hamilton's smile as he came to her desk said a lot. The conference call with Ms. Hines was for today after lunch approximately two o'clock. Sacora also got an email that she had appointment with Ms. Mays Friday at one o'clock. Maybe things would move quicker than she thought they would.

Chapter Seventy-Six

After the morning of typing and completing all the documents for the cases she had been assigned, Sacora was making arrangements for lunch. She decided on a close chicken shop for a chicken tender sandwich. After she had eaten, she texted Julie, *"Call me if you can."*

Julie called, "I am on recess from court. This is a perfect time. What is going on?"

Sacora said, "I am pursuing the adoption of Aylassa, Alisha, and Elijah Malone. I have a conference call with the Baldwin County of Department of Human Resources at two o'clock. I am anxious. I really want these children's custody to be granted to me. I know nearest relatives have to be notified, and that worries me. I know absolutely nothing about the biological father, and the man they talk about, Seth Bishop, is in prison. I have a home and love for them, and I don't know what else the State of Alabama will require for adoption."

Julie said, "I have not worked in this part of law, but I do know that the money of Barton's trust fund will be in your favor to show monetary capabilities to provide for them. I have to go, Sacora. Good luck, and will talk to you later."

Sacora said, "Goodbye, Julie."

Back at her office, sitting at her desk, she was preparing a list of questions for Ms. Hines. The biological father was first, then grandparents, and then what was next she would find out.

Ms. Hines was earlier than two o'clock with her conference call. Mr. Hamilton's motion for her to come to his office was before she had finished her list of questions. Mr. Hamilton's smile was comforting, and she thought she would take notes of the information Ms. Hines gave her.

Ms. Hines said, "Sacora, has everything been all right with the foster care this past month?"

Sacora said, "Yes, ma'am, it has been awesome, and I have interest of adopting Aylassa, Elijah, and Alisha Malone. Can you inform me if this would be possible and what steps would I have to go through to make an adoption request?"

Ms. Hines said, "As all children in foster care, the State of Alabama keeps an ongoing status of children's custody. Autumn Malone being deceased, the investigation of the biological father will be next. We do have record that the grandparents or parents of Autumn Malone are not eligible for adopting due to age and poor health. The whereabouts of the biological father at this time are unknown. The grandparents had given us the information that he had been absent from the children's home for a while. The boyfriend, Seth Bishop, is in Hamilton, Alabama, prison and will have another eighteen months to be incarcerated. Seth might have some information on the father's location. The father will have the right to them or be required to endorse documents for adoption. It is common for foster parents to adopt the children they are fostering. If you will proceed further in the process of adoption, you will need the father's permission and signatures. Also, Sacora, you have a quality life style for being an adoption candidate. You have a home that is able to provide safety and security. I will give it some research and attention and will give you a call back. Also an Email of guidelines you can study to expedite the process."

Sacora said, "Thank you for the information. I will be grateful to adopt these children, and please keep me updated. Goodbye, Ms. Hines."

Ms. Hines said, "Sacora, I will keep you updated. Goodbye."

Sacora saw Mr. Hamilton's smiling face, and she went back to her desk thinking about what Ms. Hines had said of the biological father. Where would she start? How could she find him when he couldn't be found by the State of Alabama? Even Autumn's parents did not have an address or contact information for him.

Chapter Seventy-Seven

Sacora went through the evening with day care and home business as she had done all week. When she had finished all items on her list and in her long, hot bath, her thoughts were on the adoption of the children. Sacora knew that she wanted to finish what Autumn Malone had started. Elijah making Aylassa laugh with all his unique voices and being in an advance class and Alisha needing security to know where she awakened this morning was where she would sleep tonight was very important. Sacora opened the door for Eeyore and thought even the animals were having a better life because they were here. Eeyore went to her blanket and Sacora fell asleep with so much on her mind.

Another week had come and gone. Friday morning was here. Sacora made her bed, opened the door for Eeyore, showered, and dressed for another hot day in Alabama. She started cooking breakfast, not going to the porch for coffee. Alisha, Elijah, and Jeremiah were taking care of Hugs, Kisses, Diesel, and Clover. Sadie and Aylassa were ready for day care, and Alisha, Elijah, and Jeremiah were ready for school. Out the door and taking care of school and then day care, Sacora sat at her desk with the appointment of Ms. Mays on her mind. Only a month of fostering, and it felt like she had always been with them. Lunch was a quick burger and fries and then to Ms. Mays's office.

Ms. Mays offered so much information of standard adoption. The situations of her fostering already, grandparents not being able to adopt, and the father being estranged were in her favor. Ms. Mays suggested she visit Seth Bishop in the Hamilton, Alabama, prison for any and all information he could give on the biological father. Ms.

Mays sent an email while Sacora was in her office to the prison for permission for a visit on Sunday afternoon's visitation schedule, two o'clock to six o'clock. Ms. Mays also gave her a map and the contact guard when she arrived. Sacora paid Ms. Mays's fee for continuing the case and her constant involvement until the case was settled, closed, or there was no hope of adopting. Sacora left the office feeling optimistic of the consultation.

Sacora worked another couple hours and was interrupted by a text from her mom. "*We are on our way home. We are scheduled to be at the airport around eight o'clock Gate 21. Can't wait to see you.*"

Sacora waited until five o'clock to text back. "*Yes, ma'am, I will be there looking for you.*"

Sacora texted Joe, "*Do you think Joy will sit with the children so that you and I can go the airport? My parents should be arriving by eight o'clock. Please let me know before six o'clock.*"

Joe texted back immediately, "*Yes, and we will grab some Kentucky Fried Chicken for everyone's supper.*"

Sacora being in a hurry texted back, "*Thanks, Joe.*"

Sacora went to the day care, and the children's faces were smiling. No school tomorrow. Sacora stopped at the barn and helped with the changing of water, feed, and salt. Elijah and Jeremiah shoveled the feces, and Alisha, Aylassa, and Sadie fed handfuls of feed to Diesel and Clover. Sacora washed Sadie and Aylassa's hands with wipes and buckled up in the van to park in the driveway. Sacora opened the front door, and Eeyore went in to eat. Alisha and Jeremiah went to Hugs and Kisses to feed and water them. Sacora said, "Please put Hugs and Kisses in the kennel for the night. I have a surprise. My parents are coming home tonight, and Joy will be sitting with you here while Joe and I met them at the airport."

Jeremiah said, "I thought it unusual that we did not walk Diesel and Clover tonight."

Sacora said, "Tomorrow you should have an opportunity for them to be on their leashes all day. I needed the time to get you settled in before Joy and Joe get here."

It wasn't long Sacora was at the front door waiting for Joe. The sound of loud Foo Fighters music was playing. Joy came in with

Kentucky Fried Chicken and started putting it on the table. Elijah and Alisha went to the refrigerator for chocolate milk. Aylassa and Sadie washed their hands on an antibacterial wipe and climbed into their chairs. Jeremiah sat with Sadie, and she was waiting on macaroni and cheese with her chicken tenders. Joe took Sacora's hand and said, "What about you and I get something to eat on our way to the airport? Would this be okay with you?"

Sacora said, "Yes, let me say goodbye, and we will go."

Sacora gave Joy some ideas for dessert and snacks for later. All or any homework, she would check later. Joe and Sacora were on their way to the airport.

Chapter Seventy-Eight

Joe opened the door of his Dodge Charger for Sacora and quickly gave her kiss. He started out the driveway and turned down the music before taking her hand.

Joe asked, "Where would you like to eat? I think Golden Corral is our best option for timing. What do you think?"

Sacora said, "Yes, it is an option for good timing. I do enjoy their food too."

Joe said, "Golden Corral it is. Let me have some clues about your parents. What do I need to say?"

Sacora said, "Be yourself, Joe. You are perfect, no clues needed."

Joe and Sacora were seated quickly at Golden Corral and enjoying their meal. He could tell every now and then she went into deep thoughts. He asked what was on her mind and if it was something he could help her with.

Sacora said, "I have started to pursue information on adopting the Malone children. I want them with me permanently. I have a scheduled visit Sunday between two o'clock and six o'clock at the Hamilton, Alabama, prison with Seth Bishop, the boyfriend of Autumn Malone. I hope to get information from him on any and all relatives that would contest the adoption. I also need information on their biological father."

Joe said, "I am free Sunday. I will go with you, and Joy can sit with the children. If this is okay with you?"

Sacora said, "It is more than okay with me. I would love for you to go. What time do you think we need to leave? How long will it take us to get there?"

Joe said, "I will google and let you know later, but now we need to get to the airport. What gate did you say?"

Sacora said, "Twenty-one, and I am ready to see my parents."

Through the traffic at the airport, Joe held Sacora's hand for comfort on her excitement and then looked for gate 21. They had arrived and was waiting patiently when Sacora heard her mom, "Sacora, we are here."

Sacora made her way to her mom still holding Joe's hand through the crowd. Sacora dropped Joe's hand and turned toward her mom, hugging her so tight. Corey Hill lifted Sacora up so high and hugged her so tight. Joe, seeing the reunion, realized how much Sacora's parents loved her and her love for them. Sacora turned around and said, "Mom and Dad, this is Joe McCarley. Joe, this is my parents, Samantha and Corey Hill." Joe reached out and shook Corey's hand.

Joe said, "I have heard a lot about you, and it's great to finally meet you."

Samantha said, "We need to get our luggage. Most of our things we shipped back home to avoid the chance of being lost on the planes. We have two cases to retrieve and our travel-on cases we have."

Corey said, "Joe, if you will walk with me to the luggage area, we will retrieve our two cases."

Joe nodded at Sacora, and he left with her dad. Samantha Hill looked at Sacora, "You did not tell me that Joe is the Joe McCarley, the running back for the Miami Dolphins."

Sacora said, "No, Mom, I did not. He is my friend Joe that I am very fond of. I called him for repairs at my home, he fixes my broken things, and it has been nice having him around ever since. How does everyone know about his football days and I did not?"

Samantha Hill replied, "You were only studying Barton Haynes's interests. Your dad and I watch football, remembering the days he played through high school and college. I was a cheerleader, and that is our days of falling in love. Sacora, Joe may fix more than your broken things."

Chapter Seventy-Nine

Joe and Corey Hill came to the gate carrying two cases. Their luggage reached destination. Samantha Hill picked up the other cases, and Sacora took one from her mom.

Joe said, "This way to the car." He led the way to the Dodge Charger and opened the trunk for the luggage and put them in to fit. He opened the door for Sacora, and Corey opened the door for Samantha on the opposite side of the car. Samantha was holding a bag of gifts and handed Sacora a gift. She said, "This is a bracelet for a broken heart. It is to mend your heart Sacora and give a promise for a better life."

Joe smiled and did not comment. Sacora said, "Thank you, Mom. I will treasure it always."

Joe asked, "Would you like to stop somewhere to eat?"

Corey said, "I don't want anything. Do you, Samantha?"

Samantha said, "No I am ready to meet the children and give them their gifts."

Joe slowly drove through the congested traffic and held Sacora's hand on the way home. Sacora asked her parents, "Would you like to drive my Bug home and bring it back tomorrow? I would love for you to see Hugs, Kisses, Diesel, and Clover tomorrow. You will meet Eeyore tonight."

Samantha said, "You still love Winnie the Pooh, huh?"

Sacora giggled and said, "Yes, I do, and when you met Eeyore, you will know why that is her name."

Joe stopped to turn into the driveway, and Samantha exclaimed, "No, this is not what I remember. This is totally different."

Corey said, "Look at this house, Samantha. It is beautiful."

Sacora said, "Joe and his dad, Zac, did all of the renovations and remodeling. I have enjoyed residing here. I did not have an opportunity to see it before, but I think it is beautiful too."

Sacora opened the door and said, "Surprise! This is my parents, Corey and Samantha Hill."

Joy came first to greet them. The sound of the TV's *My Hero* told Sacora the children were watching Joe's football video again. Elijah turned down the volume, and Alisha, Jeremiah, Sadie, and Aylassa went to meet Sacora's parents. Elijah followed after Aylassa with Eeyore. Sacora introduced each child to her parents and Eeyore.

Samantha said, "I have gifts for you all." She took out bracelets for the girls first. And the bracelets resembled Sacora's.

Samantha said, "These bracelets are for broken homes with a promise of a new home, a new beginning. And this is for Elijah and Jeremiah. These sticks are for the promise of being a great shepherd and lover of animals."

Corey said, "We had a successful trip and will tell you about it later. I am ready to see home and my bed. What about you, Samantha?"

Samantha said, "Yes, I am. Sacora, we will take your offer of the Bug and will bring it back tomorrow."

Sacora handed Corey the key and gave him and her mom a hug and kiss good night. Sacora watched them drive away, and so did Sadie. Sadie started crying and said, "My wike de buggy. My don't want it to be gone."

Sacora hugged her and said, "The buggy will be back tomorrow, okay?"

Sadie wiped her tears and said, "Otay."

Joe said, "Joy, it is time for us to make it home. Are you ready?"

Joy said to the children, "Goodbye. See you later, alligators." And then to Joe, she said, "Yes, sir, Dad, I'm ready to go home."

Elijah said, "After a while, crocodile."

Joy went to the Dodge, and Sacora walked Joe out to the front porch. Sacora kissed Joe good night and said, "Thank you for tonight." Joe went to the car, and Joy looked at him. She hesitated and then said, "I saw that."

Joe said, "You saw what?"

Joy said, "I saw a sweet good-night kiss."

Joe said, "I am glad you saw that. Now I won't feel bad about snooping when you have a boyfriend. I plan on seeing as much as the moon."

Chapter Eighty

Sacora came inside and said, "All right, my sweethearts, time for bed. Joy has seen to your showers and baths." Alisha, Elijah, and Jeremiah went upstairs, and Sacora followed with Sadie and Aylassa. Sacora has always put Sadie and Aylassa in their cribs first, but tonight Alisha, Elijah, and Jeremiah were tucked in first.

Sacora turned back the cover and kissed Alisha's forehead and said, "Good night, sweet baby."

Sadie said, "My wuv you, Eisha."

Aylassa kissed her cheek and said, "Good night, sweet baby." She was imitating Sacora, and this made Alisha smile, and she said, "Good night, Aylassa and Sadie."

Sacora told Elijah "Good night, buddy" and turned back his covers. Aylassa imitated Sacora again with her version of "Good night, buddy." Sadie said, "My wuv you, Lijah."

Sacora told Jeremiah "Good night, sweetheart" and turned back his covers. Aylassa didn't imitate Sacora but Sadie said, "Good night, mine butter. My wuv you."

Aylassa and Sadie walked down the stairs, and Sacora carried them to potty. She picked them up and rocked them, singing "Grandma's Lullaby." Alisha could hear Sacora singing and focused on every word. This was the first time Jeremiah and Elijah heard "Grandma's Lullaby" so plainly. The shower and hair dryer always interfered with them hearing Sacora sing so clear. Sacora put Sadie and Aylassa in their cribs and opened the door for Eeyore and waited until she came back in to her blanket.

Sacora's long, hot bath was later than usual, two hours later, but she had to wind down. It had been a big busy day. The meeting with

Ms. Mays, getting information she needed for adoption procedures, being with Joe and his offer to go to Hamilton, Alabama, prison with her on Sunday, and her parents coming home, meeting Joe, a big day. Sacora went to her bed, falling into the pillows. Exhausted, she slept until the sun shining woke her up.

She looked at the clock and could not believe it was nine o'clock and the children had not awakened yet. She changed the sheets on her bed before Eeyore came to her for the door to be opened. She showered and put on comfortable clothes for cleaning and went outside on the front porch with Eeyore and her coffee. A Saturday morning, the children had looked forward to no school. It was ten thirty before Alisha came to the front porch and almost eleven fifteen when Sadie, Aylassa, Elijah, and Jeremiah had awakened. Late for breakfast and lunch, Sacora cooked scrambled eggs for sandwiches. After the blessing, the children's appetites were noticed. The egg sandwiches, orange juice, and chocolate milk disappeared quickly.

Alisha went to open the kennel for Hugs and Kisses. Sacora dressed Sadie and Aylassa for the barn, their visit to Diesel and Clover. Eeyore went to the barn with them today. Elijah reached the leashes off the nail and handed Jeremiah Clover's leash for the walk they had planned. Aylassa fed handful of food to Clover, and Alisha fed Diesel.

The lambs were walking around the driveway and barn with disciplined instructions from Elijah and Jeremiah. Sacora started putting more salt out for the lambs when Sadie said, "Wook, mine buggy."

Sacora looked up, and her mom and dad stopped at the barn. Corey said, "This is a nice barn for the children's animals."

Samantha said, "It is different from when I was a child. Sacora, do you mind if I see the rest of the house today? I was very tired last night."

Sacora said, "Sure, Mom. We will be going to the house soon. Sadie, do you want to ride in the Bug with my dad?"

Sadie said, "Otay," and Alisha and Aylassa wanted to ride in the Bug too. Sacora walked down the driveway with the lambs, Elijah,

Jeremiah, and Samantha. Jeremiah said, "Sacora, when do we get the mail?"

Sacora looked at the mailbox, and mail was hanging out over the cover. It had been a month since she had gone to the mailbox. Sacora never even thought about the mail. She decided she would bring a bag later today and take care of the overflowed mailbox.

Chapter Eighty-One

Sacora opened the front door, and the children wanted a drink. Elijah and Jeremiah tied Diesel's and Clover's leashes in the front yard to graze while they were in the house. Samantha started up the stairs and smiling said, "Things have changed." Alisha went with her and said, "This is my room, and the other two are Elijah's and Jeremiah's."

Samantha went up the next stairs and looked around. This was the attic she played in when she was a child on rainy days. Now it was a stunning bedroom with a bathroom. Alisha looked around the room. She had never even wondered what was up the stairs. Samantha and Alisha went to the kitchen, where Sacora was putting drinks back in the refrigerator.

Sacora said, "I was getting ready to clean the bedrooms upstairs and change sheets while Sadie and Aylassa take naps this afternoon. Will you and Dad stay for supper?"

Samantha said, "Yes, we will, and I will help you with cleaning and changing the sheets. I will vacuum before Sadie's and Aylassa's nap. It will be nice to spend time with you."

Samantha went to Alisha's room, remembering her days as a child. The room was kept very neat by Alisha. After she changed the sheets, Alisha carried the sheets to the washing machine. Sacora had changed the sheets of Elijah's bed and then Jeremiah's.

Alisha carried the sheets to the washing machine, and Sacora started it. Samantha cleaned the bathroom upstairs, and Sacora cleaned the one downstairs. In the kitchen, Sacora swept and mopped. Samantha dusted the furniture in the upstairs bedrooms and the living room. They kept working until everything was done.

Corey had been outside with Alisha, Elijah, and Jeremiah playing with Eeyore, Hugs, Kisses, Diesel and Clover. He was amazed how Diesel and Clover would lead on the leashes with the children. Eeyore playing with Hugs and Kisses was entertaining too. Jeremiah told Corey his favorite thing was throwing the football, but they did not have a football at home. The football was Joe's at his mom's.

Sacora started the spaghetti, and Samantha cut the lettuce, tomatoes, broccoli, carrots, and cucumbers for the tossed salad. Garlic bread was on a baking sheet ready for the oven when the spaghetti was done. Samantha enjoyed her Saturday afternoon with Sacora, and the visit had been great in her homeplace. Samantha and Sacora talked about her visit to Hamilton's prison, and Samantha asked if she and Corey could sit with the children while she was gone tomorrow. Joe and Joy were coming for supper. Joy had been invited to a family reunion with Zac and Wendy McCarley, and Sacora would ask if she wanted to go with them and her parents sit with the children.

Sacora heard loud Foo Fighters music and went to the front door. Joe and Joy came in, and Samantha put the bread in the oven. Sadie and Aylassa heard Joy and Joe and had awakened. Corey and the children came in to wash hands and sat at the table.

Sacora looking around the table, six children, Joe, and her parents, and thought, "This is an amazing Saturday night."

Joy did decide she would go with her grandparents to the family reunion and Sacora's parents would be sitting with the children tomorrow. The dinner table was full of laughter and hungry children. Sacora's parents were the first to leave after the table, and kitchen were cleaned. Corey had gone to the barn to put Diesel and Clover up for the night, and Jeremiah and Elijah shoveled out the feces. Alisha had fed and watered the rabbits and put them in their kennel. Eeyore had eaten and was ready for her blanket.

Sacora told Joe and Joy good night and kissed Joe again on the front porch. He had planned to be back in the morning around eight o'clock. In the bathroom giving Sadie and Aylassa a bath, Sacora took the time to explain that she would be gone tomorrow and her parents would be with them at Aylassa's house. Alisha gathered her clothes and was in the bathtub when Sacora was singing "Grandma's

Lullaby." Elijah and Jeremiah were upstairs for their showers and bedtime. When Sacora had Sadie and Aylassa in their cribs, she quietly looked at them at the door and thought, "Yes, I want this forever."

Sacora tucked in Alisha, Elijah, and Jeremiah, leaving their doors opened some. She went to her long, hot bath and thought about questions she would have for Seth Bishop, praying that it would be a productive visit to result in her adopting these children she loved so much.

Chapter Eighty-Two

Sacora was up around five o'clock sitting on the front porch with her coffee by six o'clock. She was showered and dressed into cool attractive clothes. Eeyore had been sitting at her feet quietly, still resting from yesterday. Her parents were planning to be here around seven thirty with McDonald's biscuits. Still with the conversation to Seth Bishop on her mind, the sunrise was comforting and broke her attention for a minute.

Alisha did not sit with her on the porch this morning. She slept in for a while. Seven thirty, her parents parked in her driveway with McDonald's breakfast and a Walmart bag. Sacora and Samantha took the biscuits to the table, and the children had awakened from the Foo Fighters music. Joe was here. They had come to the kitchen, and Sacora had a few minutes to tell them goodbye and have a great day with her parents.

Jeremiah spotted the Walmart bag, and Corey gave it to him. He opened it and showed it to Elijah, a football. Alisha, Sadie, and Aylassa saw their surprises, stuffed bears. Samantha told Sacora that she would take care of their showers and bedtime to take her time coming home tonight.

Sacora loved on her parents and the children before walking out the door to Joe's car with him. Ready to start a long drive, Sacora buckled up comfortably with the conversations still on her mind. Joe went through the drive-through for their breakfast and started their trip north to Hamilton, Alabama, prison.

It was a long trip, peaceful, and Sacora rested some. She did not realize how tired she had been. Joe noticed her relaxing and did not talk much. Two thirty in the afternoon, they had arrived at the gates of Hamilton, Alabama, prison. Sacora was looking at her map from Ms. Mays. She gave Joe directions and then the name of the guard. They had found Seth Bishop.

After all screening and procedures to enter the prison, Joe and Sacora was introduced to Seth Bishop. He was a young, neat, nice man, no tattoos showing. He looked at Sacora and said, "Why have you wanted to see me?"

Sacora answered, "I will be blunt. I have been fostering Aylassa, Alisha, and Elijah Malone for a month, and I have fallen for them and want them with me always. I have pursued the action of adopting. I want to finish what Autumn Malone started. I can tell she put so much love and effort into her babies. I was hoping you would or could give me information on any or all relatives that might pursue adoption. I need to know about their biological father, if he would interfere with my adopting them."

Seth cleared his throat and spoke, "You are right about Autumn Malone. She was an A1 momma. Her parents were older when she came along, her mom around forty-five, and her dad, fifty years old. They did not have her spoiled but did have her feeling wanted and cherished. This was what she gave her children. I was with her six months before her brain cancer was diagnosed. Her husband, Tarik Malone, had left for some job in Atlanta, Georgia. He never returned to her, and she had started talking to an attorney about abandonment divorce. I understood he had been gone over a year when I moved in. The children and her parents were her life, and she still showed me love and appreciation. Autumn was a registered nurse and made a good income. I worked at a plant, and when Autumn could no longer work, bills of living expense and medical bills became so overwhelming. Autumn started taking Oxycontin for pain. She would take one half and give the other half to me to sell to pay mortgage, utilities, and what medical bills I could. My mom, Lana Bishop, kept the children while I worked and took care of Autumn. The last week of Autumn's life, I took all my vacation time to be with her and the children. I could not stand the thought of her leaving this world without me. We had buried Autumn on Wednesday. I had one more drug sell on Sunday before I was to return to work on Monday, and that is when I was arrested. I had planned to pay the remaining amount for her funeral expenses that her parents could not pay with this drug sell. I pled guilty because I was even though the courts did not want to hear my reasons. I would not change anything. I am very honored to have known and loved Autumn Malone and her children. I do know why you love them and want to adopt them. I wish I could do more. I would like to visit them when my sentence is over, if this would be okay? Tarik is an unusual name, and maybe this will help you find him."

Sacora was touched by his story and said, "Yes, that would be nice. Elijah has spoken of you so much."

Seth said, "I would like to know Aylassa, Alisha, and Elijah have a loving, safe, and secure home. I will help you all I can, but right now this is all I know."

Chapter Eighty-Three

S acora stood up and said, "I had forgotten to introduce you to my friend, Joe McCarley. Joe is also very fond of Aylassa, Alisha, and Elijah. Can I leave you my phone number and my email address in case you remember anything else?"

Seth said, "Yes, sure. I can read people very well, and I can tell you have good intentions. I will do my best to remember what Autumn said about Tarik."

Sacora said, "Thank you for seeing me today." She gave her contact information to Seth and also Ms. Mays the attorney for her adoption services. Sacora and Joe told the guard their visit was over and was escorted toward the parking lot area.

Joe saw a McDonald's and went through the drive-through for some lunch. In the car, Sacora was quiet again, but Joe decided to discuss the information that Seth gave them. He took her hand and said, "I know an outstanding private investigator that would not charge much to locate Tarik Malone. As Seth mentioned, he has an unusual first name and should be easier to find. I am offering assistance, not taking over."

Sacora said, "I think that is a sweet offer. Thank you."

The conversation was small talk as Sacora was thinking and Joe driving. At nine thirty, Joe parked into Sacora's driveway. Sacora could tell that the children were sleeping. All the lights were off except in the hallways and living room. Sacora asked Joe if he wanted to come in for a minute, and he declined, needing to be home with Joy. Joy was starting a new school tomorrow, and registration was in the morning. Brandie had flown in from Miami to complete forms and take Joy shopping. He kissed Sacora when he opened the car door, and she told him thank you and good night. Sacora walked in the front door quietly, and her parents were anxious to know the information she had gotten from Seth Bishop. She told them what she knew and hoped more would come. Samantha told Sacora about their day with the children and the animals and everything had been taken care of. The mail was in a bag in the kitchen. Corey had been throwing the football with them, and it was a good day. The children were ready for school tomorrow. Sacora's parents told her good night and left to their home. Sacora went to the backpacks and went through homework and put it all back for school tomorrow.

In her long, hot bath, Sacora relaxed with the thoughts, "Do what I can, when I can, and as much as I can." Eeyore was already on her blanket, and Sacora checked on the sleeping children and fell asleep with optimism.

Monday morning went smooth. The routine she had worked out well. Alisha was adjusting well to first grade and with her friend Eemonie found excitement going to school. Jeremiah and Asher were having good days, and Jeremiah was making good grades. Elijah had enjoyed his advance subjects, and his classmates loved his different voices. The children were looking for the next days out of school on Labor Day.

Joe and Joy registered for her new school and made arrangements to move Joy to Mobile. Brandie and Joy shopped for new clothes and school supplies, not moving much from Miami.

All week went smooth. Even the mail was sorted, what to keep or throw away. Friday night, Sacora went to the airport with Joe to see Joy back to Miami with Brandie to finalize the last bit of business to move to Mobile and transferring to her school. Joy and Sacora went to the restroom after Joe loved on Joy and told her goodbye.

Brandie said, "Joy told me you were in a relationship with someone outside our race."

Joe said, "Yes, I am. I married outside of my species the first time."

Brandie said, "Are you calling me a dog?"

Joe said, "Bam, you got it."

Joy came out of the restroom, and Brandie rudely grabbed Joy by the arm and walked her away to the gate. Joe snickered while he watched Brandie upset.

Sacora said, "What was that about?"

Joe said, "Nothing really, just Brandie being Brandie."

Chapter Eighty-Four

Sacora's parents had been with the children while she went with Joe to the airport, and Joe did come in after they had returned from their glorious minutes with Brandie. Elijah was the first one to speak about how he would miss Joy and could not wait until she came back. Alisha and Jeremiah also made comments of their impatiently waiting till she came back. Sacora walked Joe out and on the front porch kissed him good night.

Sadie and Aylassa had their bath and were in their pajamas, and Alisha, Jeremiah, and Elijah were on their way up the stairs. Samantha and Corey told them goodbye and "We'll see you later." Aylassa and Sadie blew kisses and went with Sacora to the rocking chair. Alisha hearing "Grandma's Lullaby" while she was in the bathtub was ready for Sacora to dry her hair when the babies were in their cribs.

Sacora tucked in Alisha, and then Jeremiah and Elijah. As she walked down the stairs, a thought hit her hard. "I am making progress on the permanency of Alisha, Elijah, and Aylassa to be with me, but what about Jeremiah and Sadie?" She looked in on Sadie and realized this baby of two years old was safe and happy here, with her brother Jeremiah saying so.

Sacora went to her bath and was thinking about Saturday and next weekend was Labor Day weekend. She thought she would go the barn and look at her decorations and plan a celebration with her parents, children, and yes, Joe and Joy. Falling asleep with her planning next weekend, she wondered if Zac and Wendy would come if she invited them.

Sacora had awakened before the children and started her day, opening the door for Eeyore, changing sheets on her bed, and having a quick shower. On the porch with coffee and Eeyore, Alisha did wake up first and sat quietly by her, Eeyore at her feet resting. Sacora was expecting Alisha to ask at any time to open the kennel for Hugs and Kisses and would start breakfast when she did.

Elijah and Jeremiah had wanted to spend most of their day today at the barn, and she would take advantage of their help deciding on decorations, tables, etc., for Labor Day holiday. Alisha asked to open the kennel for Hugs and Kisses, and Sacora went to cook breakfast. Sadie and Aylassa came to the kitchen and were ready for their cups of orange juice and breakfast.

After all children were up and their hands washed, blessing said, the large breakfast Sacora cooked quickly disappeared. Everyone dressed in play clothes for the day of not going to school, finished eating, and to the barn after the table and kitchen were cleaned. Sacora opened the storage door and looked at what she remembered from the July Fourth celebration and started taking out tables and decorations. Alisha, Elijah, and Jeremiah were helping Sacora set items out she needed. Sadie sat on the steps, and no one noticed Aylassa. Her little hands had brought her yellow school box. She opened it and took out the scissors and started cutting the wool from Clover first and then Diesel.

She looked at the wool laying on the ground and thought about what Sacora had said about the lambs needing their wool for this winter. She took out her Elmer's glue and covered both lambs with the glue and started putting the wool back on. Diesel had white wool from Clover, and Clover had black wool from Diesel. Aylassa stepped back to the steps with Sadie thinking she had finished with what was good.

Then Sacora noticed the lambs. She asked, "What happened to the lambs' wool? Who gave them a wool cut and glued it back on?"

Alisha spoke first, "It was Aylassa. I saw her when she did it."

Aylassa, with anger, replied, "Zora, Lisha not telling the truph. Her did not see me glue the lambs, 'cause I was looking to see if her was looking before I done it."

Sacora giggled and asked Alisha and Jeremiah if they would go to the house, in the kitchen, and bring her the Dawn dish detergent and the sponges from the drawer on left side of the dishwasher. Sacora got the water hose and moved it to Diesel and Clover. She saw Aylassa's yellow school box and started cleaning on it first.

Chapter Eighty-Five

Alisha and Jeremiah handed Sacora the sponges and Dawn. Sacora started putting water on Diesel first and losing the white wool and glue. The lambs had not been walked, and Clover dropped her feces, and then Diesel dropped his. Sacora moved the lambs from the feces and applied Dawn to Diesel and the wool, and glue did fall to the ground. Sacora washed him thoroughly again, leaving so much glue, feces, and water on the ground. She then started the water hose on Clover. The black wool and glue fell to the ground, and finally all the cuts in their wool were visible. Maybe not too bad and would be a few more weeks until winter.

Sacora took the leashes from the nail and handed Elijah and Jeremiah the leashes after she had connected them to the collars. They started out the barn with them when Sacora heard a car stopping at the barn. She looked to see Barton and Rachel coming toward her. Rachel knocked Elijah and Diesel out of her way. Sadie waved hello, and Rachel motioned for her to go away.

Sacora did not want them around these precious children so she immediately asked, "What do you want?"

Rachel handed her a document and said, "You will endorse this paper and I am not leaving until you do. I am Mrs. Barton Haynes now, and this money is mine."

Sacora took the paper and read that it was to waive, forfeit, deny all rights to the trust fund of Barton's grandmother. Sacora, remembering what Julie had said that the amount would help with confirming to the State of Alabama that she had monetary capabilities to provide for Alisha, Aylassa, and Elijah, took the document, printed side, and immediately placed in the feces, Dawn, glue, water, and loose wool, pressing it with her foot in the goo and pointed.

Sacora said, "I have endorsed it now, and you can leave."

Angry, Rachel bent over to pick up the document and fell in the goo, rolling around in it trying to get up. Barton came to her rescue and fell in the goo with her. Sadie and Aylassa laughed and clapped as if it was entertainment. Barton stood up first and helped Rachel up from the goo when her high heels caused her to slip in it again.

Sadie screamed, "Stinky lady do gin!"

Aylassa, clapping, laughing, and pointing, said, "You look funny with pooh in your hair."

Alisha, Elijah, and Jeremiah were ready to defend Sacora with shovels. Alisha and Jeremiah had the shorter ones, and Elijah had the longer one. Barton finally managed to place Rachel on steady ground, and he told her, "We need to leave. Our attorney will handle it from here." Rachel, showing disgust, motioned to the children to move, but Elijah took the long shovel and shook it at her. Rachel said, "I have never been treated so horrible."

Sacora looked at her and said, "And you will be able to say that again. You will never come back on my land again without me calling the local proper authorities. I will have you arrested and press charges for endangering my children."

Sacora grabbed the shovel from Elijah and put it in baseball bat position and screamed loudly, "Have I made myself clear?"

Rachel and Barton went to the Porsche covered in the goo and left out the driveway. Sacora put the shovels back on the nail and hugged all the children.

Sacora said, "I will take care of that if trouble shows back up."

Jeremiah said, "Barton is lucky Joe McCarley was not here. Joe would have given him a lesson about messing with you, Sacora."

Sacora smiled and said, "I think he would have too, Jeremiah. Let's take the lambs for a walk and put them on the front yard to graze. It won't be long until it is time for the grass to be cut around the yards."

Chapter Eighty-Six

E lijah and Jeremiah put Diesel and Clover in the front yard to graze. Sacora sat on the front porch watching Elijah and Jeremiah throwing the football. Alisha, Aylassa, and Sadie brought Hugs and Kisses to the front yard, and Eeyore came with them. Sacora was beginning to think about lunch when her parents parked in the driveway. Pizza Hut pizza and a bag from Walmart, they were carrying in their hands.

They all went inside, and the bag from Walmart had vanilla ice cream with all kinds of toppings. The children washed their hands and faces, said the blessing, and ate the pizza, suggesting what toppings would be on their ice cream. Elijah broke the laughter and informed Sacora's parents of Barton and Rachel's visit. Samantha looked at Sacora with puzzled eyes, and Sacora filled her in on the motion of Barton's grandmother's trust fund. Not only had Julie been able to avoid the money going to Barton and Rachel, she suggested that the amount would assist Sacora in adopting Aylassa, Elijah, and Alisha. Sacora still had no intentions of signing the waiver.

Jeremiah said, "Yeah, Barton was lucky Joe McCarley wasn't here. He would not have been leaving with a pretty face."

Everyone laughed. Lunch was over, and Sacora and Samantha started cleaning. Corey went with the children outside. Elijah and Jeremiah were running, catching the football that Corey was throwing them. Sadie and Alisha were playing with Hugs and Kisses. Aylassa was playing with Eeyore.

Samantha and Sacora cleaned up the kitchen and then started cleaning on the house. The vacuuming was done and kitchen was cleaned when Sadie and Aylassa wanted a nap. Aylassa climbed into her crib and fell asleep, but Sadie rocked to "Grandma's Lullaby."

Samantha and Sacora sat on the porch after everything had been finished, waiting on the washing machine and dryer. Jeremiah and Elijah were running and excited about playing football. Alisha and Eeyore played with the rabbits until the rabbits took a nap. Corey sat on the porch with Sacora, and Samantha and Elijah, Alisha, and Jeremiah walked Diesel and Clover around the front yard.

Joe's truck started up the driveway with loud Foo Fighters music. He sat on the front porch with everyone, talking and catching up on Barton and Rachel's visit this morning. Sacora took the minute to ask everyone if they would like to have a lunch for Labor Day next Saturday. Joe said he would bring the decorations and tables from the barn to the house on Friday night, and the plans for the meal were put together between Sacora and Samantha. Joe thought Joy would be back from Miami then.

Joe and Corey offered to get supper and have a picnic on the front porch. Sacora and Samantha decided on McDonald's ham-burgers, fries, and chicken nuggets. Sacora also asked to bring canned drinks for the children, and she would prepare the tables outside. Joe and Corey took the orders and left in Joe's truck.

On the way to McDonald's, Corey had some questions for Joe about his intentions with Sacora. Joe told Corey that December 2016, he had met Sacora and her husband at a Toys for Tots campaign fundraiser. Joe was very impressed with Sacora. Her eyes were on Barton Haynes only, and Joe saw Barton's eyes were on everyone else. "I thought how could a man have such a wife, beautiful inside and outside, to treat her so bad? My intentions in life were to have a beautiful wife inside and outside. Three years later, I have had the opportunity to have Sacora in my days, and the only way I am going to give it up is if she says so." Joe's answers surprised Corey, and he did not ask any more.

The orders were bought and carried to the front porch. Aylassa and Sadie awakened ready to eat. The children washed their hands and faces with the water hose and found this fun. The front porch was full of laughter and good food.

Saturday night, Hugs and Kisses were fed, watered, and put in their kennel for the night. Diesel and Clover were also walked back to the barn, fed, watered, salt refilled, and the feces were shoveled out. Eeyore went inside for a can of Pedigree and came back out.

The front porch was cleaned, and the children chased fireflies. Joe asked Sacora about church in the morning, and she said yes, her plans were to be there. Samantha and Corey also said they would be going. Samantha and Sacora finished the laundry, and baths and showers were next. Samantha and Corey told everyone good night and headed out the driveway. Sacora kissed Joe on the front porch before he left. Sadie and Aylassa had their baths and rocked to "Grandma's Lullaby" and Alisha, Elijah, and Jeremiah were tucked in before Sacora indulged in her long, hot bath.

Chapter Eighty-Seven

Sacora woke up around eight o'clock and opened the door for Eeyore, made her bed, and showered. She drank her coffee on the porch and went inside to start breakfast. Alisha came downstairs to open the kennel for Hugs and Kisses. She gave Eeyore some canned Pedigree. Elijah and Jeremiah said good morning and ran to the barn for the lambs' morning visit. Sacora had breakfast on the table when Sadie and Aylassa came to the kitchen. Elijah and Jeremiah had returned from the barn and was ready to eat, shower, and put on their church clothes and shoes.

Sacora had Sadie and Aylassa ready, and Alisha was ready for Sacora to fix her hair. They were in the van buckled up and out of the driveway at ten fifteen. Sacora parked by Joe's truck, and then Samantha and Corey parked by Sacora. Joe helped Sadie out, and Sacora grabbed the bag. Corey lifted Aylassa into his arms and Alisha, Elijah, and Jeremiah followed them into church. Wendy and Zac McCarley parked by Joe's truck. On one pew sat Sacora with her parents, children, Joe, and his parents.

Services were ended with Alisha, Elijah, Jeremiah, and Aylassa singing "Jesus Loves Me" with the other children. Sadie did not want to leave Sacora's lap. After church, Wendy and Zac had plans to attend a funeral, and Sacora's parents were going home to take care of housework and etcetera going back to work tomorrow. Samantha was teaching sixth grade this year, and Corey was going back to the office, starting where he left off before going to Africa.

Joe and Sacora were going to Golden Corral with the children and told their parents goodbye. Elijah and Jeremiah wanted to go with Joe in his truck, and Alisha, Aylassa, and Sadie went with

Sacora. Golden Corral was a good choice for Sunday after church. The children ate their favorites and ice cream with toppings again today for dessert.

Sacora told Joe goodbye with a quick kiss and went home, opening the front door. Alisha, Elijah, and Jeremiah changed into play clothes and went to the barn to play with Diesel and Clover. Sadie and Aylassa took a nap while Sacora made a grocery list. Watching Alisha, Elijah, and Jeremiah play, she decided to wait until tomorrow to buy groceries.

Sadie and Aylassa up from their nap asked for hot dogs and macaroni and cheese. After eating lunch so healthy and a lot of it, Sacora did cook what was asked for. After eating, fireflies were in the front yard to be chased by little hands and a lot of laughter. Diesel and Clover were put in the barn for the night with water, food, and salt. Hugs and Kisses were in their kennel for the night. Eeyore came in to the kitchen for food, but her surprise was not what she thought at first. It was bath night for Eeyore. Sadie and Aylassa watched Sacora give Eeyore a bath in their bathtub. Alisha helped with the rinsing, and Eeyore participated with the shampooing and rinsing. After being towel dried, Eeyore went outside to shake the extra water and came back in to her clean blanket.

Sacora thought the children's backpacks had not been checked for homework, and she looked and checked everything and put it back for school tomorrow. Baths, showers, and hair drying was over, and rocking Sadie and Aylassa, putting in their cribs, with Alisha, Elijah, and Jeremiah tucked in. Sacora to her long, hot bath and falling asleep with another week coming, and she was ready for it.

Monday morning went smooth. Breakfast, school traffic, kisses goodbye at the day care, and Mr. Hamilton's assignments for the week, but what she was not ready for was Joe's email. Joe texted her for her email address around four o'clock. He had an answer from his private investigator friend. He would send the email to her so she could forward it to Ms. Mays. Sacora sent him her address but decided not to read it until she was in the van ready to leave for the grocery store.

Chapter Eighty-Eight

S acora read the email when she was in the van after telling all her coworkers good night. She read it again just to make sure she was not making a mistake of the information.

> *I have contacted Tarik Malone in Atlanta, Georgia. He is employed by the Coca-Cola Company operating a forklift. He had not been notified of Autumn Malone's death. As for the children's custody, he will give his consent for adoption because of the large amount of child support he is not willing to pay. In return, he is asking for a death certificate of his wife to enable him to legally marry his now-live-in girlfriend. He gave me the following address to send all documents to be signed and to send Autumn Malone's death certificate.*

Sacora immediately forwarded the email to Ms. Mays. She put her head on the steering wheel and cried a few tears. How this man who was responsible for putting these precious children on this earth was willing to let them go because of thousands of dollars in back child support he was not going to pay broke her heart but at the same time gave her joy for progress of her certainty of their custody to her.

Cam came to her window and knocked. She said, "Sacora, are you all right?"

Sacora said, "Yes, I am. I have some good news that affected my emotions for a minute. Thank you for asking."

Cam went back to her car, and Sacora drove to the grocery store. She bought extra thinking about the permanency of the children's custody. She had it stacked in the back and buckled up ready to go when she got an email in return from Ms. Mays. It all sounded good to her.

> *We have just got to make sure he is all the relatives involved. The State of Alabama Human Resources normally does a thorough investigation of all or any relatives before foster care. If you are content and agree, I will start the paperwork and notify the Baldwin County Department of Human Resources of our findings. I will have a letter sent to them this week if not sooner. Congratulations, Sacora, maybe the adoption will go quicker than we thought.*

> *Ms. Mays*

Sacora made it to day care and went inside. She was ready to be home with these precious little people. Aylassa said "Aylassa's house" when she parked the van in her driveway. Elijah and Jeremiah put the groceries in the kitchen, and Sacora, Alisha, Aylassa, and Sadie put them away. Sacora had put a pizza in the oven, and she went through the children's backpacks looking at homework. Jeremiah was still making good grades, all his test on Friday had high scores, Elijah was doing well in his advanced classes with good scores, and Alisha was learning to read in advance books.

Sacora set the table and put the pizza and cups out for the children's supper. After washing hands and faces, the blessing said, everyone sat in their chairs. Sadie and Aylassa climbed in theirs without any help. Jeremiah talked about his day with Asher, Alisha talked about Eemonie's visit from the tooth fairy, and Elijah wanted to do his essay on Diesel and Clover, mostly Aylassa's day of cutting their wool.

Sacora was cleaning the table when she heard Joe's truck's loud Foo Fighters music and went to the door. He had brought some chairs that he had bought secondhand today from a client he had finished repair work. He would put them in the barn on his way out the driveway. Sacora and the children rode with him to the barn to visit the lambs. The children fed, watered, added salt, and cleaned the feces from the barn.

Joe looked at Sacora and said, "Did you find anything you could use from the email I sent? I am hoping it will go smooth and quick for you. The children have had a month here and act like it is all they know. It will be good for them when all paperwork is finished and the birth certificates say 'Mother, Sacora Hill.'"

Sacora replied, "Thank you, Joe. I am so hoping and praying no other relative will have to be notified or persuaded to give me custody through adoption. How much was the private investigator's fee?"

Joe said, "Nothing. I called in a favor that he owed me."

Chapter Eighty-Nine

Sacora had told Joe goodbye, and the children went back to the house for bedtime and getting ready for another day of school. Sadie and Aylassa were tired and went to sleep before "Grandma's Lullaby" was finished. Alisha, Elijah, and Jeremiah had finished showers and baths. Sacora tucked them in and enjoyed her long, hot bath. Thinking about Joe's comment, he called in a favor that he was owed. The information was promising and optimistic. Alisha was still putting her clothes in her backpack and not in the dresser thinking she would be leaving soon.

Sacora put all her thoughts aside and fell asleep. The rest of the week was the same routine, and Saturday morning was finally here. Sacora was ready for the lunch in the afternoon for Labor Day. The children were up around eight thirty to start enjoying Eeyore, Hugs, Kisses, Diesel, and Clover. After breakfast, Alisha went to the backyard, and Elijah and Jeremiah went to the barn. The feces were shoveled out, and the lambs walked on the leashes to the front yard to graze. Elijah and Jeremiah threw the football and then helped Sacora with the decorations.

Loud Foo Fighters music was heard first, and then Joe's truck stopped at the barn. Joe loaded the tables and the chairs he had brought Monday. Sacora and the children rode with him to the house. Sadie and Aylassa played on the front porch, and Sacora and Joe set everything up. Julie was coming home, and Sacora was ready to visit with her. Samantha and Corey parked in the driveway, and Samantha complimented Sacora on the decorations and the arrangements of the tables. Sadie and Aylassa had played all morning and were ready for a nap when Samantha and Sacora cooked hamburgers and hot dogs. Sacora cooked Sadie some macaroni and cheese and tossed salad with several different dressings were also added.

Uncle Owen, Julie, her mom, Savannah Johnson, Zac, and Wendy all came to eat and have a great time. Uncle Owen said the blessing, and Sacora and Joe looked around at all the smiling faces. Sadie ate macaroni and cheese, Aylassa ate mostly hot dogs, and Alisha, Elijah, and Jeremiah ate a little of everything.

Lemonade was on the table, and Aylassa said, "I made it." Joe spit it out, and Sacora laughed and said, "She made it from bottle water, not toilet water."

The day went by so fast, and then it was time to clean up and tell everyone goodbye. Julie and Savannah Johnson were pleased with Sacora's lunch, home, and family. Julie told Samantha, Corey, Uncle Owen, Zac, Wendy, and Joe goodbye. Labor Day lunch was over, and Joe put the tables and chairs in his truck. Corey and Zac helped Joe with putting everything back in storage at the barn.

The fireflies came so soon, and Sadie was the first to chase them. Uncle Owen told everyone good night, and then Zac and Wendy said goodbye. Samantha and Corey stayed for a while longer. Joe threw the football for Elijah and Jeremiah after Diesel and Clover were in the barn with fresh water, food, and salt. Alisha put Hugs and Kisses in their kennel for the night. Eeyore ate very little dog food because Aylassa was feeding her hot dogs. Samantha and Corey decided to leave around eight o'clock. Joe left at eight thirty. Joy was flying in from Miami tomorrow, and he would not be at church but the airport. Sacora kissed him good night and started the baths and showers, getting ready for one more day.

Sacora was singing "Grandma's Lullaby," and Alisha was listening quietly until Sacora came to the bathroom to dry her hair. Elijah and Jeremiah told Sacora good night and what an amazing Saturday it had been. Eeyore on her blanket, Sacora's long, hot bath was welcomed. Sacora fell asleep ready to conquer Sunday morning.

Chapter Ninety

Sacora was up and opened the door for Eeyore, made her bed, and showered. She drank her coffee on the front porch and looked at the clouds, thinking it might storm. She decided to wake Elijah and Jeremiah to visit Diesel and Clover before it started raining. They met her on the stairs and went to the barn running and ran back thirty minutes later. Sacora had cooked breakfast, and Alisha put Hugs and Kisses out for a while and then put them back in their kennel on the back porch to keep them dry from the rain.

Sadie and Aylassa ate breakfast slow today, being tired from yesterday. Alisha started getting ready for church, Elijah and Jeremiah were ready and in the van buckled up. Sacora left the driveway ten twenty this morning, and it started to rain. Sacora parked by her parents and Joe's parents. Everyone sat on the same pew, but it did not feel right without Joe and Joy.

After church, Sacora and the children went with her parents to eat lunch, and Zac and Wendy were going to Joe's to help Joy settle in for school tomorrow. Sadie was enjoying her chicken nuggets, and Aylassa gave hers to Alisha. Elijah and Jeremiah were ready for dessert. Samantha and Corey were on their way home, and then Sacora had the children buckled up on their way home. Sacora made the comment "No school tomorrow." Elijah was the most excited to play with the lambs and rabbits all day.

After Sadie and Aylassa took their nap, everyone went to the barn. Diesel and Clover were walked, fed, and watered and with salt added to their container. Their wool was growing back but still could see the cuts from Aylassa's scissors. Jeremiah shoveled out the small amount of feces and hung the shovel back on the nail. Sacora said it was time to go to eat supper. Alisha ran with Elijah and Jeremiah, chasing one another. Sadie and Aylassa walked with Sacora. After supper, it was the same routine of baths, showers, and bedtime. Sacora was also looking forward to a break in routine tomorrow.

The rain stopped before everyone got up on Labor Day Monday morning. Sacora opened the door for Eeyore, made her bed, and showered. Breakfast was cooked, pancakes with extra variety of pancake syrups, and the children were ready for a big day of playing. Elijah and Jeremiah went to the barn and walked the lambs to the front yard. Alisha and Eeyore brought Hugs and Kisses to the front yard to play with Sadie and Aylassa. All was going great until the car of Barton Haynes started down the driveway. He saw Sacora pick up her phone, and he decided to back out and not try anything today.

Lunchtime was a relaxed meal of sandwiches and soups with chocolate milk. Even though they played all day with the animals, the children had energy to play tag before Sadie's and Aylassa's nap. The TV and PlayStation were entertaining Alisha, Elijah, and Jeremiah. Sacora rested in her chair thinking about what Barton and Rachel were attempting now. She heard a car in the driveway, and relief, it was Joe and Joy with Kentucky Fried Chicken.

Joe and Joy came in, and Sacora took the food to the table. Sadie and Aylassa had awakened, hearing Joy. Suppertime had so many smiling faces at the dining room table.

Sacora had started cleaning the table when Eeyore started barking and they heard a car in the driveway. Sacora looked, and it was Barton Haynes. He came to the door, and Sacora was escorted by Joe. The children were looking out the window with curiosity.

Barton spoke, "Sacora, I am asking you to endorse this paper to waiver all of the trust fund to me. I have a new wife now, and none of this money is yours, it is hers."

Sacora spoke angrily, "This is not what the courts of Alabama say, Barton. I will not endorse the paper for you, and you will not harass me."

Barton then noticed Joe McCarley. He said to Joe, "Hey, I know you. You are Joe McCarley. We met you at the Toys for Tots fundraiser a few years back."

Joe said, "Yeah, you did. I did not like the way you treated Sacora then and I don't like it now. The best thing you can do is take her answer of no and get in your car. You are not wanted here. That is what attorneys are for, Mr. Haynes."

Barton said, "I won't give up, Sacora." He left out the driveway throwing gravel.

Sacora turned to Joe and said, "You met me before?"

Joe said, "Yes, I have. You were such a beautiful woman in a red dress at the Toys for Tots fundraiser, December 2016. I'd seen Barton Haynes making eyes on all the other women when he had the most beautiful wife, beautiful heart, and such a lucky man throwing it all away."

Chapter Ninety-One

S acora said, "Joe, why did you not tell me you met me before? You knew my grandmother, remodeled this house, and you know more about me than I thought."

Joe said, "Sacora, yes, I met you before, but it is now, right now today, that I have fallen in love with you." Joe kissed Sacora and said, "We have an audience, and we need to get back inside."

Sacora looked at the six faces in the window and said, "Yes, we do."

The Labor Day holiday was over, and Joe and Joy were leaving. Sacora said, "Joe, good night," and kissed him on the front porch after Joy went to the car. Sadie and Aylassa had a bath and rocked to "Grandma's Lullaby," and Alisha, Elijah, and Jeremiah were tucked in. Sacora had backpacks ready for school tomorrow.

Weeks had gone by, and no other relative had been mentioned for contesting the adoption of Aylassa, Alisha, and Elijah. Ms. Mays had the documents signed by Tarik Malone for his permission for adoption to proceed, and a copy of the death certificate of Autumn Malone had been returned to him. Sacora still had no idea on Sadie's and Jeremiah's custody information. Ms. Hines did not know anything about the certainty of their case and was continuing to work on the adoption of the Malone children.

Halloween was next week Thursday, and the children were talking about what costumes they wanted to wear. Elijah and Alisha were discussing the fall festival's talent show, and Sacora had agreed to help them participate. Elijah had decided to tell jokes in his Forrest Gump voice, and Alisha was going to sing with Eemonie.

The night of the talent show, Sacora, Joe, Joy, Samantha, Corey, Zac, and Wendy were all there waiting and giving support. Alisha and Eemonie took the stage, and in front of the microphone, Alisha started singing "Grandma's Lullaby." Sacora's heart went into butterfly mode as she did not know Alisha knew the song and had taught it to her friend Eemonie.

Chose your friends so you can keep 'em, make your
words sweet you'll have to eat 'em.
And don't forget to pray, at the start of everyday

Chorus:
And don't ever doubt a dreamer, never give up on
love
Always put the Good Lord first, he'll see you have
enough
And when you see the glass is half full or maybe half
empty chile, you just have more glass than you
need
And may you always be on an uphill path of a
downhill journey

Second Verse:
Loving hands made you, evil hands will destroy you
And there's no job great or small, to get it done it
takes us all

Bridge:
And may you always be greatly treasured and may
you have happiness unmeasured
And as you grow and years go by, remember
Grandma's Lullaby

Sacora had tears falling but applauded the loudest. Joe and his parents were impressed and applauded with Samantha and Corey. They all stood up for a standing ovation. Joy was screaming with applause, and Alisha and Eemonie were smiling so big. Next was Elijah. He cleared his throat and started his voice of Forrest Gump.

Chapter Ninety-Two

E lijah started his jokes. The first one was, "Did you hear about the two guys who got caught stealing a calendar? They got six months each. What did one mouse say to the other mouse chewing on a DVD? The book was better.

"My neighbor is such a great storyteller of his days of being a pilot. A beautiful, blond girl boarded the jet and went to first class to take a seat. She told the attendant, 'I am blond, I am beautiful, and I am going to New York.' The attendant said, 'Ma'am, your ticket is for coach, and you need to come with me.' And she refused, saying, 'I am blond, I am beautiful, and I am going to New York.'

"My neighbor, being the pilot, asked, 'What is the problem?' The attendant told him of the situation. He went to the beautiful lady and whispered something in her ear, and she laughed, walking to coach with the attendant. The attendant asked, 'What did you say to her?' He answered, 'I said that this part of the jet, first class, is not going to New York.'

"He was introduced to two immigrants from Ireland, Me Pat, and Mike. They had brought from Ireland one case of Irish whiskey. When one bottle of whiskey was left, they had an agreement that whoever died first, the other one would pour the last bottle of whiskey on the grave of their dear friend. Me Pat died first, and Mike standing at his grave said, 'Me Pat, we had an agreement to pour the last bottle of our Irish whiskey on the grave of the one that passed first. I am here with the whiskey to pour on your grave. But, Me Pat, would you mind if I ran it through my kidneys first?'

"My momma and me went to the other neighbors' house to visit the new baby. My momma said, 'Don't say anything about the baby because he does not have any ears.' I did not but did ask Momma if the baby had good eyes, and she said, 'Yes.' I said, 'Good because he could not wear glasses.'

"I want to thank Sacora Hill and all the other parents that are here tonight, teaching us children how to leave a better world for Betty White and Clint Eastwood." Elijah, changing to his voice, said, "I am Elijah Malone, and I hope everyone has a safe and happy Halloween Thursday night."

The applause was loud, but Sacora's was the loudest, so proud of Alisha's and Elijah's entertainment. The rest of the night, Jeremiah played games and won prizes. He brought them to Sacora, so many she could not carry, Joe helped her carry prizes. Sadie and Aylassa was entertained by different costumes of Disney characters and Looney Tunes. It was a great night for everyone. Sacora told her parents and Joe's parents good night. This was the first time the children realized they had additional grandparent figures and loved on them when saying goodbye.

Thursday night, all children dressed for trick or treating, buckled up in the van with Joe, and Joy went to Sacora's old neighborhood. Joe was surprised to Sacora's opinion. "If Barton and Rachel Haynes can come into my world causing trouble, I will go into their world getting the best candy on Halloween for my precious babies." The house Sacora lived in for ten years was avoided, but the others were hit heavy with six children. It was a good night, Sacora's first Halloween being a mom. So many pictures were taken, and Joe and Sacora celebrated their first Halloween together as well.

Chapter Ninety-Three

November 10, it was Sacora's birthday. After church, there was a large celebration at Golden Corral with her parents and Joe, Joy, and Joe's parents. Alisha, Elijah, and Jeremiah had given her a card and gifts from Dollar Tree, saving some school-spending money. Sadie and Aylassa sang "Happy Birthday" to her loudly. Joy had a surprise for Sacora tonight: a candlelighted supper in the dining room of Sacora's home, just her and Joe.

Sadie and Aylassa napped, and Elijah, Jeremiah, and Alisha played with Eeyore, Hugs, Kisses, and Diesel and Clover. Joe and Joy came around four o'clock with steaks from Texas Roadhouse to celebrate Sacora's birthday. Joy put hers and the children's on the back porch for a picnic and Joe and Sacora's in the dining room, lighting the candles. Joy sat with Sadie and Aylassa, helping them eat steak. Aylassa ate more A1 steak sauce than steak and had a lot on her face. Joy had set the CD player up for Joe to slow dance with Sacora. Joy heard the song "Simple Man" by Shinedown playing, and she knew the night was going more than just good.

Joe had slowed dance with Sacora, and when the song had finished, he took a diamond ring out of his pocket and held it so that Sacora could see it. Joe said, "Sacora, I am a simple man now after I have lived the life in a celebrity circle. I am asking you to marry me and to have a simple life with me. I love you, and I would like for you to add me to the adoption request to have these children mine as well as yours. I want a home, family, and a simple life with you. What do you say?"

Sacora, full of emotion, said, "Yes, Joe, I will marry you. You are a very much part of my happiness. I can't imagine how I would ever make it through one day without you."

Joe asked, "What about a small wedding on the beach with the children and our parents, Julie, and Tyler?"

Sacora said, "That will be nice and sweet. I am free the Saturday after Thanksgiving November thirtieth. What about you?"

Joe said, "I will be there." Joe kissed his sweet Sacora after putting the ring on her finger. Six faces were watching through the doorway of the dining room. Joe started the CD again, and they danced to "Simple Man." Joy carried the children to the living room to the PlayStation. Sadie said, "My wike that song."

Six o'clock, the sun was going down, and the temperature had dropped to be cooler. Elijah, Jeremiah, and Alisha had gone to put the animals up for the night with water and food. Joe asked Sacora when she would tell the children of their planned wedding on the beach. Sacora said, "Tonight, and I will tell my parents and Julie tomorrow."

Joe and Joy leaving, Sacora kissed Joe on the front porch and said, "I love you, Joe, and maybe it is time for you to start thinking about moving in. What about Joy in the upstairs bedroom and bathroom, having some privacy?"

Joe said, "I think that will be perfect. I know where I will be moving in."

Sacora giggled and kissed him again. She watched him walk to the truck where he parked the day she first saw him. So soon, Saturday the thirtieth, twenty days from today, but would seem so long. Sacora turned into the front door and took a deep breath.

She motioned for the children to come to her when she sat in her chair. She picked up Sadie and put her in her lap. Sacora started to speak, and the attention from the children's eyes were so on her. Sacora said, "Tonight Joe asked me to marry him, and I have said yes. We are going to marry on the beach Saturday after Thanksgiving. I would love for you to be there with us."

Elijah answered first, "That is great, Sacora."

Jeremiah said, "Absolutely I will be there. Won't we, Sadie?"

Sadie said, "My wike Doe."

Aylassa said, "I like the beach."

Alisha did not say anything.

Chapter Ninety-Four

Monday morning Sacora was up, opened the door for Eeyore, made her bed, and showered. Today was Veteran's Day, no school and no work. Sacora put on a light jacket and sat on the front porch drinking her coffee, thinking about her routine would be changing. Alisha came and sat by her with her jacket. Alisha asked Sacora to zip it up. When Sacora started zipping it up, Alisha busted into tears and said, "I am going to miss you when you marry Joe and I have to go to a new foster home."

Sacora, touched deep, said, "No, my sweet baby. When I marry Joe, nothing is going to change. I will take care of you and Joe will take care of me. Joy will move in the bedroom upstairs, and you will have Joy every day."

Sacora dried her tears on her jacket and put Alisha in her lap, hugging her for affection and warmth. Eeyore came from the back, and Alisha started to pet her. Sacora decided that it was time to tell Alisha of her intentions to adopt her, thinking about the words she needed to use. She took a deep breath and began. Sacora said, "You know, my sweet baby, I have loved every minute that you have been with me. Joe loves you too. We have asked the State of Alabama to complete the paperwork so you will be with us always. Me as your mom and Joe as your dad. Elijah and Aylassa will still be your siblings. We have asked for them to be with us too."

Alisha, still crying, said, "I would like that, Sacora. I love Joe and Joy too. When will you know if I can be here forever?"

Sacora said, "I don't know, my sweet baby. I am hoping soon."

Alisha stopped crying and asked to open the kennel for the rabbits. For the first time of sitting on the front porch with Sacora, Alisha kissed her cheek and said, "I love you, Sacora."

Sacora hugged Alisha and said, "I love you, my sweet baby. It is time to start breakfast." Sacora cooked a large breakfast. Sadie and Aylassa were up in a laughing mood. They climbed into their chairs, and Elijah had started to use his different voices in nursery rhymes. Jeremiah asked, "Sacora, am I going to be here when Joe moves in? Will Joy move in too? Will I have to go home? Will we be put in another foster home? Will Sadie and I go to different places to live?"

Sacora said, "As far as I know, you will be with me, and yes, Joe and Joy will be moving in. Joy will move in the upstairs bedroom, and I do not want you and Sadie to leave us."

Jeremiah said, "Sacora, I don't want to leave either."

Sadie hearing the conversation said, "My don't want to leaf eber."

After the table was cleaned and the dishwasher started, with laundry in the washing machine, everyone went to the barn to play with Diesel and Clover. Sacora's thoughts were on Jeremiah and Sadie again and decided to question Ms. Hines of their future custody.

Joe and Joy came for supper. Sacora and Alisha carried Joy to the upstairs bedroom and asked her if she would like to move her things in here. Joy was excited to have her own bathroom and level of the house. Sacora asked her what she needed for her classes with a computer and Wi-Fi. She wrote it down, and she would take care of it.

Alisha took Joy's hand and showed her her room. Joy was so surprised to see such a clean and neat room but did notice the backpack stuffed full of her clothes instead of in the dresser. Elijah's and Jeremiah's rooms are here.

Joe was throwing the football to Jeremiah and Elijah while Diesel and Clover grazed on the grass in the front yard. Jeremiah asked Joe, "So when are you moving in? I am ready to see you every day."

Joe said, "It won't be too much longer."

Sacora had called Samantha after supper to tell her the news of marrying Joe. Samantha was excited but overwhelmed with emotion when Sacora asked her if she could wear the dress she wore when she married her dad. Samantha and Sacora started discussing the details, a lot to do in the days to come.

Before Joe left tonight, Sacora kissed him on the front porch, and he handed a CD to her. A late birthday present because it was just released today. Joe bought one of the first ones released. Sacora looked at Joe with touching the CD, Backroad 48's *Your Dog Stays with Me*. Sacora said a sincere thank you and kissed him again.

Chapter Ninety-Five

The next day at work Sacora decided to text Julie to meet her for lunch. After a phone call from Julie, lunch was planned. Sacora put her left hand to Julie's face, and Julie hugged Sacora and squealed. Julie told her, "We are also celebrating today. Barton Haynes has sent your portion of the trust fund."

Sacora and Julie discussing details of the wedding on the beach, lunch was over too soon. Julie and Sacora said goodbye and would finish planning the wedding this weekend and decorate for Thanksgiving. At work, Mr. Hamilton had an answer from Ms. Hines. Information had been sent to Ms. Mays for adopting the Malone children with Joe McCarley. Maybe finalizing would be soon, no contesting relatives had been found. Sacora asked Ms. Hines about Sadie and Jeremiah Walters earlier this morning. No information was available today. Ms. Hines did understand that Sacora and Joe would pursue adopting them also.

The week went by, and Saturday morning was welcoming. Samantha and Corey came first thing with McDonald's biscuits. Julie came also, and the ladies discussed details of the wedding and decorating for Thanksgiving. Corey went outside with Elijah, Jeremiah, and Alisha. Sadie and Aylassa were coloring in the Winnie the Pooh books. It was too cool for them to play outside.

The wedding was planned with the boys wearing khakis pants with white shirts, denim jackets, and leather Clark Wallabees. The girls would be wearing denim jackets and white dresses with leather sandals. Sacora wanted the coral rose bouquet, and the songs played would be discussed later. Joe came in and asked if he could put some of Joy's things upstairs. Sacora asked if he needed any help, and he said, "I got it."

Jeremiah's smile was so big while he watched Joe bringing in Joy's things. Corey did not say much, just sat on the front porch with Alisha. Alisha looked at Corey and said, "You know, Joe and Sacora don't want us to leave. I don't want to leave either."

Corey said, "We don't want you to leave either. What about we check on Hugs and Kisses?"

Corey and Alisha played with Hugs and Kisses until lunchtime. When everyone was seated, sandwiches, chips, and drinks on the table, Corey took the spoon and hit his glass and said, "Attention, everybody. I have a toast. Today we are starting a new adventure of tying all these people in love forever. Samantha and I couldn't be more happier to have a son, Joe, and six grandchildren, one dog, two rabbits, and two lambs."

Samantha was smiling, nodding. The children's appetites were good today, and it did not take long until dessert was on the table. Julie then had her say about the happiness she had for her dear friend Sacora finding love and a family. It was then mentioned if Sacora had announced her engagement to Uncle Owen, Ginger, and Sandy.

Sacora would be calling them soon.

Joy and her grandparents, Zac and Wendy, came after lunch. Wendy complimented the Thanksgiving decorating that had been done today. It was agreed that Thanksgiving Day dinner would be at Sacora's home, and Joe's family would start a new tradition. Wendy went upstairs with Joy to see her new bedroom and bathroom. Joe had put her things on the bed, and Joy started putting them in place. When Joy finished her room, going downstairs, she looked in Alisha's room, and Alisha was putting her clothes in the dresser. Alisha looked up at Joy, and they exchanged smiles.

Chapter Ninety-Six

Corey had gone to the barn with Elijah and Jeremiah to put Diesel and Clover up for the night. Alisha attentively showed Corey how she put Hugs and Kisses in their kennel with food and water. Eeyore ate more dog food than Sacora thought after the ham sandwiches Aylassa had fed her. After all the goodbyes were said and Sacora kissed Joe on the front porch, she looked at the living room of the children. Baths, showers, and bedtime were here, and plans for church in the morning were on Sacora's mind when she fell asleep.

Sunday morning went smooth. Sacora parked by Joe's car, and the pew was full of Joe's parents and Sacora's parents with the children sitting between them. After services, Joe and Sacora were congratulated on their upcoming marriage. The lunch plans were at Zac and Wendy's. Alisha wanted to go with Samantha and Corey. She kissed Sacora goodbye and said, "See you later." Elijah and Jeremiah wanted to go with Joe in his cool red Dodge car, and Joy went with Sacora, Sadie, and Aylassa.

The lunch was Joe's favorites, barbecued chicken breasts, potatoes, green beans, tossed salad, broccoli and cheese, garlic bread, and for dessert, a blueberry delight with ice cream. All the children's hands were washed and ready to eat. Thanksgiving Day would be on Thursday, and this family would be together again enjoying food and laughter.

Samantha and Wendy have already bought dresses for the wedding, and Sacora was taking the week off to go shopping for what the children need. Her dress was at the cleaners and would be ready to pick up tomorrow. The florists would have flowers ready for the wedding on Saturday morning. Sacora would look at wedding rings for Joe tomorrow too. It was all coming together. Sacora decided on the songs to be "The Rose" by Bette Midler because it was a song her parents had played at their wedding. When she walked to Joe, Backroad 48's song "Talk to Me" was what would play. Leaving after the ceremony, Joe asked for Foo Fighters' "Walk."

Sacora left Wendy and Zac's with the children and parked in the driveway looking at her house, remembering May of 2019, when she felt so devastated moving out of her home. This house had brought her so much happiness, the moments with Joe McCarley and the precious six children. She was hoping to have good news soon about the adoption being final and the situation with Sadie and Jeremiah being permanent.

Elijah and Jeremiah changed clothes and went to the barn for Diesel and Clover. Alisha put Hugs and Kisses up for the night. Sadie and Aylassa took their nap, and Sacora made the grocery list for Thanksgiving dinner. She fixed cheese toast and soup for supper, and baths, showers, and bedtime came too soon.

Monday morning, the routine went smooth, school and day care. Sacora came home to an empty house. She looked around for a minute and then decided to drive the Bug shopping for the Thanksgiving dinner and wedding. Her first stop was the cleaners for her dress, and then everything else fell into place. She bought Joe's wedding band, and she found the children's clothes and shoes. She bought groceries for the week as well as Thanksgiving dinner. After she had put everything in its place, she sat in her chair thinking about how it all had gone so fast, but the changes had been so nice. She went to the day care at four o'clock, and McDonald's for supper.

The children's clothes fit perfectly, and Sacora took pictures of them posing for her. Alisha blew kisses and had made such beautiful pictures. Sadie liked the denim jacket and would not take it off until bedtime.

Chapter Ninety-Seven

The week of Thanksgiving had been great. When school was out for the holiday, Sacora did not take Sadie and Aylassa to day care. The children enjoyed their time with the animals, PlayStation, and just being home. Thanksgiving dinner was such a pleasant meal. It seemed like the turkey was more than just turkey, the sweet potatoes were sweeter, and the desserts were more than Sacora could eat. Sacora looked at the table surrounded by smiles of faces she did not even know last Thanksgiving other than her parents.

When the table and kitchen had been cleaned, the wedding was the conversation. Sacora seemed to think she was ready. Joy had shopped with Wendy and bought her things, even some flowers for her hair. Wendy bought smaller versions for Alisha, Aylassa, and Sadie. A photographer had been scheduled. Uncle Owen would be performing the ceremony. The plans for the children, Samantha and Corey would be with them on Saturday night, and Wendy and Zac would be with the children on Sunday until Sacora and Joe returned home. Joy would be with Wendy and Zac all weekend.

Joy had brought her computer, and Joe set it up. Wi-Fi was to be installed one day next week. Joe would be moving in and would be available the day of installation. Joy had settled in her bedroom and would be ready by Sunday night after the wedding to be moved in permanently.

Thanksgiving day was over. Sacora's parents said goodbye, and Joy left with Joe's parents. Elijah and Jeremiah took care of Diesel and Clover and Hugs and Kisses. Baths, showers, and bedtime were here. Sadie and Aylassa were sleeping in their cribs after "Grandma's Lullaby." Sacora tucking Alisha, she said, "This was my first Thanksgiving without my momma. I miss her, but it was nice. Good night, Sacora. I do love you."

Sacora, being so touched, kissed her forehead and said, "Good night, sweet baby. I love you very much." Sacora tucked in Elijah, and then Jeremiah, leaving the doors open some. Sacora in her long, hot bath thought about she had suggested going to the mountains for the holidays and how much things have changed since the suggestion.

Friday morning was the last morning of preparing for her wedding day. She enjoyed her coffee on the porch and knew she would not have time for that tomorrow. Ginger and Sandy would be conditioning and styling her hair in the morning. She cooked breakfast, and it was cooler today, so Elijah and Jeremiah left Diesel and Clover in the barn. Hugs and Kisses were out of their kennel for a while but not all day. Sacora instructed Alisha, Elijah, and Jeremiah to do extra with food and water on the animals because they would not have time tomorrow. Eeyore would be taken care of like every day. The children enjoyed their day with no school, and the cooler temperatures went outside to play for a while and inside for a while.

Sacora had cooked pizza in the oven and made tossed salad for supper. Sadie ate pizza better tonight, and Aylassa ate more salad. Elijah and Jeremiah were ready for Joe to move in Monday and talked about it through supper. Alisha still had not much to say other than she liked her dress and floral hair bow. Baths, showers, and rocking chair with "Grandma's Lullaby," tucking in Alisha, Elijah, and Jeremiah. This was the last night of being without Joe. Eeyore went outside but came back in quickly to her blanket. Sacora's long, hot bath was welcomed, and she did her planning of schedules for in the morning while relaxing. Sacora fell asleep with anxiety for her big day tomorrow.

Chapter Ninety-Eight

The morning for Sacora came so suddenly. She was up at four thirty and took her shower after making her bed and opening the door for Eeyore. Eeyore did not stay out long. After seeing that, Hugs and Kisses were in their kennel, and Eeyore came back to her blanket and went to sleep and did not bother to eat or drink her water. Sacora was to be at Sandy and Ginger's by six o'clock. Samantha and Corey were parked in the driveway by five thirty with biscuits and dough-nuts. Sacora told them bye and drove the Bug to Sandy and Ginger's. Six o'clock, they were ready for her. Sandy locked the door behind Sacora. No other client was expected until eight o'clock. Sacora was to have two hours of undivided attention for her special day. The last client was scheduled before eleven o'clock, closing for Sacora's wedding.

Sacora's hair was deep conditioned, with such a soft, manageable texture. Seven o'clock, right on time, a stylist, Stella Margaret, came in and braided a vintage braid on Sacora's hair. A unique braid was perfect for Sacora's hair under her mother's veil. Stella Margaret was young but had learned this braid from her grandmother. Sacora looking in the mirror was so pleased. She offered to pay for her hair styled, and it was declined, a gift from Sandy and Ginger.

Sacora parked in her driveway at eight thirty. Her parents were in the living room with Alisha. Nine o'clock, Samantha and Corey left to dress for the wedding and pictures. Elijah and Jeremiah came downstairs to check on Diesel and Clover and to eat breakfast. The lambs would be fine for the day without walking and had fresh water, food, and salt. Elijah was the first to finish breakfast and went upstairs to get ready for the big day. The wedding was scheduled at one o'clock but needed to be at the beach for pictures at eleven o'clock. Jeremiah went upstairs next. Alisha wanted extra attention from Sacora. Sacora took thirty minutes after Alisha's bath to dry her hair and arrange it in a french braid with the floral hair bow. Sadie and Aylassa were the last awakened, and Sacora had a smooth morning with their dresses and hair after eating breakfast.

There was nowhere on the beach to change, and Sacora took advantage of her mirrors. She had an audience of Alisha, Aylassa, and Sadie on the bed. Alisha reminding her again she needed lip gloss and not lipstick until she was older. Sacora's makeup was finished, and she put her dress on and would change shoes in the van before she added the veil to her hair.

Sadie said, "My fink you are georgous."

Aylassa said, "Bootiful bride."

Alisha said, "We are all ready now. Can we have pictures just us at home before we leave for the beach?"

Sacora said, "That is a great idea." She took the camera, and the camera on her phone and made pictures. Sadie and Aylassa imitated Alisha blowing kisses. Elijah and Jeremiah made pictures with their sisters in addition to all of them together on the stairs. Elijah took the camera and Sacora's phone and took pictures of each child with her, and then Jeremiah took pictures of Elijah with Sacora. Everyone was ready. Sacora texted her parents and Julie. She said she was leaving and would see her there. Ten thirty, Sacora parked at the beach. She was changing her shoes when Samantha and Corey came to the van all dressed, escorting large smiles. Elijah, Alisha, Jeremiah, Sadie, and Aylassa unbuckled their seat belts and went to Corey. Samantha helped Sacora with her veil.

Everyone ready to participate with the photographer did not have a difficult time smiling and laughing because of Uncle Owen's sense of humor. Sacora's eyes sparkled with happiness, and this was the first time in years that Samantha and Corey saw this in her eyes.

Each picture was so precious. Sacora with the children, Uncle Owen, Ginger, Sandy, and her parents. But the pictures of Sacora and Julie were treasures. Julie was just beautiful in her dress and denim jacket. She was so happy for Sacora, and the smiles in the pictures were so authentic.

Chapter Ninety-Nine

The morning for Joe and Joy was such eventful minutes. Joy was so excited for her dad she skipped breakfast and started on her makeup and dressing. Sacora had the bouquets for Wendy and Joy at the beach. Wendy asked Joy before she was completely ready if she did not want to eat a biscuit or something.

Joe had come in at his parents around ten o'clock to eat breakfast with Joy. Joy finally ate a biscuit and drank a Coca-Cola with Joe before finishing her makeup. Zac and Wendy were dressed, and everyone was at the beach by twelve o'clock. Wendy put the boutonnieres on Zac and Joe. Wendy kissed Joe's cheek and wished him great happiness. Tyler met Joe in the parking lot, and Sacora went to another place to avoid Joe seeing her. The photographer took pictures of Joe and Joy first. Joe's parents were the last ones taken before the wedding.

One o'clock and everyone in place, the music started of Bette Midler's "The Rose." Uncle Owen was in his place first, and then Joe and Zac joined him. Wendy and Samantha were on the other side of Uncle Owen. Tyler and Julie came from different directions and joined for a few steps to separate to stand by Zac and Wendy. Elijah and Alisha came from different directions and joined together for a few steps and then separated, then Elijah stood by Tyler and Alisha by Julie. Jeremiah and Aylassa walked straight in front of Uncle Owen, and Aylassa went to Alisha and Jeremiah went to Elijah.

Sadie walked to Uncle Owen and, remembering the pictures, were blowing kisses. "The Rose" had finished playing, and the piano started playing "Talk to Me" by Backroad 48.

Corey, Ginger, and Sandy had been standing in front of Sacora and then moved for Joe to see his bride. Sacora started walking toward Joe with Corey. Sacora's bouquet of coral and peach roses fell to her knees in length, and the breeze from the ocean made it look magical. Sacora stopped at Uncle Owen. Uncle Owen looked at his brother and asked, "Do you give this woman to this man?" Corey answered, "Yes, I do." He looked at Joe, shook his hand, and said, "Sacora is our treasure, son. Take care of her." He then went to stand by Elijah and Tyler. Joe took Sacora's hand, smiling.

Uncle Owen said, "We are here today to join Sacora Elizabeth Hill, the treasure of Corey James Hill and Samantha Elizabeth Hill, to Joseph Clay McCarley, the only son of Zachery Clay McCarley and Wendy Danielle McCarley, in Holy Matrimony." The vows and rings were exchanged, "You may kiss your bride," and then Joe and Sacora were pronounced husband and wife. The Foo Fighters' song "Walk" played, and joyfully Sacora and Joe walked a few steps from the ocean. Everyone gathered around Sacora and Joe for a happy dance. Pictures were taken behind a place in the sand that was engraved November 30, 2019. Each child posed for their picture with Sacora and Joe. All parent pictures were so happy poses. Joy showed so much happiness for Joe and in their pictures after the wedding with Sacora it showed in the poses and smiles on her face. Alisha hugged Sacora, and it made such a great picture. Sacora and Joe posed for their pictures alone after all the family ones were taken. Sacora was so happy with the wedding pictures. She could not wait to have the prints in an album. Sadie was standing too close to the water, and Sacora said, "Come here, my little darling, you are too close to the ocean." Aylassa went toward Sadie, and the waves knocked them down in the ocean. Both of them cried and, being wet, ran to Sacora and Joe. The photographer did capture it all in pictures.

Chapter One Hundred

Sacora and Joe enjoyed the moments with family on the beach until it was four o'clock. Samantha had taken Aylassa and Sadie to put dry clothes on, and then everyone left to go to Sacora, Joe, and Joy's new home. When arriving in the driveway, Sacora said, "What is this?" Aylassa said, "Party at Aylassa's house."

The church members had arranged a reception in the backyard while everyone was at the beach for a wedding. Tents were set up with food and drinks. Eeyore had flowers on her ears. The rabbits had on lace and flowers. Diesel and Clover were in the barn. No one knew about them. Sacora got out of the van with the children and went to the backyard. Joe and Joy came looking at the decorations and food. Sacora was so excited and grateful. A wedding cake and punch with brunch food and dinner food were waiting on them. Zac, Wendy, Samantha, and Corey were amazed. No one knew of the plan but the photographer. She had kept them on the beach making pictures until she was notified the reception was ready.

Again pictures were taken, cutting the cake, and the punch poses. The children standing around and the animal pictures were so affectionate. The church members were giggling as the surprise was so organized and actually a surprise.

Joe said, "This has been an awesome reception." Nine o'clock, Sacora went in to change after all the reception items had been removed and cleaned up. Alisha, Sadie, and Aylassa stayed with her while she was packing a bag for the night. Sacora was getting them ready to be with Samantha. Alisha was showing more being upset than Sadie and Aylassa. Sacora reassured them her plans were to be back tomorrow. Sacora had taken all their dress clothes to the laundry room when the children had changed.

Ready to leave, Sacora kissed the children. She hugged her mom and dad, thanking them for the day. Zac and Wendy reassured Sacora and Joe that the children would be fine with them after church tomorrow. Joy would be ready to be in her new home too.

Sacora and Joe, leaving in his red Charger, waving to their family standing on the front porch, decided it had been an awesome day. Joe and Sacora reached their room, honeymoon suite, which Joe had rented for the weekend. Joe had picked her up and carried her through the doorway. Sacora was pleased with all the romantic surroundings.

Samantha and Corey were ready for their first night of being grandparents. Sadie and Aylassa were clean and in pajamas. Alisha had asked Samantha if she knew "Grandma's Lullaby," and she answered with, "Yes, it is a lullaby I sang to Sacora." Alisha wanted to sing it with her, and Samantha and Alisha sang to the babies. Sadie and Aylassa sleeping in their cribs, Alisha went upstairs. Elijah, Jeremiah, and Corey had been to barn with Diesel and Clover. Eeyore had been fed and watered when the rabbits were and put in their kennel for the night. Samantha went to check on Alisha and tucked her in and gathered Elijah's and Jeremiah's dirty laundry. She carried it to the washing machine and started it. Samantha and Corey went to sleep on Sacora's bed, and everyone slept until the sun was shining. Samantha and Corey were up and looking around at the clean house, the entertained, very-much-loved children, and the well-taken-care of animals and wondered how Sacora had done it all for so many weeks alone.

Corey went to McDonald's for biscuits, and Samantha started getting ready for church. Elijah and Jeremiah ate breakfast and then got ready for church. Eeyore, Hugs, Kisses, Diesel, and Clover would be fine until tonight when Sacora and Joe were home. Samantha had all the children ready for church by ten fifteen, and Corey drove the van. At church, Joy, Zac, and Wendy sat on the same pew with Samantha and Corey, the children between them. Church members smiling about the surprise reception they had yesterday was the conversation and were sending best wishes to the newm blended family.

Chapter One Hundred One

Sacora and Joe enjoyed their morning with breakfast showing up at the door of their room. Sacora had been so overwhelmed how the wedding and the reception were so full of love. Her minutes with Julie and all the pictures of happiness had ended when Julie whispered in her ear, "I told you so. He is the love of your life. Joe is a genuine man with an eye for only you."

Sacora and Joe had planned on being home around six o'clock and had started packing up and headed that way. Corey and Samantha had carried the children to Zac and Wendy's after church in the van and then drove back to Sacora's for their car. Joe and Sacora went home for the van before going to Zac and Wendy's. Joe put his things in Sacora's room and looked in the bathroom. He laughed and said, "Joy has a level, a bathroom and bedroom to herself, and I share with four ladies. What a dream." He kissed Sacora and asked, "Are you ready for the family now?" The children were excited to see the van park in the driveway. Elijah and Jeremiah went to Joe and Alisha to Sacora. Sadie and Aylassa were with Wendy in the kitchen putting the last few bites of supper away.

Sacora and Joe had a conversation with Zac and Wendy, waiting on Joy to gather what she would be taking home. Alisha making every move with Joy, it was announced everyone was ready for home. Sadie and Aylassa went to Sacora and buckled up in the van. Alisha wanted to sit with Joy, and Elijah and Jeremiah sat together. The van that seated eight was now full. Sacora parked the van in the driveway, and Aylassa said, "Aylassa's house." Sacora turned off the alarm and unlocked the front door. Elijah and Jeremiah wanted to go to the barn, and Joe went with them. Sacora got Sadie and Aylassa ready for bed. Alisha was ready for bed too. When Elijah, Jeremiah, and Joe came from the barn, Sacora had the babies in their cribs and Alisha tucked in, and Elijah and Jeremiah went upstairs for showers. Joy had gone to her room and started getting ready for her week of school. Eeyore had been fed and watered, ready for her blanket. Sacora tucked in Elijah and Jeremiah, leaving the door open some for the hall light.

Sacora asked Joe, "When you were remodeling this house, did you ever think you would be residing here?"

Joe said, "No, I did not, but I am proud I did a good job."

Sacora took her hot bath and fell asleep tonight with Joe beside her. Awake at five o'clock, it was time to start Monday morning. Joe was moving his things in today and would be here for the Wi-Fi installation. The package that was ordered had a surveillance camera setup for outside around the house and would also be installed. Sacora opened the door for Eeyore, made the bed, and showered. Joe sat with Sacora on the front porch drinking coffee and watching the sunrise. Alisha came and sat with them for a few minutes and went to open the kennel for Hugs and Kisses. Sacora started breakfast, and Elijah and Jeremiah went to the barn with Joe. Diesel and Clover were growing and needed the wool cut from their eyes. After the Christmas holidays, it would be time for the veterinary checkup and immunizations. Elijah and Jeremiah went back to the house and got ready for school. Joe came in to eat breakfast with everyone. Sadie and Aylassa were up ready for day care. Sacora had kissed Joe goodbye and told Joy goodbye and to enjoy her day at school. Alisha told her goodbye when she understood that Joe would be taking her to school. Alisha, Elijah, and Jeremiah waved at Sacora going down the sidewalk at their school, and Sacora waving back at them was a good start of her day. Sadie and Aylassa kissed her goodbye. Sacora's first day at the office as Sacora McCarley, Mr. Hamilton handed her forms to sign and update with her married name. The day went by quick, and Sacora was anxious to have her little family together for the first supper tonight.

Chapter One Hundred Two

Sacora made it to the day care, and Sadie was so happy to see her. Aylassa was ready for Aylassa's house, and Alisha, Elijah, and Jeremiah had finished their homework for Sacora to check. Parking in the driveway, Sacora saw men still working on the surveillance system outside, and this made Aylassa upset. The men were doing something to Aylassa's house. Joy had made it home and was watching TV when Sacora and the children came in. Joe had started supper. The ground beef and noodles were cooking for spaghetti. Sacora settled the children and animals and started making the toss salad. Joe had walked Diesel and Clover earlier today and changed their water, food, and salt. Alisha, Elijah, and Jeremiah watched TV with Joy.

Supper was ready and on the table. Sadie and Aylassa wiped their hands and faces with antibacterial wipes, and the others washed their hands in the bathroom. The men had finished with the Wi-Fi and surveillance installation, and Joe sat down ready to eat with his family. Jeremiah was hanging on every word Joe said, but Elijah was the first to respond on the topic of Mr. Holden wanting to buy the sheep manure.

Elijah said, "That is awesome. We have a large pile already to be moved."

Jeremiah said, "And he is going to pay us for manure?"

Joe said, "Yes, for fertilizer."

Sacora looked at Joe smiling. Two young boys working for money was always a good start around Christmas holidays. Sadie asked about when Santa was coming, and Sacora said, "We will start counting the days. Today is December the second, so that is twenty-three more days. Ms. Koch has been talking to you about Santa coming too."

Joe and Joy would have their first Christmas here too. Joe asked, "When do you plan on decorating for Christmas?"

Sacora said, "What about Saturday? I have my decorations in the barn. I will put my Thanksgiving decorations in storage too."

Joe said, "Yes, I saw them. I will get them Saturday and put the Thanksgiving decorations back."

Aylassa said, "I am good. Santa Claus is watching me."

Joe asked Sacora, "Would you like to go Christmas shopping Friday night? My mom and dad would like to have the children over."

Sacora said, "That will be great. I have plans for what I would like to buy."

Alisha asked, "Will Joy be there?"

Joy answered, "Yes, ma'am, and we will do what you would like."

Aylassa answered, "I want to watch the pretty man."

Joy said, "Okay, we will play some Elvis Presley videos."

Supper was finished, and the table, kitchen, and dishes were cleaned. Alisha and Joy went to check on Hugs and Kisses with Eeyore. Sacora asked Elijah and Jeremiah about their homework to check. Sacora looked at it and signed the homework journal for Elijah and Jeremiah's paper. Sadie and Aylassa were ready for their baths and bedtime. Sacora gave them their bath and was singing "Grandma's Lullaby" when Joe stopped to listen at the door. Sacora had put the babies in their cribs and started out the door. Joe looked at her and said, "That is so amazing. Do you do that every night?"

Sacora said, "Yes, I do. The lullaby is a song my mom sang to me when I was growing up. Just so you know, I was standing right here in this spot when I knew I had fallen in love with you. Everything in this room that I see and touch is a thought of you."

Joe kissed Sacora and said, "I will always keep that in mind."

Joe went to shower, and Alisha asked to take a bath in Joy's bathroom. Alisha gathered her pajamas and went to Joy's bedroom and bathroom. Joy dried her hair. Elijah and Jeremiah showered, and then Sacora and Joe said good night to Joy in her bedroom, and then Alisha, Elijah, and Jeremiah were tucked in with an affectionate good night. Eeyore had been fed, watered, and was on her blanket when Sacora went for her long, hot bath. Sacora was thinking how everything had gone smooth tonight, and Elijah and Jeremiah were excited about the selling of the manure. Joy taking moments with Alisha had brought so much happiness that was showing in her sparkling eyes. The washing machine and dryer had been started, and Joe was sitting in the living room on his phone making arrangements for a repair job next week. Bedtime for Sacora and Joe with six sleeping children beside them and above them. Sacora's day of an impossible dream had come to an end.

Chapter One Hundred Three

S acora and Joe were awakened before the clock sounded the alarm.
Sacora made the bed and showered. Joe opened the door for
Eeyore, but Eeyore came back in suddenly to her blanket. Sacora
dressed and was on the front porch with Joe and watched the sunrise
holding his hand. Coffee was so good this morning. Alisha came to
the front porch and sat in Joe's lap. Her jacket was not enough to
knock off the chill. Joe wrapped her in his. Sacora went inside to
start breakfast, and Joe went with Alisha to the back porch to feed
and water Hugs and Kisses. Eeyore stayed out when the rabbits were
out of the kennel.

Sadie and Aylassa were up when Joe and Alisha had come in
for breakfast. Elijah and Jeremiah were downstairs dressed to go
visit Diesel and Clover. Joe went with them to the barn and put the
leashes on to walk the lambs for a while. Elijah and Jeremiah ran to
the house for it was time for school. Sacora had Sadie and Aylassa
ready for day care, their bags packed, and the backpacks of Alisha,
Elijah, and Jeremiah were ready too.

Joy was up and downstairs ready for school. Joe told all the
children goodbye. Joy said, "See you later, alligators," and Aylassa
said, "After a while, crocodile." Sacora and the children were buckled in the van and out the driveway. School traffic was smooth, and
Sacora had an opportunity to indulge in the goodbyes and waves of
the three smiling faces going down the sidewalk. At the day care, Ms.
Koch was ready for Sadie and Aylassa. Sacora told them goodbye, and
Sadie kissed Sacora's cheek and said, "My see you at Lassa's house."

Sacora said, "Yes, I will see you two at Aylassa's house." Aylassa
kissed Sacora's cheek and waved goodbye. When Sacora made it

to her desk, before she started on Mr. Hamilton's assignments, her phone showed an email from Wells Fargo Bank. Her money from Barton Haynes had been put in her account. Sacora immediately forwarded the email to Ms. Mays. This was the monetary security that would qualify her and Joe to adopt five children.

Sacora had finished the day taking a quick lunch. Mr. Hamilton approved Sacora to be finished Friday at lunch to start her weekend. Christmas shopping with Joe could be earlier to keep the children from being out so late. The day was over, and in the van Sacora was ready to go to the grocery store with a list from Joy and Joe of their favorites. Sacora put everything in the van and went to the day care. Alisha needed some help with putting her things back in her backpack. Elijah and Jeremiah had finished their homework. Sadie and Aylassa hugged Sacora ready to be home.

Sacora parked in the driveway, and Joe came to help Elijah and Jeremiah with the groceries. Joy, Alisha, Aylassa, and Sacora put them away. Hamburgers and hot dogs were the requested meal tonight, with Sadie's request of macaroni and cheese. At the dinner table, Joe noticed someone on the surveillance cameras. He got up to the back door noticing that the person was running toward the back porch. Joe left the lights off and grabbed the young man by his pants and belt.

Joe asked him, "What business do have snooping around the backyard?"

He said, "My name is Luke Goodman. I am the uncle of Sadie and Jeremiah Walters, and I had been notified of where they where. I wanted to make sure they were okay."

Joe said, "Come in. This way to the dining room."

Sadie was the one who ran to him and said, "Wuke, my wuv you."

Luke picked her up and said, "I love you, Sadie. Jeremiah, you look great. You have grown so much since I saw you last summer. Are you still liking school?"

Jeremiah said, "Yes, Uncle Luke, I love school this year. I have a friend, Asher, and I am making good grades."

Luke said, "That is great."

Sadie said, "Wuke, you want some of mine macaroni and cheese?"

Sacora got up to get him a plate and thought how this young man loved Sadie and Jeremiah and they loved him. Luke sat down to eat, and Joe and Sacora could tell he was hungry. Joe asked him how he got there when he noticed no automobile in the driveway. He replied with he had walked. Luke thanked Sacora and Joe for the meal and started out when Joe said, "I will take you home. Get in my Dodge Charger."

Luke said, "Thank you. It is getting cold."

Luke told and showed Joe the way to his sister's home, mother of Sadie and Jeremiah. Joe told Luke, "Goodbye, and you are welcomed anytime to visit."

Chapter One Hundred Four

Joy had been upstairs studying, using the Wi-Fi for homework assignments, and Alisha went to Joy's bathroom for her bath. Sacora had finished Sadie's and Aylassa's bath, singing "Grandma's Lullaby," and put them in their cribs. Alisha was ready for Sacora to dry her hair and be tucked in. Elijah and Jeremiah had showered and were ready for bed. Sacora had the baths, showers, and bedtime over when Joe came through the front door.

Joe went to shower, and Sacora asked Joe what he thought the visit from Luke Goodman was about. Joe said he was not sure. He asked to be carried to his sister's home, the parents of Sadie and Jeremiah. Sadie and Jeremiah knew he loved them and was interested about their well-being. Sacora went to her long, hot bath, and Eeyore went with her, lying on the floor. Eeyore could tell Sacora was upset.

Joe and Sacora fell asleep with questions. The next morning was the same routine, Joe helping Alisha, Elijah, and Jeremiah with the animals and taking Joy to school and moving in. Sadie and Aylassa were ready for day care, and Ms. Koch had something new every day about Santa Claus. Sacora and Joe had made it through another day. Friday morning had arrived, and Sacora would be working until lunchtime. Mr. Holden will be coming to collect the manure and leave Joe the money. Sacora told the children she would be picking them up early at school and day care. One o'clock, and Sacora went to check out Alisha, Elijah, and Jeremiah. The day care took a little longer because of the Christmas activities. One forty-five, Sacora was headed to Zac and Wendy's in the van. Joe met her in the truck at Zac and Wendy's for their night of Christmas shopping. Joe's parents had offered a bedroom for Santa's gifts, and

Joe would take care of that situation when Sacora drove the children home in the van.

Joe handed Elijah and Jeremiah their money from Mr. Holden. Joe said he would take them to spend it on Christmas gifts or what they wanted. Sacora and Joe told the children and Joe's parents goodbye. They went to eat at Longhorn Steak House and discussed what they would be buying. Sadie and Aylassa would be easy, but the games on PlayStation would take some time. Alisha wanted a certain kind of doll and clothes. She did not have a doll at all right now. Elijah and Jeremiah had not asked for anything in particular. So the guessing game has begun.

First Toys R Us and then Walmart. Sacora had a blast shopping for the children. Sadie's and Aylassa's gifts and surprises were purchased at Toys R Us. Alisha's doll and clothes were found at Walmart. Jeremiah's games were on sale at Walmart for the PlayStation, and Elijah wanted a Nintendo and games. Joy wanted jewelry and the newest, latest released Apple iPhone. Sacora thought the first Christmas shopping for five children and a teenager went well. Joe was watching Sacora glow and smile with every item she put in the cart. It was time to go, and Sacora and Joe thought they would go again next Friday night. Samantha and Corey wanted the children to be with them at their home.

Sacora and Joe made it to Zac and Wendy's after the sun had gone down. Joe parked his truck in the back so the children would not see their gifts. When Sacora and Joe walked in, Joy had Elvis Presley's video playing of the "Impossible Dream." Joe took Sacora's hand and slow danced with her. Sadie and Aylassa wanted to dance, and Joe picked the girls up, one in each arm. Alisha put her arms around Joe and Sacora while they all danced. Joy was filming the dance, and then she started dancing with Elijah and Jeremiah. Yes, tonight and every night since Joe McCarley had been an impossible dream.

Joe told the children it was time to go home. Each one hugged Zac and Wendy and went to the van and buckled up. Joe told Sacora he would be a little while at his parents and Sacora would take the time to handle the visits to Diesel and Clover, Hugs, and Kisses. Everyone waved goodbye to Joe and Joy. Joy decided to stay and help Joe put away the gifts without seeing hers.

Chapter One Hundred Five

Sacora stopped at the barn, and the children went in to pet and feed Diesel and Clover. Sacora filled the container with fresh water, feed, and salt. Jeremiah was tall enough now to reach the leashes and put Clover's on and then Diesel's. Alisha walked Diesel, and Aylassa walked Clover, while Elijah and Jeremiah shoveled out the feces. They had now been excited on the money from Mr. Holden.

After the lambs had been put in the barn for the night, shovels and leashes hanging on the nails, Sacora drove to the house and parked in the driveway, Aylassa's house. Sacora turned off the alarm, unlocked the door, and told the children to visit Hugs and Kisses. Eeyore was ready to be fed and watered too.

Sacora started baths with Sadie and Aylassa. Elijah and Jeremiah had found a jar with a lid to put their manure money in until time to spend it. Alisha wanted to go to Joy's bathroom, and Sacora asked her not to until Joy came home. Alisha took her bath in Sacora's bathroom tonight. Sadie and Aylassa in their cribs asleep, Sacora dried Alisha's hair and tucked her in. Alisha said, "Good night, Sacora. You told me nothing would change when Joe moved in, and I am so happy that it has not. Do you know when I can stay forever?"

Sacora said, "No, sweet baby, I do not, but I hope it is soon."

Elijah's and Jeremiah's showers were finished, and Sacora tucked them in. Elijah had the container of money with him. Jeremiah's idea was to keep it together and spend it together with Joe. Joe and Joy had come home. Joy went to shower and finish some assignments before going to bed. Joe went to shower, and then Sacora had her long, hot bath. Eeyore laying on the floor, Sacora thought about the Christmas decorations in the barn they would be getting out tomorrow.

The sun was shining on Saturday morning and a little warmer, perfect for decorating for Christmas. Joe and Sacora drinking coffee on the front porch was joined by Alisha all excited about her first Christmas with the McCarleys. Sadie and Aylassa awakened ready for breakfast. Sacora cooked a large breakfast, and Elijah and Jeremiah were ready to eat. After the breakfast dishes were in the dishwasher and the washing machine started, Sacora changed sheets on all beds. Joy wanted to change her sheets and clean her room. She vacuumed and dusted after she cleaned her bathroom. Sacora was so impressed with the maturity of Joy and the gratefulness she showed on the peace and privacy she was given.

Alisha left Hugs and Kisses out of their kennel today because the weather was so nice. Eeyore ran and played with them until Joe, Elijah, and Jeremiah went to the barn to walk Diesel and Clover. Joe tied the lambs in the front yard while the Christmas decorations were being moved to the house. This Saturday morning was so awesome. Joe drove his truck to the barn and turned on Foo Fighters music loud. "The Sky Is a Neighborhood" was playing, and all the children danced around in the barn with Joe while Sacora set the decorations out for Joe to put in his truck.

No one noticed Ms. Mays standing in the doorway of the barn. She was so touched to see this picture of happiness, she took out her phone and recorded the family dancing. It was Sacora who saw her first.

Sacora said, "What brings you here? Do you have some good news for us?"

Ms. Mays said, "No, Sacora. Ms. Hines called you at the office yesterday, and Mr. Hamilton informed her you had taken the afternoon off. I came instead. I'm here with bad news. The Alabama Court System has approved the request of Sarah and Joshua Walters to have Sadie and Jeremiah returned to them on Monday, December 9, 2019. The finding on the court's investigation that they have concluded all requirements for the children to be returned in their custody. Their parents will be at human resources, your office, to take them home. I am so sorry."

Chapter One Hundred Six

Sacora stopped what she was doing dead in her tracks looking at Ms. Mays. Jeremiah was the first to speak.

Jeremiah said, "Sacora, tell the pretty lady that we want to stay here forever. Sadie is happy and safe here. I am too."

Sadie took Joe's hand and said, "My don't wanna weave Doe. My wanna be at Lassa's house with Zora."

Ms. Mays said, "I am sorry, and I am still working on the adoption of Aylassa, Alisha, and Elijah. It is going well. Sacora, Joe, I have done all that can be done to keep Sadie and Jeremiah here with you. I will go and I will keep trying to secure the Malone children in your custody."

Joe and Sacora told Ms. Mays thank you and goodbye. Joe went to Sacora and held her while she cried. The children gathered around Joe and Sacora in one big family hug. Joy was standing in the barn's doorway hearing Ms. Mays's conversation and looked at Joe and Sacora and asked how the courts could give them back to their parents. When Sacora pulled herself together, she instructed Joe what to put in his truck of the Christmas decorations today. The artificial tree she had was too tall for the living room, and she suggested to put it in the hall upstairs.

They decided they would keep their last moments with Sadie and Jeremiah happy decorating for Christmas. Lunchtime, everyone decided on Subway, and Joe and Joy went to get the order. Joy cried in the Dodge car with her dad of how it was just not right to take Sadie and Jeremiah back to an unsafe home. Joy had become so attached to them. She could not imagine what Sacora was feeling.

Back with lunch, everyone sat in their places at the table. Hands washed, blessings said, and then Jeremiah's words in prayer just crushed Joe's and Sacora's hearts. He prayed that he and Sadie could stay with Joe and Sacora forever. After lunch, the tree was put upstairs, and Joy, Sacora, Alisha, and Aylassa started decorating it. Sadie was handing ornaments to Sacora. Every ornament she said, "My wike thisn."

The tree was finished, and Sacora went to the washing machine, changing out laundry. The other decorations were started on the rails of the stairs. Joy came to help. Joe started toward the barn with Diesel, Clover, Elijah, and Jeremiah to finish the care of the lambs. Jeremiah's words to Joe were, "Can you not do something, Joe? Can you not change us going home on Monday?"

Joe said, "If I could, Jeremiah, I would. Sacora and me, Elijah, Alisha, and Aylassa, us, we don't want you to go home ever."

Jeremiah said, "We will keep trying Joe, right? I am not wanting to go back to my parents."

Joe just nodded and finished putting the lambs in the barn for the night. Hugs, Kisses, and Eeyore were fed, watered, and settled in for the night. Sacora had found a stopping place on the decorations and started with supper and then baths. In the rocking chair singing "Grandma's Lullaby," the tears from Sacora's eyes fell. She put Aylassa in her crib and then Sadie. She kissed Sadie's little cheek and said, "My little darling, I will love you forever. I will think about you always."

Alisha took her bath upstairs in Joy's bathroom, and Sacora dried her hair. She tucked her in, and Alisha said, mimicking Sadie, "My wuv you, Zora. My don't eber wanna weave you."

Sacora kissed Alisha and said, "My sweet baby, I am doing my best to have you with me forever."

Joe went to shower. Sacora took her long, hot bath and was not surprised when Eeyore made a place to lay on the floor. Sacora was more than upset.

Chapter One Hundred Seven

Joe and Sacora slept restless with saying goodbye to Sadie and Jeremiah tomorrow on their minds. The sun shining, a start of a beautiful, gorgeous Sunday morning. Joe had told his parents last night of Sadie and Jeremiah going home. Sacora in her routine before church texted her mom to give them the bad news of Sadie's and Jeremiah's return to their parents. Sacora did not want her mom to be troubled all night. Everyone went to church this morning with a different emotion—sadness to be saying goodbye tomorrow.

At church, members were so supportive and had a special prayer for Sadie's and Jeremiah's future days of being returned to their parents. Wendy and Zac wanted to have a lunch at their home with everyone after church. Sacora and Joe held their composure and emotions, and tears would have to wait. The goodbyes after lunch were so affectionate and genuine. Samantha, Corey, Zac, and Wendy were so disappointed of the situation too.

At home, the minutes in the barn with Diesel and Clover were videoed. Sacora took pictures on her phone and camera. Joy made pictures of Sacora and Joe with Sadie, Aylassa, Alisha, Elijah, and Jeremiah. Supper was quiet, the children not saying much of anything. Baths, showers, and bedtime were routine, but tears were falling saying good night to Sadie, her little darling. Jeremiah's good night was so heartbreaking. Sacora fell apart when she said, "Good night, my sweetheart." In Joe's arms she cried and all through her long, hot bath. Eeyore was on the floor in the bathroom and moved her blanket to Sacora and Joe's bedroom for the night. After a restless night, the morning had come with another day of beautiful weather. Joe holding Sacora's hand, sitting on the front porch with coffee was comforting. The children were up and getting ready for school. After breakfast, taking care of Eeyore, Hugs, and Kisses were tended to for the day. Jeremiah wanted Joe to go with him and Elijah to the barn for him to say goodbye to Diesel and Clover. Sacora had showered and dressed for work, and Aylassa, Alisha, and Elijah were ready for their day at school and day care. Joy was ready for school, and Joe would meet Sacora at her office after taking Joy to school. Alisha hugged Sadie and Jeremiah goodbye with tears falling before she left the van. Elijah held Jeremiah so tight in a hug telling him goodbye.

Elijah said, "You will always be my best friend."

Jeremiah said, "You will always be mine, and I will see you at school. We have one more week of school before Christmas holidays."

Sacora watched Alisha and Elijah walk down the sidewalk waving at her. Such emotion she was having to hold back. Keeping her composure was getting harder. At the day care, Ms. Koch had been notified on Friday by Ms. Hines of Sadie's and Jeremiah's elimination or termination from her day care. Ms. Koch hugged Sadie and Jeremiah and told them bye. Aylassa, not understanding, told Sadie and Jeremiah, "I will see you at Aylassa's house."

Sacora met Joe at her office and opened the door and walked in, Joe holding Sadie and Sacora holding Jeremiah's hand. He handed Sadie over to Sacora for one last kiss and hug goodbye. Sacora handed Sadie to Sarah Walters and then reached down to Jeremiah. Jeremiah said, "I am going to be big and not cry. I love you, Sacora."

Jeremiah hugged Joe and said goodbye. Sadie had went to Joshua Walters and turned around when they walked away and screamed, "My wuv you, Doe! My wuv you, Zora!"

Jeremiah's hand was turned loose from his mother's, and he ran back to Sacora and Joe. He hugged them both and said, "When I get big, I am going to be just like you, Joe. I am going to be a great man, an awesome football player, and fix things. I love you, Sacora. Take care of Diesel, Clover, Hugs, Kisses, and Eeyore."

Jeremiah's words cut Joe and Sacora into an emotional whirlwind. They watched Sadie and Jeremiah Walters leave with Sarah and Joshua Walters. Joe held Sacora while she cried. Ms. Hines, Mr.

Hamilton, and Sacora's coworkers had witnessed such an emotional goodbye. Ms. Hines informed Sacora and Joe that she had done all she could do. It was not in Sadie's and Jeremiah's best interest to be returned to their parents.

Chapter One Hundred Eight

Mr. Hamilton gave Sacora the rest of the day off. Joe and Sacora went home. One of the first days that Sacora had been home without the children. Joe had postponed his repair job until Wednesday when all the parts arrive at Tyler's Hardware Store. He had planned on being with Sacora the rest of the day. Joy would be with Wendy tonight after school. Joe had been so understanding with Sacora crying and asked her to eat some lunch.

Sacora did eat a sandwich and started to look for ideas to cook supper. Joe asked if she would like to have Kentucky Fried Chicken for supper and get it on the way to the day care. Sacora agreed and went to Jeremiah's room. She vacuumed and dusted after she changed the sheets on the bed. She looked at the clothes she had bought him and wondered what he would do for clothes, as he had grown so much taller. When she carried the sheets to the hall, she turned around and looked again and closed the door.

Four o'clock, Sacora and Joe went to Kentucky Fried Chicken and then the day care. Aylassa ran to Joe and asked if Sadie was at Aylassa's house. Joe said, "No, sweetie, Sadie went to her mom's house with Jeremiah."

Aylassa said, "Can I go? I want to play with Sadie."

Joe said, "No, sweetie, not today."

Alisha and Elijah were ready to go. Sacora told Ms. Koch thank you and good night. Aylassa saw Sadie's car seat. She asked again about Sadie. Sacora and Joe changed the subject with, "We have Kentucky Fried Chicken for supper." The van parked in the drive-way, and Aylassa said, "Aylassa's house. Where is Sadie?"

Sacora said, "Wweetie, she has gone to her mom's with Jeremiah."

The table felt empty without Joy's, Sadie's, and Jeremiah's faces. Sacora cleaned the table and dishes and started the washing machine, folding the clothes from the dryer. Joe went with Elijah to visit Diesel and Clover. Alisha went to the backyard to feed, water, and put Hugs and Kisses up for the night. Eeyore ate Pedigree and stayed close to Sacora all night. Bath time, Aylassa cried for Sadie. Sacora cried too. She put Aylassa's pajamas on her and sang some in the rocking chair. "Grandma's Lullaby" was just not the same. Aylassa still had tears in her eyes when she fell asleep.

Alisha was ready for Sacora to dry her hair when Aylassa was in her crib. Sacora tucked her in, and Alisha was so sweet. She said, "I can only think of how your heart is breaking without Sadie and Jeremiah. Do you think my momma has a breaking heart in heaven without me?"

Sacora said, "I know my heart would be breaking without you, my sweet baby." Sacora kissed her cheek and said good night.

Joe had went to the shower, and Elijah had finished, ready to be tucked in. Elijah reached under his pillow and gave the jar with the money to Sacora. He said, "This is the money from the manure and what I saved of spending money. Joe said we could buy what we wanted or Christmas gifts. Will you please take this to Ms. Mays and buy Jeremiah's and Sadie's way back home for Christmas?"

Sacora took the jar and said, "Yes, baby, I will do what I can. I love you, Elijah."

Eeyore, knowing the sadness in Sacora, found a place on the bathroom floor, waited until she went to the bedroom with Joe, and followed her. Sacora plugged her phone in the charger when it sounded of an email. She checked the email, and it was from Ms. Mays.

After the heartbreaking day you and Joe have had, I did not want to wait until tomorrow's office hours to forward this email to you. It is the order from the judge awarding you and Joe the privilege of adopting the Malone children. Congratulations. Please call the office tomorrow to schedule the sign-

ing of documents for the completion of the adoption and the birth certificates.

Ms. Mays

Sacora was crying hard with joy. Joe took the phone and held her while she cried. He read it and was joyful too. Sacora said, "We will tell Alisha in the morning when she joins us for coffee on the front porch. Is that all right with you?"

Joe said, "That is perfect. And we will tell Elijah before we go to the barn, and Aylassa's house is Aylassa's house forever."

Chapter One Hundred Nine

S acora and Joe slept with mixed emotions. The chance of losing Aylassa, Alisha, and Elijah had been made slim, and now none after the documents were signed. December 10 and Christmas coming had some hope of happiness. Sacora and Joe were up before the clock alarm sounded. Sacora made the bed, and Joe opened the door for Eeyore. Sacora showered and dressed for work. Joe held Sacora's hand watching the sunrise, drinking coffee. Alisha came to front porch, and Sacora put her in her lap.

Sacora said, "My sweet baby, you can be with us forever. Would you like to have your name to be Alisha Beth McCarley?"

Alisha said, "I won't have to ever leave like Sadie and Jeremiah? Yes, I would like to have my name McCarley like yours, Sacora."

Joe said, "That it is. Alisha Beth McCarley, welcome to your home."

It was time for breakfast, and Alisha went to the rabbits to open the kennel. Eeyore was ready to play. It was warmer again this morning, and the rabbits could stay out all day. Elijah was ready to go to the barn. Sacora and Joe told him that he would be with them forever through adoption. Joe asked him if he would like his name to be Elijah Chance McCarley. Elijah said, "Yes, that is awesome. I won't ever leave?"

Sacora said, "No, buddy, you are here with us forever."

Elijah ran to the barn, not waiting on Joe to catch up. Elijah talking to Diesel and Clover excited that he would not be leaving the lambs. He was now a McCarley like Joe and Sacora. Aylassa awakened, and Sacora kissed her and told her, "You are now Aylassa Blaine McCarley." Everyone ready for the day, buckled in the van, school traffic was smooth. Sacora waved at Alisha and Elijah, and Alisha blew her kisses. Sacora's day went by quick, and she met Joe at Ms. Mays's office at five o'clock to sign documents and request the names on the birth certificates. They were Aylassa Blaine McCarley, Alisha Beth McCarley, and Elijah Chance McCarley. Ms. Mays addressed the issue of Sadie and Jeremiah Walters with sympathy. After all paperwork had been done, Sacora and Joe called their parents with the news of the three McCarleys. Joy was so enthused that she had two sisters and a brother.

Jeremiah looked around the house for his mother and found her on the couch passed out. He knew his dad had gone to work and he could not figure out why he was not taken to school and Sadie to day care. Sadie woke up, and Jeremiah fixed her a bowl of cereal. He helped her go to the potty and get dressed. Sarah Walters still passed out on the couch at lunchtime, Jeremiah made them a sandwich and some milk. For supper, Jeremiah made Sadie another bowl of cereal. Jeremiah's questions of why they did not go to school or day care was answered by his mom that school was out for Christmas holidays. Jeremiah's information was it was one more week. Sarah Walters passed out on the couch again after drinking something in a glass, and Jeremiah told Sadie that he would give her a bath and get her ready for bed.

Jeremiah's attention to what Sacora had done every night was what he mimicked. Sadie wanted "Grandma's Lullaby" and to be rocked. Jeremiah sang what he knew, and Sadie fell asleep, Jeremiah putting her to bed. Jeremiah's shower and bedtime, he handled himself. Sadie and Jeremiah were sleeping when Joshua Walters came home from work.

Chapter One Hundred Ten

Sacora and Joe decided to celebrate at Golden Corral. Sacora picked up the children at day care, and Joe brought Joy from Wendy's. The meal was a choice for everyone's favorites. The conversation at the table was Elijah had been doing great in his advance classes, and all his homework had been monitored on the homework journal. Alisha and Eemonie had a Christmas party planned at school on Friday, and Sacora would be taking her shopping. Joy wanted a few gifts for teachers, and as of right now her friends were still in Miami.

Joe was going to be later tomorrow night, working on the repairs getting parts from Tyler's Hardware Store in the morning. The decision to go shopping Saturday for a live Christmas tree to put in the living room made the children anxious for Christmas. Joy asked Joe, "Do you think I could leave for my mom's on Christmas Day? I would like to be with you and Sacora when Santa Claus comes for Aylassa, Alisha, and Elijah."

Joe said, "I will ask, but it is a court order you are to be with me on Christmas Eve and your mom on Christmas Day until December thirtieth."

Joy said, "Thanks, Dad, for asking. I do want to be here Christmas morning at least."

Everyone was buckled in the van, and Aylassa had finally stopped asking about Sadie. When they were home, Alisha fed, watered, and put the rabbits in the kennel for the night. Eeyore ate, and then baths, showers, and bedtime went on routine. Alisha went to Joy's bathroom for a bath, and Sacora dried her hair. Joe and Elijah visited Diesel and Clover, putting them up for the night. Joe went to shower and could hear Sacora singing "Grandma's Lullaby." Aylassa in her crib, Alisha was ready for Sacora to tuck her in.

Alisha asked Sacora, "When will my papers at school be changed to my new name? Will my teacher know my new name?"

Sacora said, "We will change everything after Christmas holidays. I will take care of it." Sacora kissed her cheek and said, "Good night, my sweet baby."

Elijah had finished in the bathroom and was ready for his bed. Elijah wanted to know if Sacora had given the money to whomever could bring Sadie and Jeremiah home. Sacora answered, "Joe and I have done what we could to get Sadie and Jeremiah with us forever, like you. Good night, buddy."

Elijah said good night, and Sacora left his door open some. Elijah could hear Sacora going to Jeremiah's room and closing the door completely. He could tell she was so sad without Jeremiah and Sadie.

Sacora took her long, hot bath with Eeyore on the bathroom floor. Eeyore followed her to the bedroom and slept on the floor. Joe was so much comfort, and Sacora was comforting to Joe. Eeyore knew they were both upset and stayed close to them.

The week went on, and then Friday morning came with Christmas parties at school. Alisha and Elijah had their gifts from the shopping trip with Sacora. Walking down the sidewalk, Alisha and Elijah waved at Sacora. Aylassa's party with Ms. Koch was also today. Five o'clock came slow with so many assignments from Mr. Hamilton. Sacora and Joe carried Aylassa, Alisha, and Elijah to Samantha and Corey's. Joy wanted to go to Wendy's. Christmas shopping tonight was different from last Friday night. Sacora and Joe finished buying for Aylassa, Alisha, and Elijah but still had some things to buy for Joy.

Christmas tree shopping tomorrow afternoon would be fun. Even Joy was going. Joe had taken care of the animals before the Christmas shopping tonight so the children had bath time, showers, and bedtime.

Chapter One Hundred Eleven

Sacora and Joe were up later today. Sacora made the bed, showered, and dressed for the shopping of a live Christmas tree. Joe had went outside with Eeyore to open the kennel for Hugs and Kisses. Alisha had slept in too and sat in Sacora's lap on the front porch while she drank coffee with Joe. Christmas was in the air. December 14 and the tree for the living room is the last decoration on the list.

Joe went to McDonald's for biscuits, and Elijah and Aylassa were up when he came back. Wendy was bringing Joy home after lunch, and she was missed at the breakfast table. Aylassa was asking Elijah to go to the barn when he visited Diesel and Clover. Sacora decided to go with them also. Alisha fed Diesel and Aylassa fed Clover. Elijah put leashes on the lambs and the girls walked them while Elijah shoveled the manure for Mr. Holden.

So much giggling and laughing around the lambs, Eeyore came to check on the situation. Aylassa petted Eeyore, and Elijah took the leashes and walked both lambs when he finished with the shovel. Another sunny day with cool temperatures made a perfect day for out of school. School was out for the holidays, and Sacora would return to work on January 2, 2020. Sacora was the last on seniority list and was scheduled off so her coworkers would be working as they requested. Joe would be on call for repairs but mostly with the family. Joy was out of school and was going to Miami with her mom on Tuesday.

Lunchtime and everyone's appetite was showing. Sandwiches, chips, soup, and chocolate milk were gone quickly. Wendy had brought Joy home and visited with Joe and Sacora for a minute. Aylassa took her nap, and Joy and Alisha were getting ready for the first live Christmas tree shopping. Sacora and Joe were ready. Joe would drive the truck for the tree, and Sacora would drive the van with the children.

The fourth lot of trees they shopped, Sacora saw it. The most beautiful fir tree ever. She showed it to Joe, and he said, "Looks perfect. It is beginning to be dark, and I think perfect timing also. It looks like rain is coming and maybe storming."

Joe motioned for the clerk to remove the tree and put it in the truck. The clerk had two boards, two-by-six, to hold the tree in place in the back of Joe's truck. Joe and Sacora went to Burger King to eat supper, and Aylassa ate the most she had ever of chicken nuggets. The conversation was again with everyone's plans for the days ahead. Sacora and Joe started home with the live Christmas tree and the children.

Saturday morning at Jeremiah and Sadie's was different from Sacora's house. Jeremiah had missed school all week, and Sadie missed day care. Jeremiah was missing Asher and his other classmates. He did not have an opportunity to tell them "Merry Christmas." Sadie was talking about Santa Claus and Jeremiah's fear that Santa Claus could not find them at their home. Sarah Walters had been drinking heavily and passed out on the couch again. Joshua did not work today and indulged in his high from pills.

Jeremiah took care of Sadie, mimicking and imitating what Sacora had done.

Joshua Walters came in the house when Jeremiah was singing "Grandma's Lullaby" after Jeremiah gave her a bath. He said, "What stupid song are you trying to sing, boy?"

Jeremiah's answer was, "It's not stupid. It is Sadie's favorite lullaby that Sacora sang to her."

Joshua said, "It is stupid, and I said so. You can stop singing it now."

Jeremiah's answer was, "I will when she goes to sleep."

Joshua Walters grabbed Sadie hard from Jeremiah's arms and threw on the bed and said, "Go to sleep."

Sadie cried because of her arm, and Jeremiah's reaction was to start hitting on Joshua. Joshua took off his belt and swung it around

Jeremiah's ribs repeatedly. Jeremiah's voice screamed loud for his mom, and she did not come. Jeremiah was lying on the floor covering his face to avoid the strikes and screamed at Joshua Walters, "When Joe McCarley finds you, he will tear you apart."

Joshua answered, "Boy, your Joe McCarley is a crippled, washed-up football player. He can't even walk. How do you think he is going to tear me apart, boy?"

Joshua swung the belt one more time and threw it down and went to the garage to finish his woodworking project. When Jeremiah heard the table wood saw start, he grabbed Sadie's jacket and his jacket. He opened the bedroom window and said, "Sadie, stop crying and be quiet. We are going to Joe and Sacora's. Come on, I will help you out the window."

Chapter One Hundred Twelve

Sadie stopped crying and followed Jeremiah's instructions out the window. They were down the street in safety when Jeremiah stopped and put their jackets on. Sadie was walking fast as she could holding her injured arm. Jeremiah's hand was holding on to her the best he could. They walked for hours. Jeremiah was noticing the darkness coming and maybe rain. He enticed Sadie to walk a little faster.

Sadie said, "My tard butter and mine arm hurts."

Jeremiah put his arms around her and said, "There is the barn, Sadie. I will carry you to the porch, and Sacora and Joe will take care of your arm."

Just as Sadie climbed on Jeremiah's back, the rain poured, the thunder sounded, and lightning flashed. They finally made it to the front porch. Jeremiah's tears fell when no one answered the door. Sadie and Jeremiah sat on the front porch, wet, hurt, and scared from the storming.

Joe had stopped for gas, and Sacora was the first parking in the driveway. At first she was startled to see bodies on the front porch. Joy said, "Is that Sadie and Jeremiah?"

Sacora said, "Yes, it is. Joy will you see to Aylassa?"

Sacora ran to the children and could see Sadie holding her arm. Jeremiah's tears stopped, and he hugged Sacora so tight. Sacora turned off the alarm and opened the door. It seemed like it took forever. Joe parked in the driveway and could see Sacora with Sadie and Jeremiah going through the door. Joy carried Aylassa, Alisha, and Elijah in and stepped aside while Sacora and Joe looked at Sadie's and Jeremiah's wet clothes, removing them for a hot bath and shower. Sadie screamed with her arm when Sacora removed her clothes. Jeremiah's blue wounds were vivid from the belt when Sacora removed his shirt. Joe, seeing the results of Joshua Walters, held back emotion and said to Sacora, "Can you take care of their hot baths and showers and take them to the emergency room? Joy, can you be here with Aylassa, Alisha, and Elijah? I have somewhere I need to be!"

Sacora was puzzled but said yes, with Joy saying yes. Sacora finished Sadie's bath and Jeremiah's shower. Dressed, they went to the emergency room. Joy had called Samantha and Wendy on Sacora's phone before she left for the emergency room. Wendy and Zac came to be with Joy, Aylassa, Alisha, and Elijah. Samantha and Corey met Sacora had the emergency room.

Corey took Sadie in his arms, holding her to protect her injured arm. Sacora and Samantha followed with Jeremiah. Sacora registered the children and discovered their Medicaid insurance had been terminated with the returning to their parents. Sacora said, "I will take care of it. Give me the bill, and I will pay before we leave."

The local law enforcement had been called to investigate the attack and results of the children. After all reports had been completed, Corey asked Sacora, "Where is Joe?"

Sacora said, "He said he had somewhere he needed to be. Oh my, Dad, I know where he is."

Sacora told the officer the address Joe had given her earlier when he carried Luke Goodman home. When the children were examined by the attending physician, Dr. Kent Bridging, he asked Sacora if Sadie's arm had been broken before. This was showing on the X-ray as an old break being broke again today.

Sacora remembering Sadie's arm in a cast when she first saw her and answered, "Yes, in May of this year."

Dr. Bridging took a minute to speak Spanish to a patient leaving and then called for the RN to consult the orthopedic on call and the cast department to treat Sadie's arm. As for Jeremiah's bruises, he had two broken ribs on the left and one broken on the right. Contusions to all his ribs and would need to be still for two weeks, no running, no physical activities at all.

Sacora paid the bill, and Samantha and Corey were going home with Sacora.

Chapter One Hundred Thirteen

Joe had decided to drive the truck. It was still warm and full of gas. His adrenaline was flowing due to being angry. Joe unattached the two-by-sixes from the tree and tossed the tree out on the ground. He did not want to lose it driving fast. Joe remembered where he carried Luke home. He drove speeding to this address. Joe parked suddenly in the driveway. He went to the front door and could see Sarah Walters passed out on the couch. He knocked loud, but she never responded. Joshua Walters, hearing the loud knocks, came around from the garage. Joe had made it back to the truck when Joshua Walters came toward him with a two-by-four.

Joshua said, "Well, if ain't the famous, washed-up, crippled, done-with football player. What brings you here? You need me to teach you how to walk?"

Joe said, "I came for Sadie and Jeremiah."

Joshua said, "They're in the house asleep. And as far as I can remember, the courts said you could no longer see them."

Joe leaned up against the truck for balance and said, "You are wrong. I saw them tonight and the bruises you left on them. I came to tell you, you will never see them again. You will never touch them again. You will never cause harm to Sadie and Jeremiah again."

Joshua, holding a two-by-four, answered, "Says who?"

Joe, grabbing one of the two-by-sixes from the back of his truck, answered Joshua, "Says me." Joshua came toward Joe swinging the two-by-four, and Joe hit his hands. Joshua dropped the two-by-four, and Joe swung again, knocking the two-by-four out of the reach of Joshua.

Joe said, "This is for Sadie." Joe struck Joshua on his arm. Joe said, "And this is for Jeremiah." He struck Joshua in the stomach, hitting all ribs. Just as Joe had lifted the two-by-six to strike Joshua again, he said, "And this is for making my Sacora cry!"

Blue lights of two police cars stopped suddenly in the driveway, and an officer said, "Freeze! Joe McCarley, he is not worth it. We will take it from here."

The officer asked Joe, "Where is Sarah Walters?"

Joe answered, "She is passed out on the couch."

The officer took out his gun and unlocked the door with one shot. This aroused Sarah Walters but still intoxicated from her day of drinking was stumbling to the door. The officer repeated the rights for her, under arrest for endangering her children.

Joshua Walters still on his high and came toward the officer with aggression. The officer was having to draw his gun, and Joe said "That won't be necessary" and struck Joshua with his two-by-six. Joshua fell to the concrete. Joe, intervening with his two-by-six said, "You will stand trial for the bruises you left on Sadie and Jeremiah."

The officer touched Joe's two-by-six and said, "Joe McCarley, you have done enough. Get back in your truck, go home to your family, and this never happened. Understand me?"

Joe said, "Yes, sir. I want to know how you knew I was here?"

The officer replied, "At the hospital, your wife thought you might be." Looking at Joshua Walters and handcuffing him, the officer spoke of his rights and then said, "I am glad that I showed up when I did. Joe McCarley would have done more to you."

Joshua Walters spit toward Joe and said, "Joe McCarley, you ain't nothing, boy."

The officers put Sarah and Joshua Walters in their police cars, handcuffed, and with the blue lights still on. Joe did as advised by the officer. He drove home, and no report of the attack or incident on Joshua Walters was recorded.

Chapter One Hundred Fourteen

Joe had parked in the driveway and, seeing his parents' car there and the van still gone, asked his mom, "Have you heard anything?"

Wendy answered, "Not yet, and I am sure it will take a while."

Joy had Aylassa settled in her crib after she cried for a while for Sadie. Elijah was so worried about Jeremiah's bruises that Wendy had a difficult time convincing him everything would be all right. He had gone to his bed but was not sleeping. Joe went to his room to check on him, and Elijah said, "You told me and Jeremiah that the money from Mr. Holden, we could spend on what we wanted or for Christmas gifts. I gave it to Sacora to bring Sadie and Jeremiah home. I will give Sacora the rest to keep them here."

Joe's smile gave Elijah comfort, and he said, "Thank you, buddy. I don't think they will be leaving us anymore. You need to get some sleep so you won't be tired tomorrow and can play with Jeremiah. He will be ready to be with his friends."

Alisha was still awake, and she asked Joe, "Will Sadie and Jeremiah's home be with us forever like me? Will we ever have to tell them goodbye again?"

Joe came to her room and said, "I don't think so, sweet baby. Sacora and I have tried to keep them here forever just like you. Good night and sleep so you can play tomorrow."

Joe walked down the stairs and saw headlights from the van and Corey and Samantha's car. Corey went with sleeping Sadie and carried her to the door. Jeremiah's arms were wrapped around Joe, hurting from his broken ribs. Joe said, "You are Sacora's sweetheart, and you will never go back, do you hear me? You will never go back."

Jeremiah's tears were dropping so heavy, and he managed to say, "Yes, I do. Thank you, Joe."

Sadie had been given pain medicine for her broken arm, and Corey had placed her in her crib. Sacora standing over her whispered, "My little darling, you are safe now and you are home."

Jeremiah's attention was on Sadie and asked Sacora, "Did Sadie take her medicine? The last time her arm was broke, my mom took her medicine until Uncle Luke took it from her."

Sacora, Joe, Samantha, Corey, Zac, and Wendy had such terrible looks on their faces. How could a mother consume pain medicine and leave their infant in pain? Jeremiah decided he would go to bed after seeing Sadie was in her crib. Sacora and Joe helped him up the stairs. His pain medicine was giving him some relief. Sacora and Joe helped him into his bed, and Jeremiah's words broke their hearts.

Jeremiah said, "I took care of Sadie just like you, Sacora. I made her food, gave her a bath, and sang 'Grandma's Lullaby.' I fought my dad just like you, Joe. I am so glad I am here, home now, and I don't want to ever go back."

Joe said, "We want you here forever too. Get some sleep and let us know if you need us. Good night, and be ready for your day with Alisha and Elijah tomorrow. They sure have missed you like us."

Sacora fell apart in Joe's arms in the hall by the Christmas tree. She pulled herself together and went downstairs to their parents. It being so quiet in the house. Their parents heard Jeremiah's words. Zac and Corey were looking at Joe and could tell he was still angry.

Joe said, "We won't be at church tomorrow. We will be here all day."

Wendy kissed her son and said, "We are a phone call away. Joy, you have been a great little momma tonight. I will see you soon."

Zac hugged his son and said, "Joe, I can only imagine what you and Sacora are feeling. We will be by tomorrow with some surprises and food. Sacora, take care of the children, and we will take over tomorrow so you can rest."

Samantha and Corey stayed awhile longer with Sacora. Three o'clock in the morning, they left with intentions of being back. Samantha's school had been closed for Christmas holidays, and she planned on being with Sacora every day.

Chapter One Hundred Fifteen

J oe and Sacora went to sleep for a couple of hours and awakened Sadie for her pain medication and inflammation medication that was given to Sacora at the emergency room. Joe had taken the prescriptions from Sacora to fill at Walmart. Sadie and Jeremiah would be needing it for a few days. Joe had googled the hours for the pharmacy and planned on getting breakfast while waiting on the prescriptions to be filled.

Joe had left when Jeremiah's voice asked for Sacora. Sacora went to him with water and his medication. Before Jeremiah went back to sleep, he asked about Sadie. Sacora reassured him everything was fine and to sleep. Sacora closed the door slightly, leaving the light shining through. Alisha heard her and got dressed. She went to the kitchen and made Sacora's coffee. Sacora's eyes had been full of tears when she said thank you. Sacora said, "You know, sweet baby, what I need is to sit with you on the front porch. Let's open the door for Eeyore first and the rabbits' kennel."

Alisha went upstairs for her jacket and went to the front porch with Sacora after opening the kennel for Hugs and Kisses. Elijah had decided to go to the front porch too and grabbed his jacket. Joe came back with biscuits from Jack's and the pharmacy bag. He opened the door for them to go inside. Joe texted Joy to tell her he had biscuits but to sleep as long as she needed to.

December 15, ten days until Christmas, the live tree had not been thought of.

After eating, Elijah mentioned it to Joe about the tree. Sacora thought it would take their minds to a better place of happiness to bring it in and decorate it. Joe had tossed it a good ways from the truck, and Elijah said he would help him bring it in.

Sadie had awakened when Aylassa did. It was such a joyful reunion of the two small girls. Aylassa ate her biscuit and drank orange juice, and Sadie ate hers. After a few hours, it was time for medication again. Jeremiah's medication was carried upstairs with his biscuit and juice. He said, "I will be downstairs when you decorate the tree. Will you please wake me up?" Sacora said she would.

Samantha and Corey came with lunch. Wendy and Zac came with pizza they could have for supper. The surprises were nail polish for the girls, and the boys had a Nerf football that would not hurt Jeremiah's ribs when he caught it.

Elijah and Joe went to the barn, and Corey and Zac followed them. When Elijah was out of hearing distance, shoveling the manure for Mr. Holden, Joe told the story of his visit with Joshua Walters. Zac said, "Maybe this time will be the last time. I could not understand how the courts would put them back in that situation again."

Corey said, "We need them here for sure. Did anyone tell you when it goes before the court?"

Joe said, "We have not heard anything today. I think the arresting officers will have a nice little chat with the judge."

Corey and Zac saw Elijah coming and changed the subject. They decided to find the tossed live tree and bring it in. Elijah helping with the tree, he stopped to open the door and screamed, "Merry Christmas to us McCarleys!"

Joy had awakened and came downstairs to eat and see everyone. Wendy and Samantha greeted her first and then Sacora. Joy asked about Sadie and Jeremiah and then ate some pizza.

Joe, Zac, and Corey set the tree up where Sacora wanted it. Joe went to get the decorations, and Jeremiah's eyes were wide with excitement. Joe dropped what he was doing and went to bring Jeremiah down the stairs. Alisha started singing "Oh Christmas Tree," and everyone's voices joined in. Aylassa did not leave Sadie's side all day, helping her with her broken arm.

After the pizza was finished, Corey and Samantha were leaving. Samantha's plans were to be back in the morning. Corey would be working. Zac and Wendy would visit Joy sometime tomorrow but would be available with a phone call if they were needed.

Chapter One Hundred Sixteen

Joe and Sacora, looking at the tree after their parents had left, decided to make pictures with all the children. All smiles were big with Sadie and Jeremiah being home. Joy wanted her picture taken with each child with the Christmas tree. Alisha wanted to sing another song before baths and showers. She suggested "Santa Claus Is Coming to Town." Sadie said, "My wike dat song."

The baths were started, and Joe went upstairs to help Jeremiah with his shower. Elijah gathered all the dirty laundry and gave it to Sacora before she rocked Sadie and Aylassa. Sadie with the broken arm, Sacora sat in the rocker for a while after "Grandma's Lullaby," and the girls were sleeping for Joe to help her put them in their cribs. Joe took Aylassa first and placed her tenderly in her crib, covering her with her favorite blanket. Joe took Sadie from Sacora, easily moving her arms, and placed her in her crib. Sacora covered her with her favorite blanket.

Sacora looked at Joe and said, "This is the place I was when I knew I loved you. I love you more and more every day, Joe."

Joe said, "I love you, Sacora. We have got to do what we have got to do to keep Sadie and Jeremiah here."

Sacora agreed, and Joe went to shower. Sacora opened the door for Eeyore, and she went out with Alisha to put Hugs and Kisses in their kennel for the night. Alisha went upstairs to Joy's bathroom and Sacora dried her hair and tucked her in. Alisha had concerns about Sadie and Jeremiah. Sacora attempted to reassure her, but Alisha still was not content with the reassuring. Elijah gathered Jeremiah's pajamas, and Joe helped him get dressed and to his bed. Sacora came to tell him good night and gave him his medication. Sacora was surprised when Jeremiah told her he had not been to school last week when she told him no school until after the holidays. Elijah was tucked in and voiced his happiness with Jeremiah being home.

Sacora went for her long, hot bath. Eeyore made a place on the floor, resting from her long day. After her bath, Sacora heard her phone with an email, and reading it, she ran to Joe. It was from Ms. Mays.

Sacora and Joe,

This afternoon an emergency meeting had been scheduled concerning the status of Sadie and Jeremiah Walters. The police officers that arrested Sarah and Joshua Walters were questioned. Ms. Hines from Baldwin County Human Resources had been questioned. I had been notified as counselor of the situation from Ms. Hines and informed a hearing concerning the custody of the children will be tomorrow at two o'clock. I am asking you to be there. It will be an advantage for us to ask for permanent custody tomorrow.

Ms. Mays

Joe and Sacora hugged each other, and Eeyore, not knowing how to respond, brought her blanket to their bedroom to sleep there all night. Sacora texted Samantha to ask if she would sit with Aylassa, Alisha, Sadie, Jeremiah, and Elijah while the meeting was in session. Mixed emotions of worry and happiness accompanied Sacora through the night.

Chapter One Hundred Seventeen

Joe and Sacora awakened early before the alarm sounded and gave Sadie and Jeremiah their medicine. Sadie went back to sleep immediately, but Jeremiah still showed worries about going back to his parents. Joe said, "If you go back to your parents, I am going too. Deal?"

Jeremiah fell back to asleep when he said, "It is a deal, Joe."

Sacora opened the door for Eeyore, made the bed, and showered for the exciting day. She sat on the front porch with Joe, watching the sunrise and holding his hand. This morning, Elijah came to the front porch with Alisha. Eeyore came around from the back with Hugs and Kisses, and no one knew how the kennel was opened. Elijah and Joe went to the barn to walk Diesel and Clover. Alisha went inside with Sacora to cook breakfast. Aylassa was up, and Joy came downstairs to eat before school. Joe came in with Elijah, and Elijah asked to ride with Joe in his truck to take Joy to school for her last day for the Christmas holidays. Sacora said yes if Joe did not mind.

Sadie woke when the door was closed with Joe leaving. She was ready to eat and was happier today. Aylassa still did not and would not leave her side. Sadie ate more this morning and seemed to feel ease with the broken arm.

Samantha had come earlier to be with the children. Samantha had started the washing machine and folding laundry. Sacora looked exhausted. Samantha took control of everything, and Sacora rested, getting ready for the meeting on Sadie's and Jeremiah's custody hearing. Joe and Elijah were back from taking Joy to school, and Wendy had made arrangements to bring Joy home.

After lunch, Joe and Sacora were dressed for court and kissed all the children goodbye. Samantha's goodbye brought Sacora some comfort. At the courthouse, a parking place was hard to find. Joe and Sacora had driven the Bug and had benefited for a small parking place.

Inside the courthouse, Ms. Mays motioned for Joe and Sacora to step inside a small conference room. She introduced the young man, Luke Goodman. Sacora and Joe had informed Ms. Mays that they had already met and left the rest of the story of how they met unknown. Luke would be testifying for Joe and Sacora in the best interest of Sadie and Jeremiah.

"Everyone in the courtroom, all rise" was spoken and the judge entered the room. The case was introduced, and each attorney had a turn in opening arguments. The attorney for Sarah and Joshua Walters mentioned that Mr. Walters would not be present as he was admitted in a hospital for injuries.

Ms. Mays's opening arguments were Sadie and Jeremiah had a safe, secure, and loving home with Joe and Sacora McCarley. The judge wanted to hear from Luke Goodman, the brother of Sarah Walters.

The attorney for the Walters asked Luke some questions. "How informed are you with the care the parents gave their children?"

Luke answered, "When my mom passed away, they moved in the house with me. I am a student in college. My sister, Sarah Walters, started drinking heavy grieving for our mom, leaving the children unsafe, hungry, and they took care of themselves. Jeremiah's school was not important, he missed a lot. Sadie needed constant attention, and Sarah was not giving her any at all. When Joshua started swallowing large amounts of Oxycontin that was my mom's, violence started. Jeremiah and Sadie were removed from them in May of 2019 to a foster home. Sadie had a broken arm, and Jeremiah had a broken nose. I fussed with Sarah and Joshua, made them move, and then after sometime I had custody of Sadie and Jeremiah. I kept them as long as I could. I ran out of money quick for food, diapers, day care, and Jeremiah's school."

Chapter One Hundred Eighteen

The attorney tried in every way possible to cause Luke Goodman to change his story, and it never happened. Ms. Mays had the opportunity to question Luke. She approached Luke by saying, "In addition to what you have been asked, are you here to request and to support the courts of Alabama to give Joe and Sacora McCarley the custody of Sadie and Jeremiah Walters as foster parents?"

Luke said, "No, ma'am. I am not."

Ms. Mays was surprised. Joe and Sacora were disappointed. Ms. Mays asked again. Ms. Mays saying, "In addition to what you have been asked, are you here to request and to support the courts of Alabama to give Joe and Sacora McCarley the custody of Sadie and Jeremiah Walters as foster parents?"

Luke said, "No, ma'am. I am not."

Ms. Mays, being puzzled, asked, "Then why are you here, Mr. Goodman?"

Luke answered, "I am here to request and support the Alabama courts with the assistance of Baldwin County Human Resources to terminate the parental rights of Sarah and Joshua Walters and give Joe and Sacora McCarley the permanent custody through adoption. My sister and her husband cannot and will not give Sadie and Jeremiah a safe, secure home of benevolence. I am stating repeatedly that Joe and Sacora McCarley can and will give Sadie and Jeremiah a home of structure, safety, security, and benevolence."

Ms. Mays nodded and said, "That is all, Mr. Goodman."

The judge spoke, stating information that Joe and Sacora did not know. "This made the fourth time that Jeremiah Walters has been removed from the home of his parents due to injuries sustained through violence. For Sadie Walters, the second incident resulting in a broken arm from the violence. I have seen a video that Ms. Mays has submitted as evidence of the children with Joe and Sacora McCarley dancing and singing in their barn. After the documents of truancy reoccurring for the week of December ninth through December ninth, I have decided to follow steps of legal process to terminate the rights of the parents. As of today, Joe and Sacora McCarley will have full and permanent custody and given the option for adoption. Court is adjourned." .

Ms. Mays hugged Sacora, and Joe was so relieved with the outcome. Ms. Mays said, "Congratulations. Celebration can be started. Sadie and Jeremiah will be with you through the Christmas holidays."

Sacora and Joe left the courthouse with enthusiasm and could not wait to tell their parents. Joe was on his phone with Wendy, and Sacora called Samantha. Wendy and Samantha would be there tonight for the celebration of two more grandchildren. Joe and Sacora went to celebrate with a dinner at Olive Garden. It was final, five children would be given a permanent home with Joe and Sacora.

The waitress could tell excitement and happiness in Joe and Sacora. She brought cake first for their celebration. Their meal of chicken alfredo and salad was so enjoyed. Sacora was upset all week, and food did not taste as good as it did right now. Joe also had an empty stomach ready for good food. On the way home in the Bug, Sacora thought about the day she bought this Bug. She was distraught from her marriage ending and the devastating thought of not ever having a family. But today December 16, 2019, she had an amazing husband with an awesome daughter and five children. Her thoughts were interrupted with an email from Ms. Mays on her phone.

Sacora and Joe,

Ms. Hines has completed the documents required for release of parental rights of Sarah and Joshua Walters. I have the GRANTED ORDER from the judge. Can you be at my office before four o'clock today to endorse and complete the forms for adoption and birth certificates? It is an hour from now, and I will have it all ready to be completed and filed today before five o'clock.

Ms. Mays

Chapter One Hundred Nineteen

Joe and Sacora went to Ms. Mays's office before four o'clock, and her assistant had all documents ready to be completed. Ms. Mays had left a financial statement showing the monetary capabilities that providing for the six children was more than enough. Sacora had never asked Joe about his income, but her eyes looked twice at the amount of his statement, five million and something. She was so impressed that he never discussed his money. She should have known that he had a good financial status from playing pro football. Barton always flaunted his finances to impress the people around him. This was one of Barton's actions she detested. Joyfully the information on all forms were completed. Sadie Azariah McCarley and Jeremiah Dane McCarley were added to the forms for birth certificates.

Joe and Sacora left the office of Ms. Mays extremely happy with reassuring the promise made to Jeremiah that he would never return to Sarah and Joshua Walters. This evening, Wendy and Samantha had surprised the family with a small party. Julie and Tyler were already there when Joe and Sacora parked in the driveway. Kentucky Fried Chicken on the table with plenty of fixings. Jeremiah's face of relief and happiness when the news was given to him that he was now a McCarley just like Sacora, Joe, and Joy.

The days before Christmas passed so quickly with Sacora and the children being home and Joe occasionally taking repair jobs. All gifts were wrapped at Wendy's and brought under the live tree in the living room. Joy had gone to Brandie's and would be coming back for Christmas Eve and Christmas Day. Joy then would fly back to Miami on Christmas Day.

Christmas morning was so full of laughing and smiles, gifts being opened. Elijah took so many pictures, and Joy took many pictures of her large family. Zac, Wendy, Samantha, and Corey came for Christmas dinner. Everyone seated around the table laughing at the words coming from the children about their version of Santa Claus's visit. It was a great Christmas day for Joy until time for her flight. Sacora decided that they would all go to the airport to see her off to Miami.

At the airport, it was a sight to see all the faces telling Joy goodbye. Sacora was watching, thinking her impossible dream was no longer an impossible dream. Joy would be back for New Year's celebration.

Sadie and Jeremiah were healing with Elijah, Alisha, and Aylassa, taking consideration of the activities they were able to do. Elijah and Jeremiah's manure money kept coming in, Elijah doing most of the shoveling. The animals were adjusting to the cooler temperatures, Hugs and Kisses being in their kennels most part of the day. Eeyore was enjoying the rabbits what time they were out.

New Year's day, Joy was home, and the celebration was a huge one. Sacora and Joe went all out with food and noise makers. Party for New Year's Day was a new thing for all the children. Pictures and videos were made with grandparents, Tyler, and Julie.

January 2020 was an amazing start for the McCarley's. The children went back to school, and Sacora went back to work. All the teachers were informed of the name changes of the children, and forms were completed with their new names. Sacora and Joe were listed as parents, and Samantha, Corey, Zac, and Wendy were listed as grandparents. The children could be released to them from school and day care.

Chapter One Hundred Twenty

Joe and Sacora had adjusted to the routine of school and animals. Saturday after Valentine's Day, Sacora had gone to the barn to bathe Diesel and Clover for their veterinarian appointment scheduled on Monday afternoon. Sadie and Aylassa were playing on the steps, watching Sacora clean the lambs for their visit to Dr. James. Joe had taken Jeremiah, Alisha, and Elijah to register for football and cheerleading. Elijah wanted be the football manager for coaches Joe and Tyler. Jeremiah's plan was to be the best football player Joe would teach him to be. Joe would be bringing Subway home for a picnic.

Sacora heard a car and thought it was Joe and the children. She looked up to see Barton Haynes. He had two dozen roses in a bouquet in his hands. Sacora had been told by Ginger and Sandy that Rachel had left him and carried most of what he had with her, house, car, money, and etc.

Joe parked his truck at the barn, opening the door for the children. He noticed Barton Haynes's car and walked to the doorway of the barn. Sadie and Aylassa went to Elijah, Alisha, and Jeremiah. Sacora had her back to Joe and did not see him. Elijah told Sadie and Aylassa to watch for them and motion when Barton was coming. Sadie and Aylassa said, "Otay."

Elijah's and Jeremiah's shovels were off the nail, and they shoveled manure in Barton's convertible Porsche. Alisha took a small Allen wrench and engraved in large letters on Barton's car "**I Don't Like U.**" She went from one side to the other until she had engraved all around his car.

Barton came to Sacora and handed her the roses with "Happy Valentine's Day."

Sacora took the roses and asked, "What brings you here, Barton?"

Barton said, "I wanted to wish you a Happy Valentine's Day."

Sacora said, "I heard Rachel is gone. You are alone, aren't you, Barton?"

Barton said, "Yes, I am, Sacora."

Sacora said, "You are lonely because you are mean, Barton, and you are mean because you are lonely." Sacora looked at the roses and asked, "What do you want, Barton?"

Barton said, "I want you to come back to me. I will buy you the house on Magnolia River you love. It is for sale, and I will double what they are asking, ten million dollars if I have to. You can drive any expensive car you would like to drive. Just come back to me, Sacora."

Sacora handed the roses back to Barton and said, **"No, thank you, Barton. I married Joe."**

Barton looked disappointed and walked past Joe to knock him off balance, but Joe was ready leaning up against the barn. Sacora turned around to see Joe standing in the doorway of the barn and went to him smiling. Joe grabbed her and kissed her passionately.

Sadie and Aylassa made motions Barton was coming. Barton had a come apart when he saw his car. Elijah could not resist the temptation and threw manure one more time in his car. Barton got in his car, moving some of the manure, and drove away.

Sacora washed Sadie's and Aylassa's hands and faces. Alisha, Elijah, and Jeremiah washed their hands and faces with the water hose. Joe put the tailgate down on the truck for a picnic. Joy had come to the barn for the Subway lunch picnic. Elijah, Jeremiah, and Alisha were eating and laughing about what they had done to Barton's car with Joy. She had seen the car from her bedroom window.

The picnic was interrupted by the mail carrier blowing the horn. Sacora went to get a package. It was a large envelope from the State of Alabama. Sacora opened it and gave some things to Joe. It was five birth certificates: Sadie Azariah McCarley, Aylassa Blaine McCarley, Alisha Beth McCarley, Jeremiah Dane McCarley, and Elijah Chance

McCarley. Mother, Sacora Elizabeth Hill McCarley. Father, Joseph Clay McCarley.

The Foo Fighters music played loud in the house the rest of the afternoon as Joe and Sacora put nails in the wall to hold the frames of the birth certificates.

THE END

About The Author

Sherry Myrick was born and raised in Russellville, Alabama, and has resided in a small community Tharptown for the past forty years. She finished high school with a GED. She attended Northwest Community College English classes with her oldest son, Jamie Myrick, sharing books. Sherry's love for writing was changed from a hobby to writing for a local newspaper. The stories she had created with her son Jonathan Myrick was twenty years later transformed into novels. With meeting co-worker Dalvin Porter, his research of Sherry's ideas became important parts of the plot. Sherry Myrick has developed a novel of inspiration of never giving up as she has lived before her children, family, friends, and coworkers.

CPSIA information can be obtained
at www.ICGtesting.com
Printed in the USA
LVHW012207290321
682892LV00010B/133